Crown Up

Esther Dale

BookLocker
Saint Petersburg, Florida

Print ISBN: 978-1-64719-572-4
Ebook ISBN: 978-1-64719-573-1

Published by BookLocker.com, Inc., St. Petersburg, Florida.

Printed on acid-free paper.

The characters and events in this book are fictitious. Any similarity to real persons, living or dead, is coincidental and not intended by the author.

BookLocker.com, Inc.
2021

First Edition

Library of Congress Cataloguing in Publication Data
Dale, Esther
Crown Up by Esther Dale
Library of Congress Control Number: 2021907199

Acknowledgements

Thank you to my mother, for reading through my
book to encourage me;
To my best friend Faith Janae for keeping me
going through this long endeavor;
To Tony Ross, for his amazing editing skills and
constructive criticism;
And to my siblings for being enthusiastic about my
passion for writing.

I wrote this book in order that followers of God will be encouraged and strengthened in Him; that they will go forth and spread the Word; that they will grow deep roots and stand against storms. I wrote this book in order that writers, young or old, will gather inspiration to weave intricate stories according to God's will, as well as to show them that they are not restricted to the way things have always been. I wrote this book to show that with God, anything is possible; that we are not limited by our talents, our skills, or lack thereof; expectations of ourselves or of our parents, or of our childhood, no matter how perfect or how broken.

This book is written to those who need to be refreshed, to all those who tire in doing good; to all those who feel exhausted; to all those who have fallen; to all those who are stuck; to all those who are lost; to all those who are confused: hear and listen to these words...

"Brothers, I know that I have not yet reached that goal. But there is one thing I always do: I forget the things that are past. I try as hard as I can to reach the goal that is before me." -Philippians 3:13 (ICB)

A note from the author

This book is an allegory for those ages 13 and above. It is however family friendly and could be read by all ages. Sometimes terms can be intimidating, so let us define what an allegory is. "An allegory is a story, poem, or picture that can be interpreted to reveal a hidden meaning, typically a moral or political one." (Dictionary.com.) This still might seem vague, so let me break it down.

Many times, people's bad moods are results of battles that you don't see. *Crown Up* depicts different characters and what they go through on a regular basis. When it looks like someone is working their job at a department store with a sour attitude, they are mentally fighting for their life, trying to overcome Pain and Sorrow, two trifling demons always causing problems.

When it looks like your sibling is being careless about their words, they are mentally drowning, trying to plead for help, attempting to escape Defeat and Chains, but no one hears their cries.

When it looks like your loved one hates you, they are mentally lost, wondering if they will be tormented by Guilt and Fear for the rest of their lives.

It is nearly impossible to fully understand someone else's life and pain, but through this allegory, I hope to open your eyes so you may heap grace, mercy, and forgiveness onto those who are struggling to simply survive the day.

This book will have two sections alternating back and forth, one showing the spiritual journey in this font and one showing the physical journey in this regular font. This system will help differentiate what you are seeing in the physical and the spiritual.

May you keep your crown up and guide others to Him.

|Chapter 1: A Child of the King|

Aneta scrambled behind a boulder as three demons prowled by her hiding place in a canyon ravine. Even though their general shape was outlined as a man except their odd hunched position and bent deer legs, their shadowy figures, seemingly half solid and half smoke vapor made up their being. Upon their head where a man's hair would have been, a black mass slowly waved back and forth, like a dreary fire with weary flames. Their face was indiscernible, as it held no features. They were without eyes, without nose, and without mouth. Their long, coarse fingers tapered off in much of the same effect as their head, giving the demons a monstrous advantage of intimidation.

As usual, the pitch black demons wore pitch black rubbery armor, dull to the look. The black armor perfectly matched their body color, and most of the time, it was hard to tell whether or not they wore anything at all, even though the demons were indisputably clad in some version of armor at all times.

None of them were chief demons, as those kind were usually in the form of gigantic wolf bears, but Aneta still knew that the lowly demons would have no trouble calling in a chief demon or two. Wincing, she stepped tenderly as sharp rock shards ripped open scabs from previous injuries. She hid her face as one demon hesitated, then continued. They must have only been traveling by, for if they were scouts, they would have investigated more thoroughly. After they were gone from sight, she waited as long as she dared, then rushed away, fleeing from the restless creatures. Those may have not been scouts, but they still hungrily scavenged for souls.

She gazed above the stony canyon walls to catch a faint glimpse of the Bridge. It was hard to see from her angle, but she knew it from any distance. It led to a lush meadow. Across the meadow was a large orchard of every fruit that one could imagine. Among the orchard, there were several cool streams that watered the ground and comforted the tired.

This Aneta knew. She had been born there, after all. But she could never get back up after having fallen down from the edge of the cliff.

She had tried for days to climb the canyon wall or find another way up. It was useless. She was lost.

At the hissing whispers of another group of demons, Aneta held back a fearful gasp and tried to hide in the canyon maze. She had barely glanced back when she spotted the chief demon who led the charge: Fear. Afraid of what might happen, Aneta nervously slipped through a narrow crevice, hiding as quietly as possible.

When evening came, she slowly crawled out of the canyon wall and sighed. She was safe...for that moment. She began walking in a general direction away from where she knew demons usually were located. Demons were not often out in the canyons in the night, as they must always have had other more important things to do in the cover of darkness. That being the case, Aneta liked to breathe fresh air as she took a walk through the canyons at night. With the night came a cool breeze and a dropping temperature, but the chill was worth it. She came out of the canyons and quietly moved through tall dry grass that made up a desert like plain near the canyon entrance.

Someone with the appearance of a man came up next to her as she strolled around in the tall grass. Depression often joined her as she walked at night, much to her dismay, although she found no reason to tell him to leave. However, even though Depression looked and acted like a man, he was not.

He was indeed a demon of sorts. For the most part, however, he kept to himself in terms of actively working with Fear, the chief demon only second to Satan. He did not answer to every wish and whim of Fear, as nearly every demon did, but that did not mean he was safe to interact with.

At any rate, Depression often looked harmless. His eyes were soft, and his chin sharp. He often left his hands in his pockets as he walked, talking quietly in his soft, lulling voice. It was so gentle and persistent it annoyed Aneta, but she could not do much. She remembered her last talk with Depression. She had had it.

Aneta stopped where she was. "I *told* you not to come back. Why are you here, Depression?"

Depression made a face. "Well...whether you realize it or not, you invited me."

She sighed again, faintly remembering the contract she made with Depression in the beginning. Until she no longer needed his services, he was obliged to come and go as he pleased. Why had she signed the contract again? Defeated, Aneta let him follow her around. Talking to him never availed much.

"I want to do something." Depression said.

"Like what?" Aneta tried her best not to say much, attempting to discourage him from talking. She herself was already tired of walking and decided to head back to her main hiding spot.

"I don't know."

"Depression, go away." Aneta walked through the desert plain and into the canyons again. Her mind raged. She was angry Depression had ruined her usually pleasant nightly walk.

A piercing screech penetrated the dry air. Aneta whipped her head around, in a scrambling panic. Depression was about to ask her a question, but she darted off, leaving him behind. She tried to conceal herself between the first rocks she could find as she held her breath.

More howling closed in. The demons' signature sound was close to a coyote's call, but mixed with a man-like howl filled with whispers. Their sound never failed to hover in between menacing outrage and nightmarish subtly. Aneta could hardly stand their controversial call, as it pierced her eardrums and sent chills down her spine.

Aneta's lungs burned. Rasping breath. Her own and the demons trailing her.

Aneta could picture their coarse fingers grabbing her ankles and yanking her down. They had done that before. She squeezed her eyes shut, trying to hold her breath. A long pause began. She could no longer hear the terrifying beings. It was eerily silent. She exhaled.

Aneta scrambled out of her temporary hiding place and ran through the canyon again. She hesitated next to a tunnel-like passage that went through the thick canyon wall and led out to a secluded place. She had once been afraid of tight places. Not anymore. Narrow crevices were how she survived. She slowly and carefully crawled on her hands and knees, going deeper and deeper.

It was dark and she could not rely on her sight. She felt along her path on her hands and knees. Soon, Depression had followed her inside, not bothering to let her focus, but filling the silence with endless, mindless chatter.

She kept silent, not wanting to entertain Depression, but he kept talking anyway. She felt the floor beneath her with her rough hands, anticipating to find a jagged fissure in the stone floor. She had painfully found it earlier when she first took the path. It was only a foot long, not big enough to fall through, but big enough for her arms to suddenly plunge until her chin caught her, cracking in the process. She soon found the fissure and gingerly clambered over it.

Aneta's head popped out the other side of the tunnel. She found herself in a small, secluded area where four walls of canyon came together, making a small square of safety that was about six feet by six feet. The night sky was visible high above the little area, fifty feet up. She sat down in relief, thankful she could rest in peace.

Abruptly, the four walls violently shook, causing the small gap she had crawled through to widen. She screamed as maniacal laughter echoed off the tight, steep cliffs around her. The small, foot-wide drop in the middle of the once-small gap she had passed through widened, and clouds of black surrounded her as she shrieked for help.

Before the dust and smoke could clear away, two chief demons stood on either side of her… Fear and Lost. Unlike other demons with a man's body, demons looked more like wispy shadows of giant bear wolves, with a discernible mouth and two gray slots for eyes. With a triumphant howl, they grabbed her, chained her, and dragged her by her ankles into the pit below. Aneta struggled until her head hit a rock, and she could not think straight with the high pitched whine in her ears. She barely noticed the cold shackles pulling her through underground caverns, and she was finally tossed into a small, cell-like place. Fear snarled a warning and pounded away.

Depression came around shortly and sat down next to her, pointing out every terrible thing that happened to her. Angry, Aneta flung herself towards him and wound up to slap him in the face. She lashed out, but Depression had moved aside and shoved her to the ground. Her face hit the stone beneath her. She cried out in pain. She slowly sat up as Depression released her in silence. She rubbed her cheek, knowing a bruise would appear.

Still bound to the contract she had foolishly signed, Aneta sighed, doomed to listen to his soft, annoying voice.

It was at least a full day before she was given water and some food. Aneta eagerly devoured the soft bread, but it became scratchy and stale as she swallowed it. Aneta found her cup of water in the dark and sighed. She knew it was not clean, but it was water. It soothed her dry throat, but it turned to acid in her stomach. After the second agonizing day in cold shackles, with Depression constantly chatting in her ear, something began to echo in her mind.

Aneta? Where are you?

Aneta slowly let tears rise to her eyes as she thought about it. At first, she wondered why she would ask herself such an odd question.

Suddenly, Lost prowled by, startling Aneta with his bass voice that rumbled her metal cup sitting on the rock floor of her cell. "You will never be found, so don't get any ideas."

Aneta slumped back, defeated.

Depression continued to talk. "He's right. You ran off and you will never be able to get back to the Meadow. Besides, these demons literally opened up the canyon fissures and shoved you in here. There is no way anyone could get down here even if they knew you *and* wanted to help...which no one does."

Beginning to sob, Aneta pulled up her knees to her chin, shivering on the stone floor in her ragged clothing. Depression leaned closer and continued to whisper in her ear. But even as Depression droned on, she heard another voice, asking the same question that came to her earlier.

Aneta? Where are you? It was more pressing this time.

Aneta straightened up. None of the demons were around, and it was not Depression's voice.

"What?" She asked aloud.

Depression sighed. "Don't make me say all of that *again*."

"No. It was someone else."

"No one else is here."

The soft voice echoed in her mind again. *Aneta? I'm waiting for you.*

Her breath was caught away. She remembered that voice. "Father?"

Depression made a face. "Aneta. Your father isn't here. He's-"

"No-" Aneta stood up, looking around. "No, that was...Jesus. That was His voice."

Fear bounded up to her cell. His voice seemed to shake the entire cell. "Quiet! Don't say another word."

For a while, Aneta quieted down, afraid that a demon meandering by might tell on her. However, the peaceful voice still sounded in her mind.

Aneta? I'm looking for you.

Again, Aneta straightened up, wondering where the voice came from. "God...*please* tell me that's You."

With angry growls, Lost and Fear approached her cell. "Say another *word* and *no one* will ever be able to find you!"

With a deep breath, Aneta stared down Fear in defiance. "Jesus? Are You there? Can You find me?"

Lost and Fear ripped open the cell door and rushed in, both trying to slash her to pieces. Aneta pushed herself away...as the canyon wall broke open behind her. Fear and Lost both froze, terrified at what appeared in the opening.

God barged in, upturning all works of the demons in the entire sub-region, ensuing chaos among Fear, Lost, and their henchdemons.

God gently picked her up, threw off her chains, and carried her back through the canyon, to the Bridge. Aneta blinked. It was sunny. How long had it been since she had seen the sun? She looked ahead of her. Across the Bridge sat the immense, lush Meadow. Beyond that, blooming orchards.

God smiled at her. "You have been trying to get up here for a while now."

Aneta sheepishly nodded.

"You can cross now, but I will not carry you across. You have to do it yourself."

Feeling like it would be the easiest thing in the world, Aneta strode forward, stepping across the Bridge. She glanced down at the ground, seeing the deep canyon. She clutched the side rails, gasping at the height. She looked up, seeing that the Bridge seemed much longer than before. Anxious, Aneta tried to keep going, striving to go back home.

Just then, the entire canyon seemed to shake as Fear and Lost, followed by Chains, pounded into the area below.

Raising their voices as angry giants, they shouted at her. "You will never make it! Those thin ropes will break! Turn back! He won't help you! He said so Himself!"

Aneta stared into the canyon below. The cries replayed in her ears. God *did* say she had to do it herself. Did He leave her to fend for herself? Did He abandon her?

"Look up, Child."

Aneta glanced up, seeing God waiting at the other end of the Bridge. As she focused on Him, the length of the Bridge did not seem to matter. Lost stopped howling. The Bridge seemed to creak and groan under her weight, but she kept walking, approaching the green Meadow. Chains quieted down. Fear could no longer say a word, or if he did, Aneta could not hear him. She at last rested her foot on the grassy Meadow's edge. Aneta embraced God, thankful she was safe and it was over.

She stepped back as she realized she now had a new dress. Aneta smiled as she lifted one side with one hand, admiring the comfortable cloth.

God smiled. In His hand, He forged a sword. "This is for you. If you allow it, it will work just as it had before in your hands. It is lightweight and immensely strong, and it will not shatter or dull. You will find that it is comparably easy to travel with; it will also guide you. Even so, you will need armor." He laid out leather and chain mail. "This, as well, is lightweight and tough; it will not be pierced by any mortal-crafted weapon, as many will attempt to combat you."

Aneta tried on the leather vest, then the chainmail, remembering how to properly fit it to herself. It was indeed light and comfortable, with the chainmail neatly matching her attire.

God next brought out a pair of sandals with a matching belt and a crown. "The shoes are for when you travel through uncharted territory. Here, there is no need for them, since the grass is soft and the ground is smooth. You will be at peace when you travel, for your feet will not tire and you will be able to cover much ground.

"The belt will gird you with strength and truth, and in the end, it will be one of the only things to help you when truth is not known from falsehood. With this crown, as you wear it, nothing can harm you without your permission. Take heed: they will succeed in convincing you that they can do harm, and that they already have taken position to injure you. That is their most potent weapon: trickery. That is how many fall. Use wisdom with great boldness, and you will not fail as long as you have the smallest amount of faith. Plant a single seed of faith and you will reap a hundredfold. My warrior and princess, go forth and make disciples and encourage My followers."

Aneta was quiet. She wanted to tell her Father something, but she wasn't sure if she could.

"Is there something you would like to discuss?" God sat down next to her.

Aneta sat down cross legged on the grass. She tried to keep her voice from wavering. "I...have a question..."

"You may ask."

She gulped. How could she ask? Would He be mad? "Jesus...I'm not sure I can."

God didn't say anything yet.

"I'm...I don't think I could fight with a sword again. I'm out of practice...and...well. You know the other reason."

"Aneta." God gently spoke to her. He was compassionate and understanding. "I know. But you are able to fight again. You are called to fight for My kingdom. When you go to the place which I will send you, you will find many hardships. It is a difficult place with difficult people. And you will have people come along to help you, but at one point, you will have to decide to fight. I know it will be hard. But your past does not tell your future what to do."

Tears brimmed her eyes. "How am I supposed to fight? I can't do this, Jesus." Overwhelmed, she sobbed. "I haven't fought since--since the day I--I--I...I haven't fought since...since Coward and I..."

"Aneta, all is forgiven. Forgive yourself. I will give you all the strength you need to fight through your hard days."

Aneta wanted to protest, but she knew He was right. God was always right.

"Alright." She wiped her face with her sleeve. "Alright God. I will do what I can for you. I'll try my best to fight for You."

With a deep breath, Aneta held up the sword, upon which she noted the words engraved elegantly on the blade.

Aneta, the Child of the One True King

|Chapter 2: Aphoticton|

The cool, fall breeze caught up the skirt of Aneta's dress and playfully tossed it about as she walked along the sidewalk. God had sent her to the quaint town of Aphotiction, but instructions as to what she was doing would come later. Aneta remembered God's warning about the difficulty to come and the battles that were to ensue. How that would happen, Aneta did not know. Everything in Aphoticton seemed calm and complacent.

Cars lazily droned by, and people leisurely strolled along the sidewalks. It was around lunch time and she was growing hungry. Aneta looked through the windows of a thrift store, a law firm, a bank, a bakery, a shoe store, and a funeral home before finding a sandwich shop with a delicious smell wafting out to meet her.

Opening the door, Aneta approached the front counter and ordered her sandwich. As the cashier rang up her order, she decided to finally ask her burning question.

"Is there a church in Aphoticton?" Aneta asked, quite bold in her question.

The cashier eyed her as she handed Aneta her bag. The woman put her palms on the counter, looking annoyed. "Are you a *Christian*?"

The cashier's question threatened her. Aneta's face fell blank. Her boldness vanished and her courage failed.

Aneta snatched her crown from her head and hastily stuffed it into her shoulder bag. The looks coming from the people in the sandwich shop stopped. At the same time Aneta's mind eased up, she immediately felt a heaviness weigh on her. God had given her that crown to wear as a testimony. It was a part of her armor. It protected her.

She still wore her other armor God had gifted to her, but the people there did not seem to notice it, especially since she was no longer wearing her crown. Feeling unsure of what to do, Aneta decided to leave.

Aneta shook her head immediately. "No. No...I was just wondering. You usually see them...in towns. That's all." She motioned with her bagged sandwich. "Thanks." She managed a smile and hurried out the door.

When she found a park in the middle of town, a heaviness settled on her heart. She sank down on a bench, defeated. Wanting to cry, Aneta kept her head down, focused on her sandwich. She squeezed her eyes closed. Why did she struggle with the thought of people judging her? Why did the cashier seem so hostile? Was that an example of God's warning?

With a deep sigh, Aneta hoped her task in Aphoticton would not be too difficult.

Sitting on a bench, Aneta pulled out her crown and looked at it. She let it sit in her loose fingers.

Depression came around shortly. He sat down on the bench next to her.

Getting weary, Aneta asked, "why are you here *again?*" With her souring mood, Aneta was thankful no one could see Depression. People leisurely walked by, holding dog leashes or holding hands. No one noticed Depression sitting by Aneta.

"Hey, you're the one who still wants to hang out with me." Depression defended himself.

"What? Since when did I say that?" As soon as Aneta spoke those words, she remembered. "Oh. The contract."

"-that you signed yourself," Depression added. "Now how are you feeling? Horrible? Good. Because you *are* horrible. Get used to it, Sweetie. Now hear me out. Sure, okay, you're not *that* horrible, but...have you seen the others? God has children who are so high and mighty, and so spiritual. They have been in church *all* their lives, never walked away once. You may not be horrible, but...compared to *them*, well, you're pretty horrible."

Aneta stared at him, a degraded look on her face. "But that's not-"

19

"Is it, though?"

Aneta fell silent. She slightly bowed her head and covered her face with one hand, letting her crown hang from her other hand. Beginning to shudder, Aneta let it slip and crash to the ground as she now used both hands to cover her face. As the gold metal clashed against the concrete, Aneta shuddered again.

For a while, she sat there, overwhelmed at the very thought of trying to live in Aphotiction. When she finally opened her eyes, she bent down to pick up her crown. It was gone.

Aneta jumped up. "Where did it-"

Depression stood there, smirking. He dangled the crown on the end of his crooked finger. Furious, Aneta reached for her crown, but Depression snatched it back. "Neh-eh," he grinned. "Remember the contract? That *you* signed? I am entitled to anything you have."

"Fine! *Keep* it!"

At those words, Depression smiled in delight. Wanting to push his luck, he reached for Aneta's shield that she held in her left hand.

Furious, Aneta pulled her shield closer to herself and stalked away, not enjoying Depression's tauntings.

Aneta sat on the park bench for an hour before realizing she still had her sandwich. She had not yet opened the bag. Her appetite had left. Not wanting to keep it or throw it away, she wanted to give it to someone else.

She soon spotted an elderly lady walking by. The woman looked homeless.

"Excuse me?" Aneta called to her. "Miss? Here. It's a sandwich. I haven't opened it yet. I'm...not even hungry. Take it."

The woman's eyes brightened. They began to shine as tears sat on the verge of falling. In a shaky voice, she said, "oh, o-hh, thank you. Thank you, little lady."

After the elderly woman left, Aneta slowly rested on the bench again. What was she supposed to do?

For the next hour or so, Aneta did nothing.

She then spotted a girl across from her, getting up from a bench and walking away. The teenager did not trudge or drag her feet, but Aneta realized something was wrong. Her countenance conveyed agony, as did her purposeless gait. From the girl's purse, a note fluttered to the ground.

Aneta waited until the teen was a good distance away to pick up the dropped note.

--Broken
Not or Seem will be able to bring you. Be at the inn by 4
--Helpful

Looking up, Aneta realized the girl, presumably named Broken, was already out of sight. Pocketing the note, Aneta decided to get moving. Her sharp self-disappointment had dulled, and she was hungry again. Aneta meandered around for a little bit until finding a place called Gray's Cafe. She stepped inside. A fresh aroma of cookies and pastries filled the air with a sweet scent. Parallel to the counter, there were five tables, each table having two chairs. However, the cafe also had a few barstools at the counter, so she pulled up one to sit on. As she did so, a clean-shaven man in his mid-fifties walked up to her.

"Hello, my name is Advisor. What may I get for you?"

With a nervous exhale, Aneta looked around to see a few demons lurking in a few booths. They acknowledged her, but did not threaten her. Aneta breathed in a slight notion of relief, but it didn't last long.

The man behind the counter patiently waited for Aneta to decide. Behind him, Aneta saw another demon standing there, almost completely morphed into the man. As the man moved, the demon moved correspondingly. But to see both a man and a demon standing in the same occupying area transparently gave Aneta chills. She saw both the man's eyes and the demon's glare at her simultaneously. When the demon controlling the man realized Aneta noticed, it gave her a playfully evil grin.

From the black, shadowy, smoke-like mist that slowly drifted from the controlling demon, Aneta concluded it was not a good place to be. Simply seeing demons that close made Aneta shudder again, making her wonder if she would have to battle demons like the one from which she sat three feet away. They used to chase her for years. Was she supposed to face them? She had never wanted to fight another demon again. Too many times, she had tried and failed. God knew that. Why did He pick her to fight for His kingdom? She was done with fighting.

Aneta stood up. "Actually, I think I'm good."

"Are you sure?" The question was stated gently, but to her, it seemed like a threat.

Aneta nodded and hurriedly left. She kept walking until she came across a place called Lyle's Diner. It seemed safe, so she sat down.

A friendly looking man with a circle beard and glasses walked up to her. He was casually dressed in jeans and a black shirt. His t-shirt was completely black except for one aesthetic white line on the front. Aneta wondered if it stood for anything.

"Good afternoon. My name is Ly. Anything you would like right away?"

Aneta ordered a small lunch. After Ly left the table, Aneta relaxed and glanced around. The diner's quaint atmosphere comforted her. The walls were cheerfully painted with soft backgrounds and stenciled quotes, such as: "Believe in yourself," "Listen to yourself," "Obey globally," and "Follow your heart."

As she ate, she watched people come and leave. Only one person caught her attention: an elderly lady. It was the same homeless woman to which she had given her sandwich. Curious, Aneta watched her.

Ly seemed to know her. "Good afternoon, Biddy. Coffee?"

"Yes, please." She sat down. Soon, she received her coffee. She sat for about ten minutes, then stood to pay. She reached into her pocket, but froze. She began quietly exclaiming to herself as she continued to search every pocket on her body. "Oh, oh. No, not there. Oh...oh no. Oh no..."

Aneta noticed she must have lost her money at some point. Ly did not seem pleased, standing there with his arms crossed and eyebrows lowered.

"Biddy." His voice warned her.

The elderly lady trembled. "Ly, I've always come with money, you know that. I...I just don't know...where it fell out." Her elderly voice shook.

With a sudden move, Aneta jumped up and hurried over to them. She handed Ly a five dollar bill. Ly took it, glanced at Biddy, and then gave Aneta her change after opening the register.

The homeless woman remembered Aneta and gasped. She gently touched Aneta's face with one hand.

"An angel has come twice today." She gazed at Aneta with love.

Aneta smiled. "Well, I'm glad I could help you." She then handed Ly her bill for her own food, and smiled again at the woman.

When Aneta walked out the door, she spotted the teenage girl, Broken. Aneta followed her for about a block. Broken eventually walked inside the Whimsicalton Inn. Aneta continued to follow.

Broken sat inside on a lobby bench. Gently, Aneta sat down next to her. Only then did Aneta realize how much she had stepped out on a limb. Her mind frantically rushed a word or encouragement to her heart. *For God hath not given us the spirit of fear; but of power, and of love, and of a sound mind.*

"My name is Aneta," she began.

The teenage girl glanced up.

Two demons, who had previously not paid her any attention, began to advance towards her. She had spotted them first when she walked inside the building. They had not been doing anything specific, except for seemingly just people watching. When she walked in and began to

23

talk to the teenager, they immediately moved. At that same time, Aneta habitually unsheathed her sword and took a fighting stance. Her brain finally caught up and she remembered how much she hated fighting demons.

"What's yours?"
"Broken." The teen replied.
Aneta had no idea where to go next. "Well...I found this note. You dropped it."
"Thanks," Broken muttered.

Aneta began to panic. She had not fought in a long time. What was she doing there in Aphoticton? What was she thinking? She wasn't wearing her helmet, her crown. Before the demons reached her and Broken, she let down her stance. The two demons who had been running towards her, suddenly skidded to a stop. She knew the demons would let her go if she did nothing. If she left Broken alone, they would leave her alone. She then would not be a threat.

Defeated, Aneta started to put her sword back in her sheath. What was she thinking?

Aneta realized she used to feel the same way as Broken: worn out, mentally exhausted, and done with life. When she felt like that, she had never admitted it, but she had always wanted someone to listen to her. A thought appeared in her mind.

God had listened to her. Had He not loved her and understood her when she was lost? Aneta knew she was obliged to save at least one soul, since God had indeed saved hers. Trying to push back previous memories, Aneta yanked her sword out again and leapt for one of the demons.

Aneta reached out of the first thing that came to mind. "Could you tell me...about your family?"

With ease of her hands, and not that of her mind, Aneta attacked one demon and sliced the other before they could react. Feeling a thrill that had cultivated long ago when she fought with a sword, Aneta stomped her foot, angry that she no longer loved it. The thrilling feeling bothered her. She exhaled sharply and moved to sheath her sword again, not wanting to fight again. But her hand did not finish the movement. She stood still as she spotted another demon just vanishing out the door, most likely retrieving reinforcements. Even though Aneta subconsciously decided to stay and fight, she hated every moment of it. She knew it was dangerous to fight without the mark of a Child of God on her head. Begrudgingly, she determined to do it once, and not again.

"My family hates me," Broken said.

This shocked Aneta. "I'm sure they don't *hate* you. Why would you say that?"

She did not reply.

"How many siblings do you have?"

"Two brothers. Older brothers." Broken nodded. "Not and Seem."

"Where are they right now?"

This opened a vein in Broken. "Supposed to be here. But they won't be. They *forget.* I feel like no one cares anymore. I look around and I see brothers everywhere. They are laughing and helping their sisters."

Aneta watched Broken's facial expressions as the teenager talked. Pain and anger showed predominantly.

"I see big brothers carrying their baby sisters and giving them a cup of water, or helping them up the steps. Everyone seemed to get a loving brother but *me.* How do I have two older brothers and they both fell short of caring? Not *never* loved me and Seem couldn't even *think* about me enough to-to-to *open a door* for me. I have the worst brothers in the *world.*"

Aneta inhaled, opened her mouth, then exhaled. She had no idea what to say.

"I have to go. No use waiting for them here." Broken stood up and walked out of the inn.

Aneta glanced around as Broken walked away. No demons appeared for a fight. As Broken walked out the doors, Aneta saw movement somewhere off to the side. When she looked around, she only saw the demon for a moment before it vanished again through the walls, out of sight. She knew it's armor anywhere. It was Fear.

Had Fear followed Broken? Had Fear followed her? To Aphoticton? Aneta shivered at the thought of fighting Fear. She could never do that again. *I can't fight them!* Aneta thought to herself, addressing God. How could He expect her to fight the very demons that had tormented her for years?

A hand gently touched her shoulder. Aneta jumped.
Courage, one of her friends, stood there.
Aneta's face lit up. "Courage! What are *you* doing here?"
"I work here," Courage laughed. "God told me you would be here, but I didn't know you would be *right* here."

Aneta realized Courage was wearing her crown. It was beautiful, fashioned in the same way as hers: simply made with a single band of pure gold, almost white, with twelve small pearls embedded all around. The metal itself looked plain at first, but when carefully looked over, the crown had multiple, intricate designs imprinted on the gold.

She also wore her armor. Her belt held her sword, and her shield was slung on her back, ready in a moment's notice. Courage's breastplate had been polished that morning, Aneta could tell. Every piece of Courage's armor looked sharp and clean, even down to the heels of her shoes.

Holding her happy facial expression, Aneta gulped. She was not wearing her crown, and she had honestly forgotten about cleaning her armor. Had she even cleaned her sword after dealing with the demons? Aneta began to remember proper care for the attire and tools her Father had given her. Would Courage say anything about it?

"What were you talking to Broken about?" Courage asked. "You know her?"

"A little. I know *about* her. She is here a lot, and Helpful the secretary knows her well. I don't know much else. I've only been here for a little under a month. So where are you staying?"

"I don't know. I...just got here and...I suppose I need a job and a place."

"Okay. Come here, let me ask Helpful."

"Oh, right now?"

"Yeah, why not?"

Aneta followed Courage to the front desk where the secretary was sitting.

"Hey Helpful, do you know of any places looking to hire?" Courage leaned on the desk.

Helpful thought about it. "I haven't seen anything lately that immediately comes to mind. But...is this for you?" She motioned to Aneta.

Aneta nodded.

"Well, I'll have to ask the owner..." Helpful nodded back. "I'm not sure what kind of work you're looking for?"

Aneta shrugged. "I guess...anything that I can do or learn."

"Okay, okay." Helpful bobbed her head. "You may be able to work *here*. That is, if you think you might like to."

"Oh, I wouldn't mind working here."

Courage grinned and elbowed Aneta, making her chuckle.

"Okay then, I will make this note..." Helpful scribbled something on a notepad as she talked. "And I will let you know what the owner says. We just had two people quit the other day because they moved out of town, so he may appreciate you." Helpful paused, "and especially if you know Courage! She has quite a reputation here."

Courage reddened and playfully rolled her eyes.

"Thanks! I appreciate that. Helpful, how well do you know Broken?" Aneta decided to ask about the teenager after all.

Helpful shrugged. "For as long as I've worked here, about seven years. Why? I noticed you were talking to her earlier."

"Yes. I don't know, just curious I suppose."

As Aneta and Courage left the inn, Aneta accidently bumped into a man coming in the door. The first thing she noticed was his brilliant green eyes. They glinted as he nodded to her, apologizing. His sharp features and clean shaven face reminded her of someone she had seen before, but no name came to mind.

Slightly sheepish, Aneta nodded, apologized as well, and kept walking.

"I haven't seen you in *years!*" Courage exclaimed. "How is everything? How are you doing? Did God tell you why you are here yet?"

Aneta hesitated, not wanting to tell Courage about her rebellious stage of hiding from God. "Yeah, it's been a long time. How did you recognize me, though? I mean," she chuckled, "it's been years."

Laughing with her, Courage said, "well, for one, He said you were coming. And I recognized you, sitting with Broken actually. Other than...you know, what you look like, you are still the same person from years ago; always encouraging and building others up who are wounded. I've never seen you do anything else."

Aneta's heart sputtered, and her stomach coiled and twisted.

"Oh no..." Failure's black form lurked around Aneta. The chief demon startled her. The wolf bear of a demon subtly circled Aneta, its breathing ragged and hoarse. For some reason, Aneta did not think it was from the chief demon running.

"You have not told anyone what you did, have you?"

Aneta placed a hand over her sword's hilt subconsciously, at the same time trying not to think about whether or not it might be dull or dirty.

The chief demon mockingly gasped in shock. "What will they think?" Failure chuckled. It's gray eyes seemed to stoop to a reddish hue, and he tauntingly snapped at her.

Nevertheless, Failure's words pierced her mind. She did not want to fight. She was done with fighting. She had fought for so long in her youth, seemingly getting nowhere. She was here to do God's bidding, not to pick fights with the Darkness. But wasn't God's bidding to fight for His kingdom? Aneta's head spun. She couldn't figure out her own self. Still, the other part of her desperately wanted to hack something to pieces. Something in her still wanted to defend her soul and her faith.

Where the Spirit of the Lord is, there is liberty. Aneta had to remind herself that she was a Child of the King. She was more than a conqueror.

Aneta finally drew her sword in front of her body, poised and positioned. Painfully, she remembered she was not wearing her helmet, the crown of her identity. Depression still had it. On top of not having the one piece of armor that would have given her a little more closure, she had not put on her breastplate that morning. While she did still have her shield, she had not practiced using a sword and a shield simultaneously in such a long time, so she didn't even bother pulling it from the strap on her back. She feared it would do her more harm than good.

Still, Failure still stood before her, and she had to fight even if she only beheld two pieces of armor from her Father. Clad in only her shoes and her belt which held her sheath, she said, "God knows all things. He judges me, not you. If He is fine with me, *I'm* fine with me. Now I'm done with you, and I never want to fight any of you again."

She lunged for Failure, but the chief demon simply chortled, side stepped, and walked away without any further tauntings.

Aneta stood there, feeling foolish and dumbfounded. Almost immediately, her mind filled with past memories. Her young self had loved a good sword fight, challenging anyone who dared to insult God. She had always entertained her sword skills. She had always strived to leave no stone unturned. Now, while her arms and feet easily engaged in a proper sword fight, her thoughts stopped short. Without putting up a fight, Failure simply left while she did nothing. How on earth was she supposed to fulfill what her Father had called her to do? Would there ever be a time when Depression would feel like giving back her crown?

Aneta spotted the old homeless woman she had already met twice that day across the street.

"Oh I saw her at the diner and the park. Do you know her?" Aneta subtly motioned in the elderly lady's direction.

Courage looked. "No, I've seen her though. There are a handful of homeless people around. Hey, maybe God would have us reach out to them."

The actual thought of going out and trying to minister on the sidewalk made Aneta uncomfortable. She had successfully and subtly changed the subject, but it had still gone where she did not want to go. She was tired of trying to reach out; tired of working. "Yeah, maybe."

As Aneta and Courage walked through town on the warm fall day, Courage told Aneta about the town, Aphoticton, even though everyone called it Whimsicalton. There was one church that she knew of in the entire town, and it was small. It stood on the east side of town near all the farms. Courage went there on Sundays and Wednesdays. There were only about fifteen people who actually attended the church.

After letting a car pass, they crossed the road, and Courage pointed out a few more things. One thing about which Courage cautioned Aneta was Gray's Cafe.

Aneta nodded, "I figured that out."

Many people stared or glared at Courage's crown, but Courage did not seem affected by it. She held her head high and strode with confidence. Courage looked so strong and ready for anything, with her shining shield on her back and her sword on her hip.

Aneta began to wonder what to do about her own crown. She did not even have it anymore. What was she supposed to do? Could she still do God's bidding without it? Aneta wanted to hope, but something told her it would not end well.

The apartment in which Courage stayed was decent. After giving Aneta the quick tour around the small area, Courage suggested they share it until Aneta could rent her own. Aneta felt intimidated already, and did not necessarily want to live with Courage's boldness.

"Oh, no, it's fine!" Courage smiled. "You won't be imposing at all. I'm just thankful for God sending you. There are lots of people who need help here. Maybe that's why God encouraged you to come here. He knows exactly what Aphoticton needs."

Aneta nodded, lost in thought. She wondered how well she could help people, having been lost herself for so long. Her mind also began to wonder why God had called her to Aphoticton. Why was she there? How long would it be until she knew *what* she was specifically fighting for? How had she been so foolish as to take off her crown in the first place?

Aneta slept in Courage's apartment and walked to work with her on Friday morning. Courage had to start at seven, and Aneta was welcome to stay for the day, or to go back to the apartment. Helpful was filing paperwork when Courage and Aneta showed up. Courage hugged Aneta goodbye and headed for the janitorial closet.

Meanwhile, Helpful beckoned to Aneta. "I was able to talk to Mr. Seem because he happened to come by right before I left. Mr. Seem immediately said if you want, you have a job here. The job is yours if you want it."

"Oh!" Aneta widened her eyes in amazement. "That would work marvelously!"

Helpful smiled, "oh, they will be quite pleased. It is hard to get good workers nowadays."

"They?"

"Mr. Seem and Mr. Not, the owner and manager."

Aneta paused.

"Broken is their sister," Helpful said.

Aneta nodded in remembrance. "I see. So...the Inn is in Broken's family. Right. Okay. Small town."

With a laugh, Helpful said, "I suppose. Well, the soonest you can start is Monday." She hesitated. "You know, why don't I ask Courage if she could give you orientation? That would speed things up."

Aneta followed Courage her entire shift. Leisurely, they chatted while Courage worked, with the occasional "I make sure to get under the nightstand" or "always check behind the dresser."

She went to sleep that night in a good mood, but she still had questions. Why was she in Aphoticton? What was she supposed to do? And there was the one burning question that made Aneta nervous. Would she be able to carry out God's work appointed to her?

|Chapter 3: Try|

"I've thought about it." Depression leaned against the wall, holding Aneta's crown. "And...if you would like, you can borrow this today. Just, you know, so you know we are on good terms."

Aneta gave him a face.

"Just an *offer*." Depression shrugged and smiled innocently. "You know, I don't have anything against you. Really. As soon as you don't need me, I'm gone. I'm just trying to help, and since I'm feeling helpful, I will lend you this crown."

Still not saying a word, Aneta ignored his confusing, contradicting comment and got ready to go.

"Are you sure?" Depression prodded.

"*Yes*." Aneta could not hide her exasperation. "Keep it."

"I'm...just *tired* of trying, God." Aneta half muttered to herself.

She grabbed her purse and headed outside where Courage was waiting. It was Sunday morning, so Aneta had borrowed some clothes from Courage and they both walked to the little church near the edge of town.

Courage had been right. The church was small. There were few people gathered in the sanctuary, making the little church almost look oversized compared to the occupants of the pews. A chorus of aged voices filled the air as the congregants began to sing. Aneta glanced around.

Everyone was wearing armor, but she noticed some people were missing a piece or two. Still, some only wore one piece of armor. Nevertheless, Aneta was more interested in their crowns. The pastor wore a crown, along with another woman who was probably his wife. Their armor was as shined and polished as Courage's. Most of the rest of the members of Whimsicalton Church wore crowns except for one man. He didn't wear a crown at all. There was also a woman wearing a large hat with her shield by her side, except Aneta couldn't tell if the woman wore a crown or not.

The pastor preached a sermon and ended the service at eleven sharp, having no extra comments beyond his notes. One or two members approached Aneta and Courage after the service, one of them being the pastor's wife. They talked for a little bit, then left.

Aneta had expected to feel convicted about wearing her crown after visiting there, but Whimsicalton Church did nothing of the sort. Subtly, she was disappointed.

She and Courage walked back to the apartment.

"So...that is the *only* church here in Aphoticton?" Aneta clarified,

Courage nodded. "The only one." She paused for a moment. "Aneta...are you okay?"

Surprised at the question, Aneta wrinkled her eyebrows and wondered if something was wrong. "Oh. Yeah...why?"

"Are you sure?" Courage raised her eyes to the top of Aneta's head,

At that moment, Aneta realized why Courage was concerned. Aneta hesitated. Her ears reddened and a lump formed in her throat. Her first thought was to make up a story, but that idea quickly faded. Aneta would have rathered to keep the fact hidden, but Courage seemed so genuine and understanding.

"Yeah...I just, um, well I have a hard time with the looks. I...don't even know how you handle it." Aneta's cheeks burned as she quickly looked at the ground, not liking her ridiculous excuse.

Courage gave her a little side hug. "I did that too."

That was it. She did not go any further. Aneta acknowledged that and felt like Courage was a true friend.

But then Depression caught up to Aneta. "Hey! See what I told you?"

Aneta half expected Courage to see Depression, but even she did not see him next to her.

Annoyed, Aneta turned her attention to Depression. "*What* did you tell me?"

"You should have borrowed my crown. You know...I can't believe you. What does Courage actually think right now?"

Aneta glanced back at Courage, who still did not see Depression next to them. "What are you talking about?" Aneta was already done with the conversation, and it had just gotten started.

"I try and *try* to help you, but you refuse. When are you going to learn? When are you going to *grow up*? When are you going to be an adult? You sure look it, but you never act like it."

Depression rattled on, and Aneta's heart sank in agony. His words grated on her ears, but she could find no actual reason to tell him to leave.

"I have nothing more to say," Depression concluded. "But. I do have a message from someone else."

"From...who?"

"Pain. He says he owes you this." Depression pulled out a dagger and stabbed her in the gut.

Aneta gasped, then gagged as she clutched her stomach. Again, she had not worn her breastplate that morning. She regretted that.

Depression roughly yanked it out again, and then waved it as he talked. "I don't know his reason...but who am I to ask? You never listen to me, or to any of us. Failure has a hard time keeping you in check, and Fear loses you sometimes...you had it coming." Even though he knew Courage did not see him, Depression cheerfully gave a mocking salute to her, and walked away.

Even though Courage could not see Depression or his knife, she noticed Aneta's wound.

As Aneta hastily staggered over to the wall of a building to sit against, Courage worryingly said, "are you okay? Aneta?"

Squeezing her eyes shut, Aneta waited a moment before replying, only keeping one hand over her stomach. "Thanks, Courage. But, uh..." she held back a moan. "It...just hurts sometimes."

"What hurts?" Courage asked.

Aneta slightly exhaled. "I don't know how to explain..."

"I'm sorry, Aneta." Courage tried to find the right words to say. "I'm not sure...Father was always better at this. He knows exactly how to make you feel better." Courage smiled sympathetically. "Maybe you should talk to Him. But whatever it is, God still wants you *here* and you are still needed. And appreciated. If you don't feel that, go to Him. I'm not sure what you're struggling with, but...let me know if you need to talk to another human being." Courage laughed in an attempt to lighten the mood.

Amused by Courage's words, Aneta allowed a single chuckle, but soon returned to her sad state.

Later, when Courage was not around in the apartment, Aneta decided to talk with God. She pushed up her sleeves and began to wash the tiny pile of dishes. She started out with a few thoughts, telling God how annoyed she was at various things, but then continued out loud.

"I'm not seven sure why I'm here. You told me to come here, so I did. You said I was supposed to fight for Your Kingdom? What does that even mean? And now I don't know what to do. I'm...not even sure why You chose me? How could I possibly fulfill the position You set aside for me? Why isn't Courage doing it? She's been here longer, she's older, she has everything rolling for her already."

"Hello. How are you doing this evening?" Depression came in, with an unusually good mood, and leaned against the wall.

Aneta snapped a glare at him. Her stomach still throbbed in immense pain. "You stabbed me. How do you *think* I'm doing?"

"Oh please, don't hold that against me. That was Pain. But, if you ask me, I think you should just stop trying."

"Trying to do *what*?"

"Live. Breathe. Exist. Whatever you wanna call it. You are always trying and trying and never getting anywhere. It would be easier to just quit."

"I *can't* just quit." Aneta scoffed, but she began to worry. Depression had a way of twisting what she thought, often sounding like he was contradicting himself or making her sound like she was contradicting herself. He usually left her completely baffled. Nevertheless, she could not just quit life. That did not make sense.

"Well you *could*," Depression said. "Lots of people do. You say so yourself that you hate trying to keep going. You don't even *have* to, you know?"

Did she say she hated trying? Aneta did not know anymore.

"I mean, if you ask me," Depression pressed her, "why *not* just quit?"

"Funny notion." Aneta was never in the mood to hear his voice. "No. Go away."

Depression walked around, talking with his hands instead of leaving them in his pockets. "Oh, just *listen* already. Quitting is easy. Just...stop living and you're good. Think about it."

"I have." Aneta's words slipped out.

"Think about it more."

Aneta paused washing dishes and considered everything. Eventually, she dried her hands and propped open her Bible, looking for encouragement anywhere. She read: "*And the Lord, he it is that doth go before thee; he will be with thee, he will not fail thee, neither forsake thee: fear no, neither be dismayed.*"

She hesitated and sighed. Again, she asked God, "what am I supposed to do?"

Aneta thought about her crown. Seeing Courage wear it all the time made Aneta regret her decision to leave her own behind.

Suddenly, she looked up. "Now that I think of it...you're just the person I want to see."

At this statement, Depression eyed her in confusion. "I...never left? What do you mean?"

Aneta stood, unsheathing her sword at the same time. "I want my crown back."

Depression shrugged, then produced a contract from his pocket. With the swipe of her sword's tip, the contract lay in two pieces on the floor. Aneta pointed the sword at him and narrowed her eyes, biting off each word as she repeated her statement.

"I. Want. My. Crown. Back."

"It's mine." Depression's voice showed no worry, but as he spoke those words, he moved out of the way.

As he did so, two demons, hidden until that moment, charged at Aneta.

Aneta gasped and ducked, surprised by the attack.

That made her rethink her objective. Was her crown worth it? Would Courage say anything about it if she put her crown back on? Courage had seemed to let it go earlier, but would there be an 'I told you so' look on her face? Aneta's mind filled with possible scenarios. What if she put it back on, only to take it off again as soon as people looked at her? That would be more humiliating than not having it on in general.

Even though she knew God would forgive her, Aneta still struggled. With a groan, Aneta rested her eyes for a moment, tired of fighting with herself. She was done fighting in general.

"God, I'm...*so* done." A sigh escaped again. "I've...fought my *entire* life until I was sixteen. Well, you know, my entire spiritual life. And...I am just *so* done. Trying is so hard and so annoying. I feel like I try and try and try without getting anywhere. And then when I was little, I would try and try and You would encourage me to keep going. So I would. But then I would keep trying and nothing ever seemed to progress. I *hate* just *trying* to fight. I hate trying to always win. It never feels like it's worth it.

Even as she spoke, partly to herself and partly to God, she knew she was wrong. She had paused her thoughts only for a moment when God seemed to tell her to keep going.

It is worth the world *to Me.*

Aneta sat and let the words seep in. She remembered a verse she had learned in Sunday school as a kid; in many cases, she had been the only one who memorized the weekly verse.

But thou, O Lord, the verse said, *art a shield for me; my glory, and the lifter up of mine head.* Aneta nodded to herself as she acknowledged the scripture.

Aneta's shield kept the demons away from her face. She flung them off, leaving the two black demons to claw the air in anger. Their shadowy forms twisted in mid air and landed on all fours. As soon as one of them touched the floor, she plowed her sword though one demon's head, and horizontally struck the other one. Both vaporized. Swiftly and skillfully, Aneta sluing her shield to her back, and turned her focus to the one who still held her precious crown, her identity.

Determined, Aneta marched up to Depression as he attempted to slip out the door and grabbed him by his shoulder with her free hand. She shoved him against the wall, and then grabbed her crown from his clutches. He proved to be too shocked to put up a fight.

"I will take this, thank you." Aneta immediately placed her crown on her head. "I no longer need your services, and I have *never* needed your services. Goodbye and stay away. I am God's Child, and I am keeping my crown."

Depression finally regained his composure. He placed his hand on the doorknob. "Aneta...I hope you realize this means war. You opened a valve you can't shut."

"You have messed with a Child of God. I hope *that* means something to you."

"Alright." With a deep breath, Aneta nodded. "Alright, God. I'll try. I'll try to do what you request."

|Chapter 4: Trouble At The Cafe|

On Monday morning, Aneta got up early and set out her armor, getting ready to clean it. She shined her shoes and polished her metal. There was a little something inside of Aneta that congratulated her on performing the small task. Her lips twisted into a small smile. When she straightened from bending over on the floor, Aneta gave a sigh of contentment. Now she was ready for the day.

However, as she walked to work with Courage, she realized she had forgotten to read her Bible that morning. She would have to do that at lunchtime.

Aneta worked with Courage from seven until noon, then walked back to the apartment by herself. Courage still worked until five. She had to fill in for someone else because Not and Seem were hosting an even at the inn.

As Aneta walked, she thought about Broken's brothers. Not and Seem bothered her. How could they toss their little sister aside? Broken was only a teenager, only a few years younger than herself. She did not know if Broken's parents were still around or where Broken lived. Did she live with her older brothers? What was her living condition? She hoped someone would be able to help Broken.

When that thought crossed her mind, she began to wonder again about why God called her to Aphoticton. "God, what am I supposed to do here?" She muttered to herself, half hoping God would audibly answer her right then and there.

After a moment, she pursed her lips. She decided to talk to Broken when she could. Aneta hoped to speak a word of encouragement to her.

From what she heard, Broken spent a lot of time at the inn, and Aneta was working there again the next day. There was a good chance she could meet up with the troubled girl.

Eventually, after rehearsing a little pep talk and failing to even satisfy herself, she wondered if she should bother at all.

When Aneta glanced up from the sidewalk, she blinked in alarm. Broken was on the sidewalk, heading towards her, head down and earbuds in. Slightly nervous, Aneta stopped when she was close enough and said hello.

Broken looked up and took out one earbud. "Hi." She seemed more addled than anything. "What are you doing here?"

"What are you doing *here*?" Depression, who was walking at Broken's side, hissed at Aneta.

Aneta bit her lip. She was not entirely sure she was up for the task. "Move." She tried her best to sound like she knew what she was doing. If only she had cleaned and sharpened her sword that morning! "I want to talk to Broken."

"Well *she* doesn't want to speak to you. What do you want?" Depression's agitated tone sounded more irritated now.

Placing her hand on her hilt, she flattened her eyebrows. In a serious voice, she said, "let me talk to Broken."

Depression smirked. A dagger appeared in his hand, and he lunged at Aneta.

Aneta opened her mouth, but she was in too much of a hurry to avoid the blade to actually inhale. Instead, she sharply exhaled as she whipped her shield in front of her body in defense. The dagger clanked off the unyielding metal. As soon as she could, Aneta lifted her sword and struck back at Depression. It was difficult though. She hadn't touched her sword in a while, and she had almost forgotten how to properly handle her sword *and* shield while fighting. He was swift and agile, cunningly avoiding all of her attacks. They were at a standstill though, neither of them getting the upper hand.

Breathless, Depression said, "*no one* speaks to her without my permission. I have that right." Depression snarled. "You only speak lies to her."

"I'm not the one speaking lies!" Aneta began to pant herself. She was not nearly as practiced as she used to be.

"What do you mean?" Aneta slightly tilted her head, wondering what Broken meant by her odd question of what she was doing there.

Broken did not answer.

"Do you...want to get something at the bakery? Or the diner or...are you hungry for an early dinner?" Aneta cringed at her horrible conversation making skills.

"Wait." Broken stepped forward, seeing Aneta was struggling.

Depression glared at the teenager, obviously annoyed.

"I mean, if she wants to talk, then...she can talk. Why not?" Broken stepped closer to Aneta.

With a ghastly look, Depression stood motionless, wondering why Broken simply walked past him without his given permission.

Aneta sheathed her sword again, catching her breath.

Broken shyly smiled at her. "Actually...there *is* a cafe I really like."

"That works." Aneta shrugged, congratulating herself in successfully planning something with Broken.

Aneta's heart sputtered a little when the two of them had walked down the sidewalks and ended up at a cafe. The cute, familiar cafe sign reading *Gray's Cafe* taunted her.

Struggling to keep a relaxed expression, Aneta gave a single nod to herself and followed Broken inside. *God, give me strength and wisdom.*

As Aneta walked inside, she shuddered. Half of her rejoiced that she was wearing her crown, but her other half shrunk in fear. Demons were walking around, probably scanning the perimeter inside. Another one was hovering over a booth with two men who were conversing. Others were simply watching the slow activity in the cafe and occasionally moved about. Nevertheless, when they spotted her, they scowled. One took a step towards her, threatening her with a murmuring growl.

She spotted one customer who looked familiar. Then she recognized his brilliant green eyes. She had bumped into him at the inn the other day. He had seemed friendly at that point, but now, he just stared at her. His face showed little emotion. He wore a black suit coat with black jeans, one arm resting on the table, and the other holding a coffee cup handle. His black, sleek eyebrows hung over his glinting eyes. His black, ruffled and gelled hair almost perfectly matched the menacing darkness of which the demons were made. Black looked good on him, but it almost terrified Aneta.

In front of her, black fog, the same substance seemingly from which the demons were made of, crawled from the kitchen doors, seeping into the room. With a deep breath to steady herself, Aneta kept walking. If that was where Broken wanted to go, she had to go as well.

Broken sat down at the counter as the barista, Advisor, walked out of the back kitchen. He smiled at her, but then saw Aneta standing there. He stared at her for a moment, motionless.

She stared back. Aneta then realized his eyes were on her crown. Aneta shifted uncomfortably. Her mouth dried up. She had not worn a crown the last time she was inside. Despite herself, she was thankful her armor was clean and stately.

When Aneta moved her gaze and sat down, Advisor did so as well. Nevertheless, Advisor then hinted at a small smile, seemingly knowing something that she did not. Advisor leaned on the counter, ready for the girls' orders.

"Aneta," Broken began, "this is Advisor. He helps me when I need to talk to someone.

"Nice to finally meet you...Aneta." His pause before saying her name made Aneta shiver. "I'm glad to know your name."

"You as well." That was the only answer Aneta could give.

She regretted walking into the place. Aneta knew she was in over her head. She should have thought it through first. *God, help me. Oh, please help me. I need you to be my strength, Jesus.*

"I would like my peppermint tea," Broken said, then turned to Aneta. "Do you want anything?"

"Um, I am...still deciding."

Advisor eyed aneta and left to fill Broken's order. Broken stood up. "I'll be right back. I'm going to the bathroom."

Aneta watched the teenage girl leave the counter. With Broken's peppermint tea in hand, Advisor slid back in front of Aneta.

"Aneta, I am so glad you are here." Everything in Advisor's voice sounded sarcastic in a smooth, subtle way. "You know, last time I saw you...you didn't wear *that*." The demon controlling the barista seemed to recognize her, and knew something that Aneta did not. With vicious hatred, the black, scaly demon stared at her with its featureless face. But it did nothing yet.

"What of it?" Aneta hoped she would make it out alive.

"I have been meaning to tell you something. Just so we're clear." He set down Broken's drink. "Broken is *mine*." When he spoke that, Aneta was almost certain the demon said it at the same time. "If you would like to keep your head, I suggest you don't come near her or this place. Understand?"

Knowing she could not let Advisor think he could win, Aneta replied with the best she had. "Why? Are you afraid of what I might do?"

With a stone-set face, Advisor carefully chose his words. "Oh. No. Just be afraid of what might happen to you."

Advisor said nothing more, but the demon standing over the barista spoke up. "He would hate to be responsible for another death."

Holding back the urge to run, Aneta simply lifted her chin at the demon's sly statement.

Broken came back and sat down, enjoying her peppermint tea. Aneta tried to converse with Broken the best she could.

Even so, Aneta found it hard to ignore the stares of other customers eyeing her crown. Advisor's demon, and other demons continually hissed or glared at her with the black faces of nothing. It chilled her to the bone. The black smoke swirling around her feet, floating from the air disruption, would have been in it of itself the only reason she would have had needed to stay away from the cafe in general. But Broken was there. And she needed to stay by Broken's side. But why was Broken oblivious to the demonic danger surrounding her and physically lurking beneath her feet? Did the other customers see it or simply ignore it?

As Broken finished her tea, Advisor came and picked up the cup. He secretly gave Aneta a hatred-filled death glare.

His warning left a mark. Aneta tried to keep a straight face. *Jesus, please keep me safe. Please show me that it was not a mistake to come here.*

With all she had, Aneta smiled at Broken. "Hey, almost ready to go? Oh! Can I get your phone number?"

"Yeah. Thanks for a good chat. We should do this again." Broken inserted her number into Aneta's contacts.

Aneta smiled again, but she felt Advisor's eyes boring into the back of her head as she and Broken headed for the door. "I haven't looked at my work schedule, but I think sometime in the next week should work. Hey Broken?"

"Yeah?"

Aneta leaned in for a hug. "I love you. I'll be praying for you too. See you soon." She gave Broken one last warm smile and headed back to the inn. She did not know how Broken would take her statement, but she had mostly said it to let Advisor know she was not going to give up on Broken.

Aneta got back to the apartment and started up the stairs. Lost in thought, she accidentally rammed into another young woman who was coming down. The book the woman had been holding tumbled down the steps.

"Oh. My. *Goodness*. I am so sorry!" Aneta apologized and scurried back down the stairwell to pick up the book. She glanced at the title. A Bible.

The young woman gently grinned as Aneta sheepishly handed over the Bible. "Thanks, but don't worry about it. My name is Faith."

"Aneta."

"Are you in these apartments too?"

"Uh, yeah. Well, technically. I...just moved to Aphoticton and I'm staying with my friend--her name is Courage--until I can afford my own apartment."

"Oh, cool. How do you like Aphoticton so far?"

Aneta paused. "You also call it Aphoticton? I thought everyone here called it Whimsicalton."

Faith shrugged. "They usually do. People have used that nickname for as long as I could remember, I think...but the name is Aphoticton. That's what my parents called it, so that's what I'm calling it. Mom said they only began to call it Whimsicalton in the last fifteen or twenty years. So how long have you been here?"

"Only the last few days."

"Ah, I see."

"I...have a question," Aneta began. "So...the Bible. You're a Christian? Do you go to church here?"

Faith shook her head. "I don't. I usually listen to online sermons on Sundays. They have one church here, and it isn't very good. We really need another good church here."

Aneta nodded in agreement. "Yeah, Courage and I went to that church and it's..." She felt embarrassed about her comment, so she left her sentence where it was. "You grew up here then? Was it always like that? As in, just one church?"

"Oh, no. No, when I was younger, we have at least three or five good churches around. But one by one they died out...well, one got sued for no reason and they couldn't pay it. Everyone other one, either the pastor was killed or run out, or retired, except for that last church, Whimsicalton Church. It used to be called Holy Hands Assembly, but probably a decade ago now, they were threatened. So they had to change their name or stop existing, so they just called it Whimsicalton Church. They lost half their members to...anything and everything. In other words, someone doesn't want any effective churches here."

"Oh...wow. That's really...sad. Actually. So you know lots of people here?"

"You could say that. But...why did *you* move to Aphoticton? You are a Christian as well?"

"Oh, absolutely." Aneta beamed, feeling much more comfortable talking with Faith. "Well, I'm...I moved here because God told me to come here. I'm not sure why though."

"What do you mean?"

Aneta playfully displayed an annoyed face. "Well, God told me to wait here until He tells me what to do."

Faith bobbed her head in understanding. "Ah, well, I have to say, that is His favorite game. What apartment are you in?"

"18."

"I'm in 3," Faith said. "I..think I've probably seen Courage once or twice. Haven't officially met. We could get together in my apartment for coffee or something sometime. Or lunch or dinner or something. I work at Chef Chava's, if you know where that is. I'm a cook there, so if you ever feel like it, we might be able to meet there...or any other place here in town. Here..." Faith flipped her Bible open until she found a paper note from another time. She wrote a phone number on the corner of the paper and tore off it off, giving it to Aneta.

"Call me if you figure out a good time to hang out. Or just call me in general," Faith laughed.

Aneta smiled. "Thanks, I'll let you know."

Faith gave a little wave and walked into her apartment. Aneta continued upstairs and promptly put Faith's number into her contacts.

On Tuesday, Aneta finally got around to cleaning her sword. She shined it twice over, and held it up to admire her work. Good as new. Satisfied, she slid it into her sheath, feeling confident about the day.

Aneta worked a morning shift at the inn, from seven to eleven. As she was in the lobby, checking her purse and getting ready to leave, Broken walked inside.

"Hi Broken!" She cheerfully greeted the teenager and gave a little wave.

"Hi Aneta." Broken was not as bubbly as Aneta, but she still smiled in a good mood. "So what are you doing here?"

"I work here. I'm just finishing my shift. You?"

Broken's mood dropped. She said flatly, "waiting for something that will probably never come. I have to ask Helpful if it's here yet."

"Are you--do you have plans after that?"

"Not...really. Why?"

"Do you *want* to do something? I heard there is a new movie coming out, and I kinda want to watch it. Do you want to go to the...11:30 showing?"

"Maybe."

"Okay...oh wait a second...I forgot my wallet in my locker. I'll be right back." Aneta hurried to the back and walked back to the lobby. Broken was still there at the desk, looking glum.

"Did you get what you were waiting for?"

Broken half rolled her eyes and half shrugged.

"Did you want to go to the movie?" Aneta did not want to push anything, but if they *were* to go to the movie, they had to leave immediately to make it in time for the next showing.

"Sure. Why not?" Broken shrugged again and led the way.

The girls watched the movie, and afterwards, Broken suggested they get lunch at Gray's Cafe. Feeling she should probably say yes, Aneta almost reluctantly agreed.

As they neared the cafe, Aneta's stomach began to twist. Advisor had clearly told her to stay away from both the cafe and

Broken. She was about to openly defy him, and she had no clue what Advisor could or would do to her. He had been pretty clear about what he *wanted* to do to her.

Jesus, I'm...kinda scared to be honest. This is a risk I don't usually take. Please...protect me. And Broken. I'm just trying to do something while I wait for Your instructions. As they walked down the sidewalk, Aneta did not stop pleading with God for her own safety.

Even though she never took it off, Aneta double checked to make sure her sword was still on her hip before walking into the cafe. Before walking in the door, she readjusted her crown, moved her braid to the back, and strode inside after Broken. A small part of her wanted to run when she saw the demons rasp at her, but seeing Broken without armor, a sword, or a shield, and knowing her's were in good shape, Aneta knew she should stay to at least protect Broken.

She and Broken sat down at the counter like last time.

Advisor walked out of the back, drying a cup with a towel. He smiled and then stopped in his tracks when he spotted Aneta sitting there as well. He only jerked his stare away from her when Broken greeted him.

"Hello, Advisor. Can I have one of those cupcakes? The one with the blue frosting?" Broken hinted at a smile.

"Sure." Advisor bent down and gave Broken the cupcake. He still glanced at Aneta, not showing any particular emotion. "Don't worry about paying for it. This one is on me today, Broken." At that statement, Aneta noticed Advisor had changed his mood for those two single comments. He seemed genuinely sweet about Broken's cupcake. But as soon as Aneta ordered, his mood soured again.

"Advisor," Aneta asked, "can I just have a cup of coffee please?"

He scarcely nodded and walked into the back to fill her order. He soon returned with a steaming cup of coffee and set it in front of her. Without acknowledging her thanks, he swiftly moved away to carry on with his other duties.

Aneta did not know if Advisor was nervous around her, or if he just decided to let it slide. But she did not mind Advisor staring at them the whole time.

"So Broken," Aneta made conversation, "how has your day been going so far? Have any plans for the rest of the day?"

Broken stared at her cupcake, then bit into it. "It's fine so far. I don't have anything planned after this, except for dinner at five-thirty."

Aneta proceeded to hang out with Broken the rest of the day. They went to a book shop--one of Broken's favorites--and Aneta bought a journal that Broken had admired. After that, they simply chatted the rest of the time, walking in circles around the park. Around five, the two girls parted ways, and Aneta went back to her apartment.

She smiled, it had been a good day.

Chapter 5: A Message From The King

As Aneta was walking back to the apartment from a full day with Broken, Courage called her, asking her to come in to help clean up after an event.

When Aneta made it back to the Whimsicalton Inn, Helpful was excited to see her. "Hi, Aneta! How was your day?"

Aneta smiled at her perky friend. "It went well. You?"

"Oh, just swell!" Helpful gave an authentic laugh. "Mr. Seem missed an appointment, and he yelled at me because I never sent him a reminder, even though he told me not to interrupt him during the awards event." She rolled her eyes. "Then, a bathroom flooded, and people were complaining at me. I missed lunch. Later, Mr. Not came here and got mad at me for something else..." Helpful laughed again and shrugged her shoulders as if all was well.

Aneta wrinkled her eyebrows. "So...how is that all...*swell?*"

"Well, because *you* took out Broken for her birthday! As long as I have known her, I have never seen her smile...when she was here, she was grinning almost the whole time, and then--well, her brothers ruined her birthday by planning a separate event today, and *that's* why she wasn't smiling when you came back, but the other day, she was here and just talking and talking about how much she enjoys chatting with you."

"Wait, wait! It's her *birthday?*"

Helpful's smile dampened. "You...didn't know? What were you *doing* all day?"

"Oh, I mean, yeah, we went to Gray's Café, watched a movie...we did stuff..."

"And you didn't *know* it was her birthday?"

"Well, no. Now I feel kinda bad..."

"Don't feel bad!" Helpful stood up and hurried around her desk to give Aneta a hug. "I don't think anyone has ever done that for her, and I think she knew you didn't know, which probably made it even better! You treated her so kindly without any special reason!"

Aneta blinked, as if still trying to comprehend everything. "It's her birthday?" she repeated.

"Yes. She's turning nineteen."

Aneta sighed wistfully. "Oh, my...well, I hope she truly enjoyed herself. I wish I could have said happy birthday."

"Oh, I am just so tickled pink that you spent the day with her!" Helpful smiled again, then sat back down. "Well, what do you have planned for the rest of the day?"

"Courage asked me to come in to help clean up. I think her other co-worker got sick."

Aneta and Courage, along with another co-worker, worked to finish cleaning up from the event, and finished around seven. Faith called Aneta as the two of them walked back to the apartment and asked if they had dinner already.

"No. Courage and I just got off work. What's up?"

"*I am meeting up with my brother and his friend at a Chinese buffet; the one right behind the post office.*"

Aneta glanced at Courage, who nodded in agreement. Aneta smiled, "I think that would be fun. What time?"

"*As soon as you can. They are headed there now and I'm leaving my apartment.*"

"Okay. We are almost to the apartments. Courage and I are going to change, then we will meet you there. Thanks for inviting us!"

"*Sure thing! See you soon!*"

Courage and Aneta rushed back, passing Faith on the way, and after throwing on a change of clothes, they hurried to the Chinese restaurant.

When they got there, it took them a moment to find Faith. However, Faith came up beside them and motioned them to their table.

Upon seeing the two boys at the table, Aneta's stomach twisted. She almost panicked.

Faith did not notice Aneta's countenance. "Boys, this is Courage and Aneta." She indicated which girl was which, then pointed to a young man with square features like her own, complete with thick, black hair. "Girls, this is Bold, my brother. He is twenty-six." Faith then motioned to the other young man. "This is Theo, Bold's friend. He is... twenty-four? Yes. Yes, he is my age. I remember now."

Courage smiled and gave a little wave to each of them as Faith introduced everyone, but Aneta had a hard time keeping an amiable face. She knew who Theo was. But she had only known him by the name of Coward. What was he doing here? Did he recognize her? Surely he did. It had only been a couple years.

Courage chatted for a moment with Bold and Theo before leaving the table to get food. Aneta hurried next to Courage, biting her lip. A small part of her raced in excitement. However, she tried to remain sensible and desperately wanted the night to be over. What would Theo say about her to Bold? Or Faith?

Courage leaned over, "Theo looked nervous. Did you notice?"

Feeling like Courage already knew, Aneta began to sour her mood. "Notice what?"

Courage grinned. "Maybe he saw someone who's cute."

Aneta whacked her. "That's not what I meant."

Still amused, her friend elbowed her. "I know, I know. But, no, he looked super pale when we walked up."

Shrugging, Aneta ignored the comment, hoping it would all go away very soon. Courage apparently did not seem to notice. That would surely change, but for better or worse, Aneta did not know.

The girls got back to the table and sat down. Bold and Faith conversed with ease, their conversation helping everyone else chat as well, but Theo seemed tense the entire night. Aneta knew he knew. Nevertheless, annoyance and anger took over her nervous thrill. After all those years, the rebellious boy had decided to become a Christian? Yet, even in her anger, Aneta thought she had felt relief. However, she was not sure from where that emotion originated. Finding herself flustered, Aneta excused herself and hid in the bathroom for a few minutes before composing herself again.

Aneta walked back to the table. Theo did not at all act like her previous engagement, but his physical appearance bothered her. He had cut his hair, taken out his piercing, and was wearing decent clothing. No skulls. She could not get over that.

In the end, Bold paid for everyone, insisting that it would be his pleasure, despite their protests. When the waitress picked up the bill, she shook her head in amazement. "You are all such wonderful friends, arguing over who pays."

Courage and Faith chuckled and for the first time, Aneta saw Theo smile in humor. Immediately seeing Aneta look at him, Theo's mood dampened again. At that point, Aneta realized he may have been in a bad mood because of her. Had she been giving him an evil eye the entire night without realizing it?

"This was fun!" Faith grinned. "All in favor of getting together again?" She raised her hand.

Courage lifted her hand along with Aneta, and Bold shot his hand up. They all walked home around nine that night.

"Are you okay, Aneta?" Courage asked once they were almost to the apartment.

Aneta shrugged. "I don't know...it was kinda weird. I'm not sure what to think. But...Theo reminds me of my ex-boyfriend." As soon as she said that, Aneta decided to tell Courage anyway. "Well. He was my boyfriend. Uh, Theo...uh, well I'm surprised that...he...looks and acts the way he does."

"Oh. Interesting. Is that why he looked nervous?"

"I think so." Aneta rubbed her forehead. "Um, I'm pretty sure he knows who I am. I mean my *name* never changed. Uh, but, uh, he was uh, quite rebellious. Not a Christian. At all." As Aneta began to describe her ex-boyfriend, she soon felt sheepish about sharing his life story, acknowledging it was not entirely hers to give. "Uh, but uh…"

"So how many years were you two dating?" Courage spared Aneta from finishing her thought.

"About three years." Aneta sighed in dismay. Deciding to let it out while it was still in her own control, Aneta said, "well…it was not specifically a secret that I was dating him…but I didn't really want anyone to know. I was actually missionary dating him. I mean, I knew it was a bad idea…but I was sure I could change him. But um…it actually went the opposite." Aneta lowered her voice as she ended her sentence. When Courage did not show any sign of harsh judgement, Aneta continued. "And…the day after we broke up, I…I suppose that was the day I left God."

"What?"

Aneta cringed. It was out. And Courage now knew her past. But to her own surprise, Courage's question was not judgemental or critical. It was soft, almost a whisper, when Courage folded her eyebrows together and gave Aneta a gentle questioning look.

Slumping her shoulders, Aneta then shrugged. "I only became a Christian again in these last few months."

Courage looked ahead. They walked for a few steps before she spoke again. "I'm sorry, I hope I'm not sounding rude or anything. I just…never knew. I'm…surprised, to be honest. Don't get me wrong, I'm not mad." She tried her best to explain. "I'm, I'm just…surprised. Just surprised. Is all. But…wow. So what if you end up doing lots of stuff together? I mean…Theo is friends with Bold and Faith, and you just raised your hand meaning you are still wanting to get together like we just did…"

"Yeah. Um, I *hope* not. C-Theo didn't raise his hand when Bold asked everyone if they wanted to hang out again. so…Im hoping he won't be there next time? I don't know. I'm…kinda nervous about if he will tell Bold or Faith something."

"Like what?"

"I don't know."

Courage wrinkled her mouth in a cute way as she unlocked the apartment door. "Well, I'm not sure what to say to all that, to be honest. But maybe pray about it? Maybe God would like you to do something about it?"

Feeling slightly overwhelmed, Aneta nodded.

In the morning, Aneta and Courage both stepped outside, their mouths exhaling small clouds. They decided to leave early and buy coffee before work.

Aneta told Courage about her day with Broken. Since they were on the topic of Gray's Cafe, Aneta asked about the atmosphere there.

"Why is it so...so..."

"Creepy? Alarming? Disturbing?"

Aneta nodded, "Yeah. And why doesn't Broken see it? She says she goes there all the time. It is one of her favorite places, and I have a feeling that I'm going to end up there. A lot."

Courage thought about it. "Well, maybe God wants you here to help others fight battles they don't know how to fight."

"What do you mean by that?"

"I don't know Broken very well. Helpful says she is adopted, feels left out, unaccepted, et cetera. Maybe Broken...doesn't know how to stand up because she has been knocked down too many times. Maybe God wants you to help her back up."

"But how am I supposed to do that?"

As Courage shared her own experience with that type of situation, Aneta saw the elderly homeless lady from before.

"Hey, Courage. Look, that is the woman that came into Lyle's Diner."

"Why don't we invite her to coffee with us?"

Aneta agreed with the snap decision, and they both introduced themselves.

"We are going to get coffee. At Gray's Cafe." The last phrase Courage added with a hurried tone, just deciding where they were going to go. Aneta gave her friend a look, but Courage kept talking. "And we would like to buy you a coffee as well."

"Oh, well, well...well, well." The elderly woman kept wringing her hands and stuttering, trying to hide a big smile. She finally found her words. "Well, thank you. They call me Biddy."

"Hello, Biddy." Courage smiled and set the old woman in between the two girls, still ignoring the look from Aneta.

"If they call you Biddy, then what is your real name?" Aneta asked, focusing on the elderly woman.

"Oh." She waved her hand in front of her face. After a moment, she said, "Lovely. My name was Lovely."

"Well, it's nice to meet you, Lovely. Have you ever been to Gray's Cafe?" Aneta eyed Courage, silently asking why they were going there, of all places.

"I don't believe so."

"Well, they have good coffee." Knowing she had to be truthful, Aneta said they had good coffee. And it was good. When she had a cup when she was there with Broken, it was some of the best coffee she ever had, only the atmosphere ruined her experience. Still, Aneta shot Courage another questioning glance.

They made small talk until getting to the cafe. Aneta took a deep breath to prepare herself and opened the door for Courage and Lovely. There was a woman behind the counter this time. She stood ready with a notepad and a pencil as they approached a table.

After sitting down, the three of them ordered coffee. As the waitress filled their cups, Advisor walked out with a tray of clean coffee mugs. He saw Aneta and froze. He leaned over to their waitress and whispered something in her ear.

Courage was busy talking to Lovely, but Aneta looked at Advisor the whole time. The waitress walked over with two coffees, set them down, and walked away. Advisor delivered the third cup, which was Aneta's, and remained at the table.

"You're Aneta, right?"

Aneta nodded. She kept her facial expression open, but she wondered if something would go wrong.

"You...remember last time you had coffee here? With Broken?"

"Yes."

Advisor rubbed his hands, looking around. He finally left their side. Courage pointed a thumb at him, and Aneta shrugged. She inwardly sighed in relief. But it did not last.

A man walked into the cafe and sat down on the barstool at the counter on a far end. He ordered a coffee and steadily turned his head, looking straight at Aneta. She almost visibly shivered at the sight of his brilliant green eyes. The villainous man wore the same attire as before: a gray shirt, a black suit coat, black jeans, and shiny black shoes. As before, every shade of black he wore perfectly matched his pitch black hair, still styled the same way. After almost glaring at Aneta for what seemed like an eternity, the man received his coffee, and ceased looking at her after that.

However, she saw Advisor whisper to the waitress again, then disappear through the back. After a few minutes, the waitress came around, refilling coffee.

She addressed Aneta. "Are you Aneta?"

"Yes."

"My name is Dr. A. Theist. I am Advisor's wife. Are you feeling okay?"

Aneta looked at Courage with an odd face. She stiffened her back. "Yes. Why do you ask?"

"*Have* you been feeling well? The whole day yesterday too?"

"Yes...is there a problem?"

Dr. A. Theist said "no" multiple times before leaving.

"What was *that* about?" Courage asked.

Aneta shrugged. "I have no idea."

As she left their table, the man with the brilliant green eyes stood up and left without paying. Aneta wondered if she had missed his payment and she was just being skeptical now.

After spending as much time as they could without being late to work, Courage and Aneta bade goodbye to Lovely and hurried to their job.

After talking with Courage and Aneta, Faith decided to go to Whimsicalton Church with the girls, as well as Bold and Theo, for the Wednesday night Bible study. Theo once again seemed overly nervous around Aneta, but it seemed to fade away as the minutes went by. Aneta herself had been slightly awkward, but she forgot about that when she looked over the sanctuary. There was a person there she had not seen on Sunday.

Despite being about seven feet tall, he still sat with a straight posture. Even though Aneta had not seen him there before, he looked confident and well acquainted with the service. However, his odd, pitch-black hair clashed with his pale white skin. When the Bible study finished, people began to leave, but the towering man walked up to the group of young people when they were in the parking lot.

"Hello, how are you this evening?" He shook their hands, starting with Theo and going around the circle. "Did you enjoy the study?"

"Oh. It was good." Faith replied.

There was not much to say about the service.

The man nodded. "Well, Theo. I actually have a message for you from the King."

Theo visibly stuttered, turning his head in the man's direction, wondering what that could possibly mean.

"God wants you to build a good church here. You saw this church. Aphoticton needs help. God is calling you for the task. And now He has sent Aneta and yourself to start the job."

"A-a church?" Theo repeated. He stole a glance at Aneta.

Aneta's eyes widened at the man's statement. She failed to see Theo look at her.

"Yes. God has chosen you. Do not worry about your qualifications. The King has already taken care of it. Be of good courage. Do not fear what lies ahead, rather, run the course to the best of your ability." With that, he bowed his head, turned and left.

The young people standing there stared. Bold and Faith stared at each other, Courage and Aneta stared after the man had left, and Theo stared at his shoes.

Faith was the first to speak. "Are you going to build a church?"

"I don't know." Theo gave something that resembled a horrified look and began to leave.

Everyone else followed behind him in silence. Once on the sidewalk, Bold smacked Theo on the back. "Come on. God wants *you* to build a church? I'm jealous. That is one amazing task."

Theo shoved his hands in his pockets and thought about it as the group walked along.

Bold said, "Hey, man, we're right here along with you."

"But, you see, I *can't*. I don't have any experience in planting churches or... or talking to people about Him or... or business and finances, or... look. Bold. I can't *lead* a church, okay? It would fail miserably."

He glanced at Aneta, who also happened to be glancing at him at the same time. He gave her a subtle face, but Aneta couldn't tell what it meant. They both looked down.

With a quiet voice, Faith spoke up with her calm attitude. "Theo, by God's grace you are here. God called *you* and Aneta. He does not call you because of what you can do to plant a church; He calls you because of what you are *willing* to do, whether or not you physically can. He will do the rest."

"Don't worry about any details," Courage added. "As you go along, He will put everything into place for you. You just gotta listen to Faith; she's got a point."

Theo glanced up at Courage, then glanced behind her. He gave a single, silent chuckle, seeing Bold stick his thumbs in the air in quiet, reserved excitement.

"Alright, I'll think about it." Theo shrugged the whole thing off.

"That's better." Courage smiled. "But I know your answer." The group began to part ways to their separate apartment buildings. "Good night, boys."

Faith glanced at Aneta. "You okay?"

"I...think I agree with Theo. I can't...*lead* a church! And lead with Theo? I hardly even *know* Theo!" She gave Courage a look that reminded her friend of their conversation the night before. She did *not* want to work with Theo. Did she?

"Don't worry about that." Courage waved off the issue. "Just focus on what God wants. Now you know why God sent you here. You *have* to accept. Bold, Faith, and I are here and ready to help."

Aneta sighed. "I don't know. I just...don't know..."

|Chapter 6: Broken And Aneta|

When Aneta started work on Thursday morning, she was busy thinking about planting a church. It seemed like too big of a task. How could it be accomplished? How would they find a building? And musicians? And people? Would Theo be the one to give sermons? She almost scoffed.

"Aneta!"

Aneta looked up, seeing Broken running for her with a big, excited grin. "Guess what! Guess what! Not and Seem *gave me presents* and they even *apologized* for not being able to do anything *on Tuesday* because they were busy and they forgot, but like, their surprise party last night made up for all of it! And they made me breakfast for dinner! I have never seen them even trying to make toast, but it wasn't burnt, so that was good." Broken giggled. "Fair didn't even help them or anything! And then they gave me such cute presents! Not gave me a kitten, and then Seem gave me an amazing book series and..." She sighed deeply. "I had the *best* belated birthday." She hugged Aneta again. "Oh! Here...let me text you my address. Can you come over tonight?"

"I'd have to look. But I probably can. Is there-"

"I want to show you something! And Fair will have dinner ready by 5:30."

Theo exited March Coffee, a coffee shop across the street from his job. He noticed an elderly woman who sat at the table outside of the shop. It was cold out. Why would she simply be sitting there without any drink?

"Are you lost, ma'am?"

She looked up, saying, "Oh, no; I am quite alright."

Theo glanced at his coffee, then at the white haired woman. "Are you sure? Do you need anything?" Without an answer, he handed her his coffee cup. "Here, take it anyway. I didn't drink from it or anything."

The narrow face full of wrinkles lit up in delight. "Oh, oh my...oh my. Thank you so much, young man!" She gratefully took the hot cup and clutched it tightly.

Theo walked back inside, re-ordered his coffee, and bought two pieces of pie as well. He brought them out to the old woman, sitting down on the cold chair.

She began to tear up when she realized the other slice of pie was for her.

"Oh my. It's just like my girls used to do. They used to bake the day away. Always had pie on hand."

"Where are they now?"

"Oh, I haven't seen them in years." Her watery eyes closed. "I have four daughters and a truly handsome husband. Well...I *had* a handsome husband. But he grew abusive, and I ran away with the girls. And now here I am."

Theo shifted uncomfortably as the old lady's voice thickened with emotion and she began to share her backstory.

"The girls and I lived here, but Cheer was in a car accident. She died."

"Oh-h. I'm sorry."

"And my other three girls got married and moved away. I haven't seen them since...since...well, it has been quite a while. Well, thank you for this pie. It tastes so good. I can't wait to bake when I have a house again."

"Are you at an apartment right now?"

"Heavens, no! I hurt myself on the job years ago. After I rehabilitated, I could not get another job. I lived off my retirement money for a while, but my bank account was hacked. I couldn't afford my house or even an apartment."

Theo's throat tightened as he studied the weathered lines and wrinkles of an old woman living an old life. Her tired eyes and worn arms showed the prolonged strain of an exhausting life with no shelter. "Oh, I see. What is your name?"

"My name is Lovely, but most people call me Biddy. Young man, you have made my day." She cheerfully smiled. "What is your name?"

"Theo."

"Good to meet you, Theo. How is it that I get to meet such a wonderful young man? I am so lucky. Someone just bought me coffee yesterday too." The woman sighed. "It is nice that you have someone in your life who cares for you."

Slightly distracted, Theo nodded.

Aneta looked over her shoulder as Courage brought in the laundry and began to fold it on the couch. Courage's expression told Aneta something was wrong. Aneta wondered if she should ask about it. It was possible she could help Courage with the issue by which she was bothered, but Aneta was unsure. Courage was much older than her, and much more experienced.

Aneta sighed and glanced behind herself again, then turned fully to face the conflict her friend was dealing with. Aneta gave a small, helpless moan, knowing she should help, but felt like anything she could offer would be useless.

Courage pushed another demon off of her chest and cracked another head, letting it vaporize into nothing. With a grunt, she swung her sword and knocked a demon against the wall. She kicked it in the head and it disappeared. She did not look at Aneta, completely focused on what she was doing.

With a gulp, Aneta turned around again, letting her hand hover over her sword's handle. Should she help Courage? Did she *need* to help Courage? If Aneta decided to step in, she would have to interfere with those demons that were attacking Courage. With a look of defeat on her own face, Aneta decided not to do anything. If she did decide to help Courage, she might do more damage by getting in the way. It was better not to risk it.

With pursed lips, Aneta decided not to do anything. If Courage wanted help, she could ask. If not, Aneta had nothing to do with Courage's problems. Aneta convinced herself

Courage knew what she was doing. She finished the dishes and quietly slipped into her room.

Aneta got a text from Courage, saying that she was not feeling well, but they needed groceries. Aneta grabbed her purse and put on her shoes at the door. The pile of laundry was only half-folded, and Courage's door was closed. Looking forward, Aneta walked to the store with the grocery list.

When she stepped inside, Theo was at the checkout. She immediately felt disdain, but checked herself. After a moment of hesitation, she knew she should at least be polite.

"Hi." She gave a single wave as she walked up to him. She wanted to use the name Coward, but decided against it.

Theo looked up. When he saw her, he looked slightly alarmed. "Hi."

"Have you...thought about if you're going to accept?"

"Have you?" He sounded closed.

"Well, yes. But-"

"Look. On top of everything, how could He want me to build a church? He *knows*, yet He still decided to rub it in my face and ask if I wanted to *build a church!* It's ridiculous!" When Aneta did not immediately reply, Theo scowled. "You don't think I can do this."

"I am thinking nothing of the sort. Don't put words into my mouth."

Dropping a cereal box inside a plastic bag, he looked down. "I'm serious! I barely have enough money to pay rent *here,* much less try and go out and witness to a bunch of heathens. I simply *can't* build a church, and I don't have the time anyway, or the resources."

"Like it or not, you were a heathen yourself!" Aneta shot back her reply, using his own terminology. Nevertheless, she could not help but see herself as a heathen as well.

Theo's rage burned. "I know!"

"You should..." With a fierce look in her eyes, Aneta scowled. "You know, maybe you *can't* actually build a church.

Maybe Father has to get someone else who is more able than you." Her red face now matched Theo's countenance.

Theo glared at her, grabbed his two grocery bags, and left the store. Uncomfortable, the cashier took back Theo's receipt that he left behind and slowly put it in the trash can. The other customers around them cleared their throats and continued their own business.

Aneta clutched her grocery list and walked through the store. The more she thought about it, the more she realized how much she wanted to put a light in Aphoticton. She desperately wanted to reach out. However, the more she thought about it, the more she felt like it was an impossible task. She began to rethink her own decision about accepting the calling of building a church. Bogged down with numerous contradicting thoughts, Aneta tried to busy her mind with something else.

In the middle of the cereal aisle, Aneta realized something else. That was the reason God had called her to Aphoticton. She was supposed to put a good church in that city. She exhaled. It seemed slightly insane. Her thoughts hung in the balance. She now stood indecisive. Again.

Aneta swallowed. With butterflies in her stomach, she walked up the white porch, decorated with beautiful pillars. After timidly ringing the beautiful-sounding doorbell, a man wearing a suit and a bow tie answered.

"Good evening."

"I'm Aneta. Uh, Broken told me to, uh...she invited me to hang out...here for dinner...which is at 5:30? I'm a little late."

The man smiled. "Ah, yes. Welcome, Miss Aneta. We were expecting you."

Aneta slowly entered. The man closed the door behind her. She gently slipped off her shoes. Intimidated, Aneta looked in awe at her luxurious surroundings, slightly fearful that anything she touched would break. She had gone to the address Broken had given her and found herself in front of a large house in a rich neighborhood. It took a moment for her to realize that

Broken's brothers owned the Whimsicalton Inn. What did Broken's parents do? Was the man who met her at the door the butler or her father?

"Broken will be down shortly," the man said.

Aneta smiled. The man was polite and respectful, but not in a highly sophisticated way that made her feel inferior. Rather, he displayed a loving attitude that showed Aneta she was welcome in the household.

From somewhere in a nearby room, a woman called out, "Diligent! Is she here?" A woman wearing a white apron and a dress appeared. Her plump figure made Aneta smile. She immediately liked her. The woman gasped daintily at Aneta.

"Oh, you must be Aneta. Good to meet you! My name is Fair. I will be pulling dinner out of the oven shortly...didn't burn it yet." She gave a small wink. "Even if I did get a little distracted getting caught up on laundry."

Fair hurried across the room and into an adjoining room. Aneta followed her into the kitchen, not wanting to stay by herself in the living room. She was almost positive now that she'd just met the butler and the housemaid.

"Are Broken's parents here today?" Aneta asked.

Fair pulled on oven mitts. "Oh, they aren't here at all. Mr. and Mrs. Operose died several years ago."

Aneta gasped, "Oh my! I am so sorry."

"It's quite alright." Fair smiled at her. "I can't believe Broken has finally found someone she looks up to other than us."

With a friendly smile, Diligent, the butler, set water on the table. "Broken has been a sorry sight for years. I have never seen her more ambitious than during these past few days."

Aneta smiled, beginning to feel more comfortable. "Well, I'm very blessed, so I figure it is nice to share." She felt bad for not specifying who blessed her. Could she really start a church with a timid attitude like that?

Fair gasped, putting a hand over her heart, "Oh, bless your heart many times over! God always knows what He is doing."

Aneta almost felt like crying. "Thank you." She had neglected to speak of her Father, yet Fair had brought out the truth.

Fair continued to talk until Broken came bounding down the stairs.

"Hi, Aneta!" She plopped down next to her at the table. "I'm so glad you're here. After dinner, I want to show you what I've been doing upstairs."

Aneta smiled in relief. Everything seemed to be working out okay.

After dinner, Broken promptly led Aneta up the stairs. Aneta kept her arms by her sides, feeling small in the huge house.

They came up to a room in the middle of the hallway. Broken opened the door, revealing a mostly empty room. Colors lit up the walls and painting supplies were everywhere.

Upon seeing the walls, Aneta gasped. "Oh my..."

On one wall was a field of flowers and a river running straight through it. Another wall depicted a type of abstract art of yellows and blues. Another wall was in the making and the last one was gray.

"I did not know you could paint so well." Aneta ran out of words.

Broken beamed. "I have been working on this over the past few days. Do you like it?"

"Like it? I *love* it! This is all so beautiful! You have so much detail in that—is that a...silhouette of a trout in the river?"

"Yes."

"Whoa."

"Thanks."

"Where do you get your inspiration?"

"People I meet, places I go. Stuff like that."

"So the room was originally gray?" Aneta glanced at the one gray wall.

"No. Sorta. It was white, and I painted it, then I painted over that with gray, and now I'm painting this."

"What was the last painting?"

"Just...stuff. Nothing I'm proud of. It looked horrible."

Aneta chuckled. "I wish I could paint this well. How long have you been an artist?"

"Since I was painting on construction paper."

The girls laughed.

"That's a long time. This is so cool. It literally lights up the whole room."

"Kinda like you."

Aneta turned around, completely thrown off by the compliment. She stuttered before finding her tongue. "Thanks. But...why do you say that?"

"Because you have a beautiful smile. And your laugh. Do you go to church? The last person I knew like you went to church."

Broken's plain and simple compliment caught Aneta off-balance again. "Uh, yes. Yes, I go to church. I uh, actually go to Whimsicalton Church right now, but I will be building another church with my friends. Aphoticton doesn't have a very good church."

"You call it Aphoticton? I don't know of anyone who uses that name, except for Fair and Diligent."

Aneta did not know what to do but smile. "Would you like to come to church when we start?"

"Sure. I bet Fair and Diligent would like to as well."

Aneta's soul soared. God made a way. And the only thing she could do was smile. But then she nearly gave herself a small heart attack. Theo had not yet decided. Slightly fearful, Aneta determined to build the church even if he did not participate.

Around eight p.m., Aneta decided to leave. After goodbyes to Fair, Diligent, and Broken, Aneta walked home. A chilly breeze blew in her face. She hugged her arms tightly to her sides, hands deep in her pockets.

Her mind began to wander as she braved the cold, and wondered if she should talk to Courage when she got to the apartment. What would she say? What would Courage say? As Aneta kept walking, she began to wonder how they would gain members in the church. Where would they find a place to hold their church services? What if she could not work with the others? What if Theo did not want to work with her, highly assuming he would, in the end, accept his call? What if she herself could not work with Theo? What if she did not get along with Courage at some odd turn of events? Or Bold? Or Faith? What if she could not keep her job? She really needed a separate apartment from Courage, but she could barely make enough as it was. What if the job did not work out for her?

Aneta reached the apartment buildings, and shivered, thankful she was almost home. It was almost dark. By one of the street lights, Aneta spotted someone walking. She saw the figure in black attire, and immediately began to hurry faster. If it was that same man with those deceiving, brilliant green eyes, she did not want to be near him in the dark.

Aneta placed her hand on the doorknob to the apartment, troubled at every thought. She opened the door. What if she failed? What if she disappointed everyone else? Was she even able to carry out the task God gave her?

Tears filled Aneta's eyes as she slid her jacket off.

"Are you okay, Aneta?"

Looking up in surprise, she realized Courage was sitting on the small couch, holding a book, sitting next to the folded pile of laundry.

Aneta wiped her eyes. Of course Courage would be there. Why did she think Courage would not be inside the apartment?

"Yeah, I'm fine."

Courage did not refute Aneta, but did not seem convinced. "Are you sure?" Her tone of voice relayed genuine concern.

"I just...I have a hard time with...stuff." Aneta leaned against the wall and folded her arms.

"Is there anything you want to talk about?"

"No, I was just..." Tears filled her eyes again. Aneta wiped them away, but they came back. "I don't know what to do, with things and people and..." Aneta began stuttering and began to cry. When Aneta could no longer finish her sentences, Courage immediately stood up and hugged her.

Meanwhile, Aneta tried to wipe her eyes. "How am I supposed to build a church? I've already told people I'm gonna do it, but what if I *can't?* What if...what if we don't...have much...what if..."

Aneta covered her face, beginning to cry. A demon lumbered closer to her. She pulled up her knees and buried her face as she sobbed. The demon crouched beside her and began to whisper horrible things in her ear, driving her further into discouragement and despair.

Courage turned her head and saw Aneta's dilemma. She kept a straight face, hiding the righteous anger that flared in her eyes. Courage unsheathed her sword and raised it up, swiftly advancing on Aneta and the demons. The demon saw her and squealed, calling for reinforcements.

She sliced the demon in half before it could escape. After checking again on Aneta, Courage took a steady stance, ready to defend Aneta from the other demons that suddenly appeared.

The demons raged. Her sword flashed. They fell one by one.

Courage kept holding Aneta. "Shh, shh. Hey, hey. Listen to me. It's okay. But you're asking yourself the wrong 'what-if' questions. What if God does a miracle? What if God suddenly intervenes here and gives us more than we could ever possibly need? God sent you here, but He won't leave you alone. God is *right here.*"

Bending down, Courage gently touched Aneta's shoulder. "Are you okay?"

Aneta straightened her legs a little bit and let more tears roll down her cheeks. "I'm so sorry!"

"About what?"

"You needed help earlier and I didn't help you." Aneta wept.

"Hey, hey. It's okay." Courage sat down next to Aneta. "It's alright. I'll always be here to help you. But God is also here helping us too. Don't worry about that. Just keep being the person God created you to be. He will take care of the rest."

Courage stood up and offered a hand to Aneta. They hugged again.

|Chapter 7: Daunting|

Around six in the morning, Theo stepped outside, taking a walk before starting the day. With his hands in his pockets, he strolled along the sidewalk, wondering what to do. Before he could say anything to God, his mind ran to his opportunity to plant a church. Aneta's words echoed in his mind again. *Like it or not, you were a heathen yourself!*

Theo knew he could not build a church. He was too young; he did not have enough wisdom on how to start, much less finish. How could someone as young and spiritually immature as him carry out such a huge task?

He had not engaged with many people in Aphoticton. That alone would get him off to a slow start. Why had God asked him in the first place? How could he begin to think *he* could build a church? Why was Bold not asked to plant a church? Why not Faith and Courage?

Theo scoffed to himself. He had messed up years ago, before all of the current happenings. Aneta would be a much better fit for the job *without* him. He had never thought he would see Aneta again. Now, they were supposed to be planting a church together. He kicked at a pebble on the sidewalk. She had been a Christian for her whole life. He had become a Christian only days before meeting her in Aphoticton. One thing that almost scared him was how Aneta acted. She had not yet spoken of their previous relationship.

Theo sighed in annoyance. "You know I can't do this." He began speaking to his King as he walked along the empty sidewalk. "And I also know You just love a good challenge, don't You? Of course You do. Can't You ever pick someone who actually *wants* to do something like this? Or even someone at least *worthy* to do the job?"

A soft voice replied, breaking through the turmoil in his mind. *Who defines worthiness? You, or I?*

Theo softened his face. "Alright, alright. I get it. You think I'm worthy to do this...but it doesn't help. Look, You know what I did." Theo turned towards the street, talking to thin air. He pointed a finger at himself. "You *know* what I did! Stop trying to pick me! I don't *want* to be Your 'chosen one.' It's always a big deal in novels and movies, but being a 'chosen one' isn't as fun as it seems! It isn't as epic either!"

You have an opportunity. Decide.

After running his fingers through his hair, he exhaled and stuck his hands in his pockets again, resuming his walk. "Well, I still can't believe You are still asking me. If I try to do this, it's gonna fail miserably." He slowly smiled, in spite of himself. "I can't do this. I doubt I will ever be able to do this. Why do You pick the most unlikely of every person or group of people? I would make ten times the amount of mistakes that someone else would. Yet You *still* want me? I don't get it. I don't get *You*. Well...looks like I better go and plant a church. You got me here. I suppose I better let You do the rest."

On his brisk walk to work, Theo stopped when he heard a pitiful animal crying. He found a kitten in an alley, under a trash bag. Its eyes were infected. With a melted heart, he picked up the kitten.

There was not much he could do. He could not keep animals in the apartment. Upon looking up, he spotted Lovely, the old homeless lady.

"Miss Lovely!" He called her, running up to her. "Here, look."

"Oh!" She held the kitten and hugged it closely. "You have a sweet li'l kitten!"

"You can have it. I just found it, but I think its eyes are infected. I can't have animals in my apartment. I can get you milk and some eye drops, but I don't have time to care for it. If you would like it, I can-"

"Oh, isn't it cute?"

Theo grinned. "Sure is." He glanced at the kitten, then lifted his eyes to Lovely. He gulped, suddenly realizing he had bigger things to discuss with her. "Hey...have you ever been to church?

She cradled the squeaking kitten in her arms, acting motherly towards it. "I have, decades ago. We left when I told a friend about my husband, and how abusive he was. She told me, 'Lovely, if you get in a situation like that, you need to leave. You can come to my house if he scares you, but you need to get away from that.' So I left to her house the next day with my little girls. I think he saw me leave, because he was chasing me in the car. I could not make it to my friend's house, so I hid until he went away, then I ran here. I don't think God can help me. The church here in Aphoticton didn't really help me either." She looked sad, most likely remembering a lot of her earlier life.

"God *can* help you. Hey...do you want a Bible study? We can look at where Jesus says that."

She looked at him with searching, hopeful eyes. "I would like that, Theo."

"Awesome. Uh, Thursdays? Starting tomorrow. Yeah, tomorrow is Thursday..."

"Thursday will work nicely. Buh-bye, Theo."

"Bye, Miss Lovely."

Theo walked back down the sidewalk, heading to work.

Theo widened his eyes. He unsheathed his sword, but lost his gumption and immediately bolted, dropping his shield in the process. From its immense stature and deafening roar, Theo recognized the miscreation before him as Daunting. Memories flashed through his mind; times of when he himself had sent Daunting to intimidate others by the order of demons above him. He had never seen the monstrous demon up close, but badly wished for something to protect himself against the flying projectiles of Daunting's whiplash tail. If only he had not dropped his shield!

The gigantic winged demon landed with a thunderous impact. As it did, it laughed, remembering Theo from before. With a swipe of its forearm, it knocked Theo off his feet. Theo grunted and rolled to the side before getting up, trying to avoid being trampled. His sword now laid five feet away, out of reach.

"You can't build a church here. I know you of old, boy. You can't succeed. We know your every weakness." Daunting towered over Theo on two powerful legs. Its arms were embedded in its strong, thin wings. Lurching forward, it tried to impale Theo with its two-foot claws.

Theo made a narrow escape from giant foot and the the spear-like thorns coming from Daunting's pointy tail.

"You think you can, little one, but you are *wrong!*" Daunting seethed at Theo, laughing as he tried to escape punctures. "You will *never* put a church in Aphoticton!"

Without bothering to refute Daunting's words, Theo darted away from the beast, trying to put something in the path to slow down the demon.

It was a short chase. Without protection or weapons, he was unable to defend himself, much less fight back.

The giant demon pinned Theo down with one foot, leaning over with a sly grin. "It is too hard. You will fail, and *then* what will happen? You become the boy who tried to build a business, but did not have enough wisdom to keep it going. You don't have enough resources or time or money. Who will come then? A lowly angel? Aneta?" Daunting scoffed. "I think *not!*"

With all armor stripped from his body except his helmet, Theo laid there, vulnerable to Daunting and unable to answer. Daunting was right. He could not build a church.

Bold called Theo's name, and caught up to him. "Hey, Theo."

"I'm sorry," Theo mumbled, looking anywhere but at Bold. "I'm not building a church."

"Oh," His friend rubbed the back of his neck. "I...wasn't going to ask about that. I was going to ask if you got coffee yet. I'm early for work and decided to...but, Theo. The church. Man, you can't...but God wants you to raise one up. Our King-"

"I know. I don't care."

"You already decided 'no'? That's it? Your final decision?"

Theo had no way to answer. "I don't know." He mumbled his reply, but Bold seemed more adamant.

"Then decide. Now." Bold was not having it. "So many people are lost. They have nowhere to go. It's up to *you* to guide them now."

Daunting's laugh chilled Theo to his bones. "Grace is wasted. Mercy does nothing. God's love is cheap. He doesn't care for you. You can't build a church, remember?" The beast reveled for a moment, gloating in his victory. "But I can't have you running around, thinking you can." With an open mouth, Daunting would have bitten his head off if not for Bold, who came running across the street in the full armor of God, wielding a sword.

"For the word of God is quick, and powerful, and sharper than any two-edged sword, piercing even to the dividing asunder of soul and spirit, and of the joints and marrow, and is a discerner of the thoughts and intents of the heart." Bold caught Daunting off guard and slammed his sword into its leg.

"In the Bible, it says, '*Be strong and of a good courage, fear not, nor be afraid of them: for the LORD thy God, he it is that doth go with thee; he will not fail thee, nor forsake thee.*' God says the same thing--'be strong and courageous--' multiple times." Bold stared into Theo's eyes, dead serious. "You need to do God's bidding. Otherwise He must find someone else to carry out the task. And you'll live long enough to see that other person take your blessings. But who knows how long that will take? God needs a church in Aphoticton *now.*"

"I can't-"

"What happened to '*Ye are of God...and have overcome them; because greater is he that is in you, than he that is in the world*'? Listen to me! Don't throw away the opportunity that God gave you. You may never get another chance."

Daunting screeched in agony as the wound sizzled. The blood evaporated into a red mist. That gave Theo a chance to stand up and move away.

Bold stepped forward as Daunting stepped backwards. "Daunting, get out!"

"Mark my words and remember them well," Daunting glared at Theo,"I *will* be back to finish my job." It brought down its wings, carrying itself upward in a mighty rush of wind.

Only one person stood as an onlooker across the street with his hands in his pockets. His brilliant green eyes shone out of place with his dark attire. He did not seem bothered by the fact that a demon had almost killed someone, or that the demon got away.

"Are you okay?" Bold sheathed his sword.

Theo looked annoyed. "Oh, just perfect. I just got pummeled by some dragon of a demon." He stomped away.

Grabbing Theo's sword and shield, Bold hurried to his side, "Hey, don't feel-"

"Are you going to finish that sentence?"

"Okay, okay. Fine. But seriously, it happens to everyone."

Theo paused and faced his friend. "Oh, *really?*" He spat out the remark. "And I suppose this happened to *you* before, too? Father just asks everyone to build a church, and they get a weekly reminder from Daunting that they can't *do* it?"

"Not that. Losing your shield and sword. You know, it's quite surprising that-"

"You should stop talking. Like, now." Theo kept walking.

Turning serious, Bold sighed, "Hey look. A 'thank you' would be nice."

Theo grudgingly came to a halt. "Thanks."

"Well, it's a start. But really, Theo, are you going to build a church or not?"

"Obviously not, because Mr. Man-Eating Daunting might come back to visit."

"Hey! You still have to plant a church!"

Theo threw his hands up. "Then why didn't God ask *you?*"

"Because He has His reasons; He chose you, Theo! He wants *you* to build this church. There are things He has designed for you to do, but only through His power. There are probably lots of reasons; I don't know what they all are. He doesn't tell us everything, and He doesn't have to. He is our Father; we are His children. Trust Him. Theo, if He asked you, He's got good reason."

Theo gave a deep sigh, and wiped his face with his palms. "Okay, well...that encounter with Daunting was plain embarrassing, and besides... I'm not prepared. Daunting may be a demon, but he is right. I don't have enough resources, or time, or money."

"Well, yeah." Bold shrugged. "Does anyone?"

"Aren't you supposed to still be convincing me to plant a church?"

"I am. But Daunting is right about those things. And I doubt you will ever have enough of any of those three crucial items. But...you don't need them anyway. Just grab a little time to spend with Father, and some people, just step out in faith, and badda-bing badda-boom. Father will be right there to get you everything you need to start a church. But you gotta begin with *yourself*. Yeah, it's work; but if this is your calling, it'll be doable. Not easy, but doable."

"Wow. So encouraging."

"If you don't put a church here, all these people will never see the Light. They will be lost in a dark world for eternity. God wants you here for a reason, man."

Theo softened his stressed face.

Bold waited patiently to hear Theo's decision.

Theo did not say a word. He looked pale, staring absent-mindedly at the ground. The two young men stood in the middle of the street, neither of them moving. Bold held out Theo's belongings while Theo hesitated to accept them.

Swallowing hard, Theo slowly took his sword and shield. He had no sheath or sling for them though. After Daunting ripped his shoes, breastplate, and belt off his body, they were lost somewhere on the streets. Nevertheless, Theo fought to hide a smile.

Theo nodded. "Thanks Bold. I... guess I'm still building a church."

Bold grinned. "See you after work?"

"I don't know yet."

"Hey, the squad has to get together soon! We gotta start planning."

"Squad?"

"You know. You, me, Faith, Aneta, Courage."

"Aneta too?" Theo blinked.

Bold gave him an odd look. "In case you forgot, that's the girl who is building a church with you. Yes. Aneta too. Why?"

"See you later, Bold. I'm gonna be late to work." Theo waved and kept walking.

"You're still early!" Bold called, shaking his head.

Theo breathed in relief as he got away from Bold and his questions. When he got to work, he was over an hour early. He sighed. He could have slept in. Why did he get up so early in the first place?

Silently landing on the ground with a monstrous rumble, Daunting appeared. Theo backpedaled, unprepared for a second attack this soon.

"You are mine." Daunting blocked his path. "No one is here to save you this time."

Theo fumbled as he gripped his sword. "I am never alone. I have Father's spirit within me, and through Him I will defeat you."

"Those are tall words coming from a pile of stubble." Daunting stepped forward, shedding projectile spikes from his tail as he forced Theo backwards.

Theo deflected everything, but could not hold his ground. He should have practiced with Bold. He was almost caught off guard when the gigantic demon kicked him.

His shield took the blow, but Theo's entire arm vibrated from the impact, and he flew backwards.

He had to get his armor back! Where did it get ripped off before? Theo stood up, gathered his courage and rushed back into the fight, mostly trying to get back on the street where his armor laid.

"Fool!" Daunting swung a massive claw, knocking Theo onto his back. Theo was still trying to get his bearings when the beast drooled over him.

Daunting said, "*The fool hath said in his heart, There is no God.*" Daunting's intimidating snarl froze Theo in place. "*They are corrupt, they had done abominable works, there is none that doeth good.*" What makes you think *you* are any better? Your heart is corrupt." With another kick, Daunting launched Theo several feet away, against a building's wall.

Theo tried to stand to escape, but there was no way out. His gaze drifted to his left. Shocked, he spotted his armor sitting on the sidewalk twenty feet away.

"You are a vile thing; an abomination to God Himself." Daunting stood defiantly in front of Theo, keeping him alive only to wear him down to his lowest point. "You led people astray for years. You sold souls; you traded souls; you left souls to their plagues. You led souls straight to the depths. You escaped once. Your Father had saved you. You escaped me once. But you will *not* escape again. You have not yet achieved complete freedom."

Grabbing his legs and dragging him onto the street, Daunting sneered at Theo. "You still owe a millennia's worth of work."

In defeat, Theo stopped struggling. Daunting was right. He had lost many souls. Too many. He could never win. Out of his misery, a verse of scripture came to mind.

For even the Son of man came not to be ministered unto, but to minister, and to give his life a ransom for many.

God's voice came through so clearly. *Child, pick yourself up. The battle is not yours, but Mine. Fight. Win.* I will *build a church in Aphoticton.*

Daunting spread its wings and took off, dangling Theo in the air.

"Whom the Son sets free is free indeed," Theo told himself. With all his might, Theo used all his upper body strength to arch up and slice Daunting's feet. A pair of deep incisions leaked red mist.

Daunting shrieked in pain and rage and released Theo.

Theo fell for a second before straightening out and going down feet first. He dropped out of the sky, and hit the ground with a roll. His armor was right there. It was mended and neatly waiting in a pile on the concrete. He didn't know who found his armor and fixed it up, but he was simply grateful. He barely had time to put on his breastplate when Daunting growled and plummeted right towards Theo.

Raising his sword, he stood his ground as Daunting sailed directly for him. He sidestepped three seconds too early, giving the impression of a false move. The beast fell for it and changed as well, giving Theo the opportunity to move aside again, drop to his back, and completely chop off Daunting's leg.

The demon's roar shook the ground.

Daunting tried to land, but stumbled and tumbled, leaving a deep trench in his wake.

Theo stood over the fallen demon.

"God is our refuge and strength, a very present help in trouble. Therefore will not we fear, though the earth be removed, and though the mountains be carried into the midst of the sea; though the waters thereof roar and be troubled...Come, behold the words of the LORD, what desolation's he hath made in the earth. You will no longer haunt me, Daunting. I have made my decision."

With all of his remaining strength, and more from his Father, Theo plunged his sword into the scaly chest of the demon.

Daunting's body vaporized into a red mist.

Without any other delay, Theo donned the rest of his armor. Exhausted, he sat down and sighed. He had several rub-burns, along with multiple bruises and some nasty scrapes on his legs. They could have been avoided if he had all of his armor, but he was thankful to have made it out alive.

He was just relieved he would not have to face Daunting again. His thoughts turned towards building a church..

"I...guess I'm building a church for sure now." Theo shook his head as he muttered to himself. His eyebrows lowered. "But...I still have to work with Aneta." He partly glanced upwards. "God, how is that even supposed to work? How are we supposed to work together?"

"Who?" Bold came up to him. He then took a step back seeing Theo's scratched up state. "Woah, what happened?"

"Daunting came back...but I decided to build a church."

"For real?"

"For real."

"Hey, that's awesome, Dude! What were you...uh, talking about Aneta about for?"

Theo leaned his head against the wall on which he was leaning. Still weary, he said, "she...was my ex-girlfriend."

|Chapter 8: Gracefully Broken|

On Saturday night, Theo walked into Chef Chava's Restaurant with Bold.

"Do you have a reservation?" the lady at the front desk asked, pen in hand.

"Faith Elysian. I'm Faith's brother." Bold nodded.

The lady nodded back, and then motioned for them to follow. The two guys sat down at the table and ordered food. Courage soon arrived with Aneta, and they also ordered.

Courage and Bold helped balance everything, making small talk until all of their food arrived. Around eight, Faith plopped down next to Courage at the end of the table, exhausted and hungry.

"Thanks Faith, by the way, for paying for us." Courage side-hugged her friend.

"Oh sure! So, what is the plan?"

Theo set his fork down. "I rented out the old town hall that's kinda on the corner of Lyle and Officer. I think it might work well to start at eleven, and then end right around noon. Everyone who comes can bring a little something for the potluck, so we can have lunch there and mingle with the crowd. I'd probably just do a Bible study the first few times, then we could maybe add a song service later. What do you think?"

"I think that works, but..." Faith gave him a suspicious look. "You didn't come up with the potluck idea, did you?"

"That would be me." Courage answered.

Everyone laughed.

"Well, I think it sounds pretty good so far." Aneta nodded. "So we have Miss Lovely coming, Helpful--the secretary at the Inn--thinks she might want to come, and Broken wants to come with Fair and Diligent. And then...it will grow from there."

"And Marvel and Chava might come." Faith piped up again.

"Who are they?"

Bold answered for his sister. "They own this restaurant."

At that point, Theo's nervousness caught up with him. He realized what was expected of him and everything he had to accomplish. It seemed too much to even start.

He glanced up, eyeing Aneta. Her face was flushed and her eyelids blinked rapidly. He was uncertain about everything, but so was she, it seemed. Should he say something? After all, didn't she say she didn't believe he could actually build a church? With mixed feelings, Theo remained silent for a moment.

Theo saw Aneta darting away and rushing out the door, hiding from a chief demon that was trying to sniff her out. He took a deep breath. She looked like she needed help. It was odd to him, though. Aneta had changed somehow. She no longer strove to beat down every demon in sight. She was *running*. Why was she running? Six years ago, she would have charged them head on, and then chased them some more. Maybe he should help her.

He raised his shield as two demons attacked him, forcing him backwards, away from Aneta. Their attack only motivated him further to help Aneta.

Slaying those two, he rushed forward, but was soon stopped by Chains. It was a beastly miscreation that stood four feet tall at the shoulders, but on its hind legs, it towered over him. He grunted and wasted no time in engaging his sword. It took longer than he would have wanted, but he finally prevailed and shoved the dead carcass over as it disintegrated.

Theo darted in the direction he had seen Aneta. He soon spotted Failure trailing Aneta. The chief demon leapt to the top of the building and bounded across the roof. Aneta must have been on the other side of the building.

Theo bolted. He found Aneta just as a second demon did.

Aneta trembled. The demon slowly stalked closer to her, looking at her with its formless head. This one was taller than the average man, with longer legs, and longer fingers that almost looked like talons.

Failure had been chasing her, but this was not Failure. Where was that demon?

The demon attacked. Aneta barely moved fast enough to block it and vaporize it.

Then Failure came. He pounded to the ground from the rooftop. Aneta jumped and tripped. She caught herself before she fell. Nevertheless, her sword sank in her hand as her arms ached. She began to sweat, knowing she was in trouble. She had not yet begun to fight, but her limbs had nearly given up. Was it even worth it to fight?

Aneta's heart skipped a beat. Her sword slipped.

"Back off. Now." A new voice came in.

Aneta looked to her left to see Theo walking towards Failure, sword and shield in hand. He looked worn out, with a bloodied hand and a bruise appearing on his face. Sweat dripped from his hair. What had he fought through to get there?

Upon seeing him, and recognizing his spirit, Failure growled and reluctantly fled.

Theo stood posed for a moment, making sure it was gone for good, then resheathed his sword.

He glanced at Aneta. She still trembled slightly, but nodded to him in thanks. He nodded back.

"Are you okay?"

Aneta looked at Theo, who had asked her a question. Her tongue tripped up and she could not answer.

"It's okay." Theo smiled. "God will get us through this."

Though mostly an impersonal statement, Aneta's soul soared as his words reassured her that God would help them. She smiled and nodded, mentally thanking him for the encouragement.

On Sunday morning, Aneta walked to the old town hall, Bible in hand. They did not meet until eleven, but she had nothing else to do for the whole morning.

The caretaker of the hall had left it open for them and had left the key inside, in a kitchen drawer.

Once inside, she looked around, familiarizing herself with the tiny building. It had a main room where she first walked in, a kitchen off to the side, along with a room opposite of the kitchen, probably used for voting. She found a closet that had chairs and tables. Seeing the opportunity, she began to set up everything. She wiped the tables off with a washcloth and wondered how the day would turn out.

She was a little nervous, even though she was not the one in charge. She thought about Theo. He was probably completely ready to get on with it.

She ended up being there for an hour before a man and woman walked in. It was only ten in the morning at that point.

"Hello!" The woman seemed to know her, but Aneta was clueless as to who she was. "My name is Chava," the woman said. "This is my husband Marvel. Are you Aneta or Courage?"

Aneta smiled and shook their hands, realizing this was Faith's boss, the owner of Chef Chava's. "Aneta. It's nice to meet you."

"Hi, Aneta! We know service starts at eleven, but we decided to come early. It is pretty amazing that you are starting a church. We used to attend one a long time ago, but ever since the pastor died at Truth Bible Assembly, and the church moved, it hasn't been the same."

Aneta nervously laughed. "Well, for right now, it's just a Bible study."

"It will be a church soon. You'll see. And we are praying every day that this church will spark some light here."

Chava's determined refutation gave Aneta a sense of hope.

Miss Lovely arrived, later followed by Fair, Diligent, and Broken. They all seemed to be excited for the Bible study.

Theo's opening prayer was simple, but he seemed confident. Nevertheless, Aneta could tell he was shaking.

To her surprise, Theo started off by recalling how Father asked the five of them to come and start a church, following up with how gracious God had been. He then went on to God's grace in general, and how important it was to realize that, while anyone may have had an ugly past, they could still come to God, and He would redeem them.

He ended his lesson on God's grace with a closing thought, restating what he mentioned in the beginning of the Bible study. "God's grace never ends. It doesn't matter what happens. We could have had the worst life ever. But He still cares about us and He wants us to know that. I invite all of you to come back next week here, at the same time. God wants to work here. We have to let Him."

Aneta breathed in relief as everyone started to mingle, then lined up to eat. Fair and Diligent complimented the five young adults on how well they were doing. Everyone seemed to want to come back next week.

As Aneta finally sat down to eat, Broken put her plate down next to Aneta's.

"Aneta." She quietly spoke, as if she was unsure about herself. "I think...I want to change my name."

"What?"

"God's grace can change my name, right?"

Aneta blinked. Her mind seemed to process everything as slowly as an internet router in the country on a stormy night.

"Of course."

"I don't want to be Broken anymore if God will let me be someone else." Broken looked into Aneta's eyes. "I don't want to be Broken. By God's grace I'm alive. I am gracefully broken. I am Gracefully Broken. And I want to be His child. I know He can help me."

Aneta laughed, almost crying with joy. She had been able to spread light. She had led one soul to the Lord.

|Chapter 9: Daunting Again|

Aneta woke up early on Monday morning, cheerful and thoroughly encouraged from yesterday. With a bounce in her step, she walked along the hallways of the inn, changing the sheets and washing laundry. Everything was going as planned and everything seemed to be working out. She repeatedly thanked God for everything that He had done and everything He was about to do.

Gracefully Broken found Aneta in the laundry room. While Aneta folded sheets from the dryer, the teen chatted with her. As the two girls talked, Aneta marveled at how Gracefully Broken thought of their Father, being so amazing and so gentle and so merciful. Gracefully Broken carried on talking, magnifying every small thing in her own life, in awe of God's grace. This made Aneta wonder at herself. Why did she not remind herself of God's goodness like that every day? Gracefully Broken made God sound so much more loving and amazing than how Aneta thought of Him. How had she let the greatness of God pass so quickly from her mind?

During her lunch hour, Aneta took a walk with Gracefully Broken. The teen talked and talked, mostly about what she was learning in her mornings with Father, studying the Bible.

Gracefully Broken unsheathed her sword and whirled it around a few times, smiling. "This is so awesome! I love fighting! I hope I am good enough by the time I have to fight demons."

Aneta smiled in reply, but inwardly groaned as her heart retched. How could a new Child love to fight for the Kingdom, yet Aneta could not bear to do anything with her sword? It seemed counterproductive. How was she supposed to pick up fighting again? Lately, she had only been fighting to protect herself, or when her conscience refused to let her do anything else. Yes, she had protected Gracefully Broken before, but she did not enjoy it one bit. Defense proved difficult. She could not imagine even attempting to switch to offence.

It had been years since she truly practiced with anyone with her sword. Faith had offered one time, but she had somehow avoided the question without much notice.

Even then, Aneta's hand habitually hovered near her waist where her sword sat. What if she decided to stop fighting altogether? Could she actually do that and still fulfill what God had called her to do? What would she do? What could she do? What *should* she do?

They ended up in a little corner of a street where an old building used to be. Gracefully Broken told Aneta how the town had replaced it with a little park, a few saplings, and a few benches. A mother sat on one of the benches while her two little kids ran around in circles in the small corner park, holding kites.

Aneta and Gracefully Broken watched the sky for a few minutes, amused at the kites circling and fluttering.

When she spotted Miss Lovely walking close by, Aneta walked over with a smile. "Hello! It's a very nice day to be out."

"Oh yes. Look, Lil' Cuteness is doing well!" Miss Lovely showed Aneta the kitten sitting in her pocket, sleeping. "She will sleep in my pocket all day until she is hungry. Look at that."

Aneta smiled, "Well, she is awfully cute. But how have *you* been doing?"

Miss Lovely sighed. "Oh, I have been doing better."

One of the little girls waved at the two young women. Gracefully Broken chuckled and wiggled her fingers back. She then walked over to the mother and began conversing with her.

In short notice, Gracefully Broken was spreading the Light and talking about all that her Father had done for her and Aneta.

Long after Aneta finished talking with Lovely, Gracefully Broken was still busy chatting with the young mother. Aneta slowly pulled out her sword and gazed at the wording on the blade. Could she ever use it again in good conscience? Aneta glanced up, seeing a cloud cover the sunny area. However, it was a clear day. All except for something diving towards her almost vertically.

Daunting.

Oh, no...

When she spotted the enormous beast bowling straight towards her, she gave a terrified scream. The nightmare did not go away. She picked up her feet and fled the scene. She had only made it to the middle of the street before Daunting shoved her to the ground as it landed, rolling her over and over. She lost her breath.

Scandalous chortling echoed in her ears as Daunting towered over her. Her sword had dropped and slid to the other side of the street. She was on her own.

Overwhelmed, Aneta's eyes began to water and sorrow-filled tears streamed down her cheeks. However, she could not make a sound.

"Still trying to win, are you? I told you before..." Daunting stomped over her, "they will *not* allow a church to be built here. Not now. Not ever. He may have defeated me, but I still have a round with you." It placed its foot on top of her, its separated toes leaving room for her shoulders and head, but pinning both arms down. "Will you stop this foolishness and forsake this void endeavor?"

Her palms were skinned. Her knees were bleeding through her clothing. Her head ached from landing on the ground. Her neck didn't feel right. But her voice was clear and strong.

"No."

Her mind screamed at her. *Why* did she say that? Her other small, shy voice answered back, saying God could still help her. Aneta gulped. What had she gotten herself into?

Daunting frowned, a terrible sight. "You have chosen death."

Scared for her life, Aneta cried out and tried to scramble away. Daunting lifted his foot only to grab her again and drag her away."Just like Coward, you are worthless. You don't owe any work like he does, but I'm sure they will find some use for you."

Her question slipped out almost as a whisper. "Coward?" Unpleasant memories trickled in one by one as she stopped struggling.

Even though she had been quiet, Daunting still heard her. "Ah, I remember. He does go by another name. Theo was it? He will always be Coward to me though."

Offended, Aneta began to struggle again. She desperately wanted a sword with which to defend herself. "He is bought with His blood. I don't care what you say. I don't care what he did. He is a Child of the King." Even though her words came bold and strong, she didn't know if she believed herself. Had she forgiven Theo yet?

Daunting tossed her up, and caught her again, still walking on three legs. His moist breath engulfed her as he gave a single laugh. "So...do you yourself believe that? Or are you just divulging what they tell you?"

She would have loved to counter Daunting's words, but she couldn't. Upon realizing she had not been willing to give Coward a second chance, Aneta began to cry.

"Oops. I said too much." Daunting gave a mocking, disdainful look. "Meanwhile, you can't escape. Someone didn't talk to Him this morning. You failed your pitiful Father...and you can't go back now."

"No...but...*stop!*" Aneta began to struggle again. "He *will* forgive me, I *know* it! Let me go! You have no place here in Aphoticton!"

"Such strong words for such a weak girl."

Aneta's heart nearly faltered. She had forsaken God, and He had now forsaken her. She tried, but failed.

Daunting widened its wings to lift off the ground.

"Daunting!" A voice stopped the demon from leaving the street. Faith ran up, sword brandished. *"Fear thou not; for I am with thee: be not dismayed; for I am thy God: I will strengthen the; yea, I will help thee; yea, I will uphold thee with the right hand of my righteousness."*

With a powerful stroke, Faith slashed at Daunting's leg. It screamed, dropped Aneta, then whipped its tail about. When Faith proved to be too powerful for it, the demon took off, leaving a trail of red mist.

Aneta covered her face, starting to weep. Faith walked over and embraced her. "It's okay, it's okay."

"No it's not!" Aneta broke out of the hug. "Can't you *see?* I am a complete failure! Daunting may be a demon but he is right! I could not even fight back for a second..."

"Aneta..."

"Stop it, alright? Just stop it! Even Gracefully Broken is more convicted and dedicated than *me*! God should not have picked me to plant a church; I can't do it! I just *can't!*"

"Aneta! Stop that right now. What am I hearing? What is *wrong* with you? *Listen* to yourself!"

"I *have* been! I can't go on like this. God will have to find someone else to build this church...because I can't. I tried. But I can't. Gracefully Broken is probably who Father wants-"

"Then why did He pick you in the first place?"

"What?"

"Aneta." Faith took a deep breath and stared Aneta in the eyes. "God Almighty chose *you* knowing all your little quirks. Those don't matter to Him. You just do what you can to the best of your ability, and God will fill in the rest."

Aneta began crying again. This time when Faith hugged her in the middle of the street, she did not push away. "Listen," Faith said, "Gracefully may seem completely passionate and devoted and engaged and all...but God did not choose her for this task. He chose *you*."

"But I can't-"

"Stop *saying* that! Sorry for being so blunt and a little rude about it, but stop beating yourself *up!* Don't you *dare* discount what God has ordained to be enough. You are filling your head with lies while blind to the truth that you are *completely* enough because in God, you have all that is needed to get your job done."

Aneta burst out crying again. For a few minutes, the two girls stood in the middle of the street, hugging. Faith bent down and picked up Aneta's sword, handing it to her. Aneta accepted it.

"Do you want to practice?"

Aneta let out a shaky breath. "Maybe…maybe not right now."

Faith knew what Aneta meant, and nodded. "Soon, Aneta. Soon."

Aneta nodded, exhaled again, and offered a small smile.

"See you later, Miss Lovely." Aneta smiled and waved at the elderly lady. Gracefully Broken was still talking to the woman on the corner park. She checked her phone.

<Fear thou not; for I am with thee: be not dismayed; for I am thy God: I will strengthen the; yea, I will help thee; yea, I will uphold thee with the right hand of my righteousness.> -Faith

Aneta smiled. It was just what she needed. How did Faith know to text her an encouraging verse right then? She replied:

<Thanks :)> -Aneta

"Hey, Aneta! Come here!" Gracefully Broken waved her over. "This is Candid, and her two cute little girls, Rise and Wonder. They are coming to our study on Sunday! Candid, this is Aneta, one of the women who started this whole thing. She is so amazing!"

Turning red with embarrassment, Aneta sheepishly smiled, but inwardly began to panic, fearing that someone might come to see that she was struggling in her relationship with God.

"Nice to meet you," Aneta blurted out, shaking Candid's hand, realizing she still had to be polite. She glanced at the time and gasped. "Oh my, I have to get back to work! See you later!" She took off down the street, hurrying towards the Whimsicalton Inn.

Aneta got back just as her lunch break ended. She would have brooded over what just happened, but her work distracted her. Helpful took her aside and told Aneta how to handle clothes going to and coming from the dry cleaners, as well as how to keep track of inventory on it all.

Almost absent-mindedly, Aneta nodded, taking mental notes of what to do. "So, how come you know so much about all of this?"

Helpful laughed. "Well, before being receptionist and then secretary, I used to be the laundress."

"Ah, yes. Well, thank you for helping me out. Mr. Seem is very nice to let me work full time without much training in this."

"Oh..." Helpful glanced at the papers on her desk. "Certainly. Alright, well, get on with it."

After her shift, Aneta walked back to her apartment and sat down on her bed. She sat staring at the wall for a few minutes.

Finally, Aneta broke free of her trance and quickly closed the door to her room. After a second thought, she locked the door. Trying to compose herself, Aneta slowly inhaled. When she had taken several breaths, she kicked at the pillow on the floor, then plopped onto the bed, screaming into her blankets.

Tears splashed out. Aneta curled into a ball and cried her heart out, overwhelmed by her thoughts and emotions. Why was everything crashing down? *How* had it crashed? What was even crashing? Did she really know? Unnerved that she did not know the source of her cries, Aneta wept harder. However, she kept it contained within her blankets.

She was disappointed in herself. How had she assumed Coward could never change? Yet Theo was there, building a *church* with her and three other Christians. Had she really forgotten about God's grace to the extent that she could not bring herself to completely forgive Coward and welcome Theo?

Even Gracefully Broken, with such a rough life as she had, seemed so joyful and peaceful. What was different about her own life? Why had it gone wrong? What even had gone wrong? What was so bad about her life? What caused her such misery? Why did she feel embarrassed? What was there to be embarrassed about? When did she start to feel this way? How had she let herself sink so low? Who could make her feel like this?

"Why is your soul cast down, Child?"

Aneta immediately closed her eyes and bit her lip, knowing to whom the voice belonged. "Father... not right now, please. I don't want to talk."

"Why is your countenance dismayed?"

"I don't know."

The gentle voice continued. "Then why is your beautiful soul cast down?"

"I don't know!" Aneta shouted back. With a confused tone, she said, "Why do you call it beautiful? No, stop, don't answer that. God, just...just *stop!* You're too good and You're too...too perfect and You're too amazing to deal with me! I know You are trying to help but I really don't want this right now." She wiped her face of tears.

"Who made the heavenly bodies? Who made the rising sun? Who made the mighty wind to pass through the earth? Who made the lilies dance in the breeze? Who raises the trees to great heights? Who paves the way of the whale? Who makes the galaxies shine in the evening sky? Do not say what I have made is not beautiful."

God's rumbling voice quieted into a soft, soothing hum. "Do not say you are not beautiful, My child, for I make all things good and full of beauty. Do not say you have no worth, for I create with purpose and dignity. Do not say you are what you are not."

Shocked, Aneta sat back with widened eyes. Quietly, she replied, "I'm sorry. I didn't mean to...discount what You created."

"You have a beautiful soul. Live to the fullest, forgetting all behind and running to that which is ahead. You have much work to do. Work diligently to receive your reward."

Amazed at her Father's encouraging, strengthening, and sincere words, Aneta fell into a soft cry, astonished at how perfectly, yet gently, He touched her wounded heart. She wiped her face again, almost shaking as she stood. When she had washed her face with cool water, Aneta straightened and made an early dinner for herself.

Her phone soon rang.

"Hey. What's up?"

It was Courage. "*Aneta, Faith was supposed to take dinner to the boys at work. But she just texted me that she has to work longer because they are busy, and she can't get a break for another hour or so. Could you run the lunchbox over? I'm still at work too.*"

Aneta glanced at the clock. It read five p.m. She had nothing much to do. Even though she sort of wanted to avoid Theo, part of her desperately wanted to see him again. "Sure."

"Thanks! The lunchbox is packed up in her apartment."

Aneta grabbed the lunchbox and walked to the dealership where the boys were working. When she walked inside the lobby area, Aneta asked the person at the desk about Bold and Theo.

Theo's face went blank as he saw Aneta walk in. The awkward silence ended as Bold also saw Aneta holding a lunchbox and grinned.

"Food! You know how to cheer a guy's day." Bold winked at her.

Aneta chuckled and set the food down, setting it out on a mostly clear toolbox top. Aneta smiled and left. The sun had begun to set, giving the air a chilly feeling. On the way back to her apartment, Aneta saw a girl, probably around fifteen or sixteen years old, sitting in Aphot Park.

She would have kept walking...if not for something nudging her to talk to the girl.

Aneta gulped as she saw a familiar figure sitting next to the girl. Depression. Almost angry, she put her hand on the hilt of her sword and walked over to the girl. Depression saw her and gave an annoyed look. But there was not much he did.

Aneta gently approached the girl, asking to sit down.

The girl stared at Aneta. When she said nothing, Aneta sat down, introducing herself.

"My name is Aneta."

"I am Sorrow." The girl did not want to talk.

"Are you enjoying the sunset?" Aneta looked up at the sky.

Sorrow shrugged.

"It is so beautiful...it reminds me of what my Father says. He says all things He creates are good and beautiful, just like the sunset. The sunset always reminds me that I have tomorrow to try again."

Aneta faced Sorrow, but the young teen was already staring at Aneta with Depression whispering in her ear.

With a quiet voice, Sorrow said, "I hate the sunset. Everything that comes with the sunset is always bad."

Appalled, Aneta sat back, wondering how to reply. "Well...I'm not sure what your schedule is...but if you like, you can come to the old town hall. Do you know where that is? You are welcome to come on Wednesday night at seven. I will be there, spending some time with a few others, and you are more than welcome to join. We do a little Bible study that night."

Sorrow's expression suggested that she wanted Aneta to leave. "I don't know."

Aneta paused. "I hope you can come. Have a good evening, Sorrow. It sure is beautiful."

As Aneta walked away, she hoped everything would work out. She licked her lips, realizing she just signed up for doing midweek meetings as well. They had not planned anything for Wednesdays, and she did not know if the old town hall could be rented that quickly. It was already Monday evening. Nevertheless, she would have to tell Theo to prepare a lesson for a Wednesday night Bible study.

|Chapter 10: Fire|

After work on Tuesday, since Aneta got done at four, she walked to the laundromat to get her clothes. She had already called the town hall, and the owner said they did not have pay rent on Wednesdays as long as they cleaned up the bathrooms and such. But she had to tell Theo. Fair, Diligent, and Gracefully Broken knew about Wednesday night and were coming. That was three people. Helpful got off early that day and would try to make it. She had not seen Miss Lovely to tell her about it yet.

Theo was there with his laundry as well when Aneta arrived. Aneta gulped, knowing it was the best time to tell him.

"You said *what?*" Theo spun around, eyeing Aneta as she folded clothes from the dryer.

"Well...we were going to have midweek services at some point...and I guess-"

Throwing a shirt into his mesh bag, Theo sighed in annoyance. "I can't do that, Aneta! That's just another thing on my plate."

Aneta folded her arms with a frown.

"I can't just go off doing midweek services!" Theo groaned. "Why do you have to spout off about this stuff?"

"Spout off?!"

"I didn't sign up for extra work! Sundays are plenty enough to-"

"Theo! I just told Sorrow that we would be there. You *have* to do it. I can't just tell her 'never mind!'"

"Then *you* do it!"

"What?"

Theo picked up a dress shirt and folded it.

Rolling her eyes, Aneta grabbed a hanger and took the shirt from him, hanging it and setting it on the chair..

"You don't have to hang it up."

"Yes, you *do*." Aneta protested in annoyance. "You hang up dress shirts. Fold it up, and it gets *wrinkled*."

"It won't get *wrinkled* if you fold it right." Theo grabbed a pair of pants from the dryer.

"*If.* Yeah. Right." She folded another shirt. "What do you mean 'I do it?'"

"You do the midweek lesson. You have time. I don't. You're the one that signed up to do it."

"I can't do that!"

"Then you have to tell Sadness to cancel."

"Sorrow. I can't tell her that!"

Theo gave Aneta a look that implied aggravated exhaustion and a desire to be left alone.

With a sigh, Aneta folded her hands behind her back and leaned against the wall. "Alright. Alright, okay. Fine." She closed her eyes for a second. When she opened them, she sighed again, straightening up. "Okay, if you're gonna fold your t-shirts, at least do it right."

"I *am*!"

Aneta snatched the shirt from Theo's hands. "Oh really? Crumpled heaps don't count."

"You know you don't have to do *my* laundry."

"I don't *want* to."

"Then don't."

"Who else is going to do your laundry?"

"Me!" Theo jabbed a finger at himself.

"If you don't stop talking, my ears will start to bleed."

"No, they won't. They are already used to your own voice."

Humphing, Aneta dumped out Theo's bag, then rolled her eyes. "Theo. Just so you know, you *are* supposed to buy new socks...periodically. These better not be the socks you bought that one time with me."

"What's wrong with mine?"

"Every other sock has a hole in it. That's why. There...is no way these are the same socks. Right?"

"They are fine. Leave my socks alone."

"No. That's just...a rule of thumb." Aneta finished folding Theo's clothes and neatly put them in his bag.

Theo grumpily took his bag, and a few hangered shirts in the other hand. "Bold drove me here. Want to hitch a ride home?"

Aneta looked at him. "As a matter-of-fact, I would love one. Thank you."

Bold was in a car, waiting in the driver's seat. When Aneta opened the back door, he grinned. "Hey, Aneta. What's up? Going home?"

"Soon. Yes. But first, we are going to the store."

Theo closed the trunk and got in the passenger side door. "Why are we going to the store?"

"You need new socks."

"Right now?"

"Yes. You can't be going to church with holey socks."

"We're supposed to be holy, remember?"

Rolling her eyes, and ignoring Bold's amused look, Aneta sighed. "Oh, shut up."

"But we're actually going *right now?*"

"Yes."

Theo looked at Bold.

With both hands still on the wheel, Bold shrugged. "Man, I can't argue with her. I...we gotta go to the store."

In agony, Theo sighed.

When Theo, Bold, and Aneta made it to Sign's Store, they ran into Faith and Courage as well.

"What? So who planned this meeting here, anyway?" Bold laughed. "What are you two here for?"

"Just a few things." Courage lifted some boots. "Should I buy these rain boots? They are cute and on sale, but...I don't think it has rained here very much."

"Oh, talk 'bout rain." A new voice spoke up. A farmer stood there, holding a a basket with a few things inside. "If talkin' 'bout rain hailed much, I'd would'a gotten rain weeks 'go."

Bold nodded. "How are the crops doing? Seen much rain over there lately?"

"Oh, you ne'er know de way *this* weder has been actin'. This has been de whorst dry sehson we got. So dry. Hasn't rained in weeks. Gotta water my own crops. It'd bedder rain soon, son."

"I see. Thanks." Bold turned to the group and shrugged. "I guess there's a bit of a drought going on. Been kinda nice though. It kinda sucks when you're working on a car and it's dripping water from driving through half a dozen puddles and water drops mixed with oil and rust get in your eye. Man it's rough. I'm gonna die when it snows."

"You think?" Faith folded her arms and chuckled.

"Oh, by the way..." Theo gave Aneta a look. "We are doing a midweek service now. And *Aneta* is leading it."

"Oh, that's awesome, Aneta!" Courage smiled.

Aneta frowned. "*Yeah*. I'm gonna go find those socks."

Faith and Courage followed Aneta, leaving Bold and Theo to themselves. When Aneta found the men's socks, she stopped. "We can forget the socks."

She began to turn back, but Courage stopped her. "Wait, why?"

With a whisper, Aneta said, "Advisor is over there."

"Well, what does that mean?" Faith raised an eyebrow.

"Come on. Let's go." Aneta turned around.

Faith put her hands on Aneta's shoulders and turned her friend around. "Yes. But that way. Come on. We are getting socks."

"Ehh." Aneta made a face as they walked over to the sock section.

Just as Aneta feared, Advisor turned to them, "Hello, Aneta." His tone did not imply any sort of hidden scheme as Aneta thought.

"Hi." Aneta focused on finding Theo's socks.

"Hello, Advisor." Courage smiled. "How are you?"

"I am doing well." Advisor paused. "Aneta, I would like to apologize for the way I acted before."

Caught off guard, Aneta looked up. "Wha...oh. Um, thank you...I forgive you." From behind, Faith nudged Aneta's ankle with her foot. Aneta cleared her throat. "Uh, well, we...are having a midweek service on Wednesday...well, tomorrow...at seven. You are welcome to come if you like."

"Oh, thank you for the invitation." Advisor seemed surprised. "But I have to say... my wife is quite beside herself with you five young people. I'm not sure I agree with everything you do, but...it isn't with bad motive." He nodded and left.

Aneta groaned after he left and snatched up a package of black socks. "Alright. Let's go already."

"Good job, Aneta!" Faith grinned. "That went well!"

"Easy for you to say..."

"Alright, alright." Faith raised her hands.

Courage said, "Hey, have you figured out a place for Miss Lovely yet? She needs a place to live."

"I think so." Aneta sighed. "I'm not sure. Theo found some cheap apartments but...it would be hard to rent, even with our combined incomes. I feel like we are hardly scraping by. I'm not sure I like being an adult."

Courage laughed. "You are a pretty good adult. I'm pretty sure Bold, Faith, and I can pitch in to get Miss Lovely moved in tonight."

"Tonight?"

"Yeah. Why not?"

"I suppose..."

After buying Theo's socks, and a few other items, the five young adults walked over to the Whimsicalton Apartments, where the girls rented, and knocked on the landlord's door. After a few minutes of explanation, Courage ended up signing the paper, and they paid for the month in cash. Bold and Theo put a few things in the apartment as the girls went to find Miss Lovely.

It was around nine at night when they found her sitting on the park bench, looking at the sky. "Hey, Miss Lovely! We have a surprise!" Aneta grinned.

They walked the little old lady through the town, revealing their newly rented apartment. Miss Lovely cried for an hour, as she walked through the little room, seeing a blanket on the floor with a pillow, and a bag of groceries sitting on the countertop.

They got her settled in, then left around nine-thirty. Theo retired promptly to bed, and Bold did the same. That left the three girls standing in Faith's apartment.

"Aren't you girls going to bed?" Faith asked.

"Sooner or later." Courage winked at her. "You got a little lesson for tomorrow night?" She looked at Aneta.

Aneta groaned. "I forgot about that."

"Hey, you'll be fine."

"You got this, Aneta." Courage added. "God knew you would be doing this, and He has something for you to say. Don't worry."

"Yeah. Thanks. Good night."

Aneta woke up at four in the morning and could not go back to sleep. Her eyes ached, but her mind refused to rest. Her stomach was too uptight. She reluctantly unfolded herself from the blankets and showered. Immediately, she got herself some coffee and sat down at the table.

Aneta plopped down with her Bible and flipped through page after page, looking for something to speak about that night. Nothing. She could not find anything. That bothered her. Everything seemed so boring or too shallow. She could not do it on God's grace. Too cliche, and Theo already did that. She did not want to do it on mercy, since that also seemed too shallow.

The fact that most everyone was relatively new to the concept of a loving Father struck her, but she found it harder and harder to think about what to say. Finally, as it was almost time to go to work, she hastily chose a topic: how God protects His children. She did not like it, for it seemed still too boring, but she also knew it would work for a Wednesday.

As she ironed clothes at the inn and walked other suits to the dry cleaners, she thought long and hard on what to say about her chosen topic. There seemed to be an infinite number of possibilities, but at the same time, hardly anything to choose from. Courage joined her for lunch at the inn at their cafeteria.

"So, have you decided on what to speak about tonight?"

Aneta reluctantly nodded. "Yes. I think so. I think it's a little boring, though. About how God protects His children."

"What? I think that's a very good topic right now! Perfect, actually, for our group that we have."

"You think so?"

"Um, yeah. Really, it's *not* boring."

"If you say so." Aneta glanced towards the doorway. "Yeah. Alright, I gotta get back to work. See you later, Courage."

"Sure. Hey, whenever you need to, feel free to chat with me." Courage winked.

Aneta laughed and walked to the washroom. She gasped to see Gracefully Broken sitting on the floor, against one of the washers, sobbing.

"Gracefully Broken! Oh, Gracefully!" Aneta hurried and kneeled down, "What's wrong? What happened?"

"I just can't *do it* anymore!" Gracefully Broken burst out. "Life is too much. Everything is going wrong! I ruined my favorite shirt, and people keep attacking me, and girls are rude just because of my parents, and girls are *nice* just because of my parents, and no one wants to be friends for the sake of friendship!"

Aneta, wide-eyed, sat down on the floor next to Gracefully Broken. She had no clue how to react. "Do you...want me to listen...do you want my advice?"

"I don't know. You're the only friend I know of who doesn't care about my money...it's not even mine. A girl at school is just being nasty...rude. Whatever. And telling me...stuff that doesn't need to be repeated. What am I supposed to do?"

"Is...everything happening at school?"

"What?" Gracefully Broken wiped her face on her sleeve and gave Aneta a questioning look.

"Well, is this all at school, or does other stuff happen elsewhere?" Aneta inwardly pumped her fists in the air, excited that the words coming out of her mouth sounded so smart and confident.

"Well...there's a lot of stuff I hear that I probably am not supposed to know about Mom and Dad."

"To be honest...I'm not sure how to help. But, if you just want someone to listen, I can totally do that."

With a deep breath, Gracefully Broken began, sniffing. "My brothers...I think they try. But they forget so often. I know there is a huge age gap, but I still want my brothers to be my brothers. They are both so busy being busy they forget that I just want to hang out. I guess I'm just the annoying little sister."

Gracefully Broken talked on and on about how much she missed her parents, how her brothers did not do brotherly things, how the kids at school were snooty and stuck-up or overly nice and prying, how she kept feeling overwhelmed at the thought of getting a job, and how she constantly felt awkward at different places in town.

"I go to Lyle's Diner, and I just feel *weird* and...I keep...not acting like I should. It's hard to be a Christian at school sometimes. The kids think my parents got converted or something dumb. I doubt they actually know...about..."

Aneta sighed, at a loss for words. Something was going on that Gracefully Broken was not revealing. Gracefully Broken's parents were dead, so whatever came up about them must have been excruciatingly hard to deal with.

"Gracefully...I'm not sure how to reply. I..." Aneta nervously chuckled, "I'm just not sure. I have never struggled with the same things as you, but I know that...God protects His children. Your Father is a God...well, He is the only God there is, and God loves you. It doesn't always feel like it, but He also knows how it feels to go through all this pain. I don't know how to answer you, but...just know that He wants to make sure you know He just wants to hold you."

Gracefully Broken broke down into tears and side-hugged Aneta. Meanwhile, Aneta hoped that, in everything she had said, her words made sense and helped the teenager. She could not begin to wonder how Gracefully Broken was coping with her parents' deaths, or her brothers being mostly oblivious to her, or having little to no real friends, or living like she did.

Eventually, Gracefully Broken wiped her tears and spoke up again. "You know, I have never heard anyone speak about God in such a loving manner. You...you and Theo, and Courage and Bold, and Faith...you all have such an amazing relationship with...with-with each other and Father, and I am so far behind. I-I can't—I can't just...I feel so far behind. You just... are so graceful every day, and you're so elegant and you have everything going your way, because you are just so amazing and I am so far behind."

Aneta's heart almost fainted. Is that how Gracefully Broken compared their lives?

"Well, Gracefully Broken, I want to say I have deeply admired your beautiful spirit and soul for Father. He is so pleased with your heart and your want to love Him. I go through some rough spots too, and I'm still nervous about leading tonight's lesson."

"What?"

"We are having a midweek service...and I'm giving the lesson."

"Really?"

"Yeah. I'm not very pumped about it."

"Are you kidding? You're...you're *Aneta!* You're...nervous?"

"Yes."

"Whoa."

Aneta let out a single laugh. "Well, I *am* human. Now, Gracefully, you can come tonight, right? Are Diligent and Fair still coming?"

"I sure hope they can come. By the way, you are really good at listening."

"I try." Aneta wished she really was incredible and as dedicated as Gracefully Broken thought she was.

Gracefully Broken hugged Aneta again. "See you tonight! What time?"

"Seven."

After Gracefully Broken left the room, Aneta remained on the floor, leaning her head against the washer. She sighed, feeling a cold flash tingle across her face. "Father...how is it that you use us broken people to build each other up when we couldn't do it by ourselves? That...well, that's...pure genius, isn't it? Well, I suppose I expect nothing less." Aneta laughed at herself and got up, continuing work.

As the day drew closer and closer to evening, her stomach twisted tighter and tighter, making her doubt herself more and more. Eventually, she made an outline of what she wanted to say and briskly walked to the old town hall. She was the second person there, the first being Theo.

"You ready?" he asked.

Aneta sighed. "Yeah. I have something..."

"Oh, good. I...didn't know if you were actually going to bring something, so I brought a little lesson, just in case."

Aneta gave him a funny look. "Oh, really? What's it about?"

"Oh, well, I *am* glad you brought something, for the record. This was just a backup...uh, it's about how God protects his kids."

"Shut up."

"Hey! That's not very nice."

"I have the exact same lesson!"

"Whoa, really? Let me see."

Aneta produced her notebook, showing him what she wrote out.

"That's cool. Hey, yours is better than mine. Good thing you're doing this, not me."

"Hey, Theo?"

"What?"

"I'm...glad you...*made* me do this."

"Well, I didn't make you do it, but I'm glad you stepped up to the challenge. Do you know who all is going to be here tonight?"

"No clue if anyone will actually show up."

"Hey, I'll be satisfied with however many people come."

Courage, Faith, and Bold walked in just after six, and by 6:30, Miss Lovely, Fair, Diligent, and Gracefully Broken had arrived, followed closely by Candid with little Rise and Wonder clutching her hands. Gracefully Broken had invited them. Chava and her husband did not show up, but Aneta did not mind. The fewer, the easier. At seven, Theo prayed and people helped themselves to the doughnuts and coffee he brought before sitting down. Aneta chatted with some people first before deciding to start.

However, Faith walked up first followed by with Diligent holding a guitar. "I don't know who all knows these songs, but if you know them, sing along!"

To Aneta's surprise, the gray-haired butler began playing and Faith began singing a song. As Faith led the songs, Aneta's heart warmed up and almost melted. The songs they had picked filled her with peace and comfort.

When they were done, Aneta stood up and faced the small group of people. Before she began, she watched as Sorrow walked in with a sullen and embarrassed face. She lingered in the back, not sitting down as Aneta started talking.

Aneta fumbled with her notes, losing her place so many times that she eventually closed her notebook and just spoke without them.

"God loves us all. It doesn't always feel like it, but He is there. We run away, but He is there to welcome us back; He picks us up, hugs us, and points us in the right direction. We may feel like everything is against us, but God protects us too. We belong to His family and... and He is our Father. We cannot fathom His love for us, and He *will* provide, whether or not we are confident in that fact."

At that point, Advisor walked in, also standing in the back. She kept talking, marveling at how she could now speak without the notes and still sound decent enough. She hoped Advisor could gain something from what she said. Even though the lesson was going well, Aneta slowly began to feel odd as she heard sirens in the distance. Not the police, but fire truck sirens.

The town hall did not have windows behind her, only on the two sides of the buildings, both of which had curtains over them. However, the small group of people were polite enough to keep their attention on her as the sirens screamed closer and closer.

Aneta finished her message, and Theo closed with prayer. As he said "amen," an explosion sounded close by.

Some people twisted their necks to see what had happened, but a couple people jumped up to go outside. When Bold and Advisor announced there was an explosion at a house and two houses were now on fire, Theo decided to pray again.

People began to spectate outside. As the sun left the sky, the fires blazed hotter and hotter. Eventually, people retreated back inside the building when the fire kept spreading. Fire trucks constantly shrilled and people were shouting and crying. Fair and Diligent joined Theo in prayer. After a little bit, Candid joined them in prayer as well, making sure her girls sat quietly with two books. It was a short time before most of the people were praying. Some knelt down, others paced, and some were louder than others, but they all remained in a serious tone.

Sorrow looked slightly concerned, but after watching the fires for a while, she began to inch towards the food on the table.

"Hey, Sorrow." Aneta walked up to her.

Sorrow glanced up and nodded in greeting. "Hi. This is free, right?"

"Oh, absolutely. Have all you want. I'm glad you could make it! How are you doing? The explosion was crazy."

The girl nodded and turned her attention to the food.

"Would you like me to pray for you?"

"Prayer doesn't do much."

"Well, from my experience, prayer is quite powerful. God listens *and* understands, and that right there says a lot."

"How do you know He listens?"

"Because He also responds, plus the Bible says so. God is quite amazing; He's never too busy for me. He wants to talk with you too, you know."

Sorrow's voice was soft and sarcastic, but tinged with sadness. "Sure He does." She bit into her doughnut. "I've never heard that kind of song before, though. I didn't know they made those kind. Kinda slow and boring, but the words are...I don't quite know how to describe them. Fulfilling, maybe."

Aneta smiled. "Oh, yes, yes they are. I love them. Hey, thanks for coming. You know, we do this on Sundays too, from eleven to 12:30 or so. We have lunch, too, if you'd like to come."

Sorrow seemed to like the idea of food on Sundays as well. "Maybe."

"Aneta!" Bold hurried up to her. "Are you not aware of what is going on outside right now?"

"What happened? Did they contain the fires?" Aneta asked.

"The fire spread across the street. Two business are burning right now."

Aneta gasped. "What?"

Bold pulled her to a window. "You've *got* to see this. The fire...is *not touching* our building...not in the least." He smiled.

Aneta gawked at the sight. Thick, choking smoke filled the night air. Roaring flames shot into the sky behind the old town hall, and three buildings had been engulfed already. Firefighters ran in all directions, racing back and forth, shouting orders. Civilians gathered around and pressed as close as the police would allow, watching the night light up, but soon turned back as officers directed people to the southwest part of town. Many people were ushered out of their homes from the other side of the street as well.

The old town hall stood untouched. It was a little past eight p.m. The flames rose higher and faster. Embers began to fall halfway across the street, but most of the fire expanded behind the town hall and moved away.

After a while, a police officer ran over when he realized people were in the old town hall, telling them to get out, but then stopped himself. Instead, he squinted his eyes.

"Actually...stay in here..." He walked away, confused and perplexed at the phenomenon.

A few civilians had come into the town hall, all strangely feeling that it was safe there, despite being dangerously close to the fires raging all around.

Dr. A. Theist even hurried inside next to her husband Advisor, thankful that the building was safe, but angry at all the reasons why.

They remained there until midnight, and many of them began to pray after Bold and Theo's example. Others, especially the younger kids and a few teens, fell asleep on the floor. Some adults quietly conferred, wondering about the strange events. Some, who likely hadn't prayed in years, sat down, hands folded, lips silently moving.

Aneta eventually sat down in wonder and awe at the power of her Father.

|Chapter 11: Daunting Defeated|

On Thursday morning, Aneta slowly opened her eyes. Many people had sought refuge in the old town hall. Most of them had slept there through the night. Others had sat up, worrying and watching the fire until it had dissipated. She left the town hall and walked back to her apartment to prepare for the day.

After taking a shower, she stopped to talk to God for a few moments before rushing off again. His presence gave her peace. Feeling refreshed, Aneta walked back to the old building of refuge, finding Theo and the others who were trying to figure out what to do. They asked the firefighters how they could help and soon began passing out different blankets to the people whose houses were too dangerous to stay in.

The billowing fire had consumed the three buildings around the old town hall, and devoured another building beyond that. Three houses had been affected, aside from the one that exploded. The two houses on either side of the destroyed house were badly scorched and melted in many places, but somewhat salvageable.

The exploded house belonged to a family of ten, but they were gone on a two day trip to see family, so no one was injured when it happened. The family had arrived back from their trip around one in the morning amid the chaos.

They were offered places to sleep in the old town hall that night by Theo.

After work, by the time Aneta got to the old town hall on Friday afternoon, Theo and Bold had been able to acquire some supplies: food, hygiene, cots and blankets for the big family. Aneta was then able to meet the family, the Nepenthes. The oldest boy was seventeen, and the oldest girl was fifteen. When Aneta was introduced to Irk, the eldest boy, he seemed extremely put off and sullen about everything. The oldest girl was on a walk with the two youngest to get them out from underneath Mrs. Bloom Nepenthe's feet.

Jar Nepenthe was only thirteen years old, but he enjoyed hanging around Bold and Theo, following everything they did. However, he had a habit of speaking loudly and occasionally made Aneta jump at his holler or shout. The eleven-year-old girl and the nine-year-old boy did little to help and sat on the cots, reading, plainly bothered that their house was burned along with their belongings.

Feather was the eight-year-old who silently followed her mom wherever she went. She did not get in the way or complain, but she simply and silently kept close to her parents. Aneta soon liked Feather and her gentle, almost mute nature and made an effort to be kind.

To Aneta's surprise, Miss Lovely soon came in holding brownies. That caught the attention of every Nepenthe, even Irk. While they munched on fudgy chocolate bars, Aneta introduced Miss Lovely to Mr. and Mrs. Nepenthe.

They got into a conversation about their life journey coming up to this point in their lives. The Nepenthes had lived in Aphoticton (Mr. Prime and Mrs. Bloom Nepenthe called it Aphoticton, not Whimsicalton as most of the people of the town) for their whole lives, just like their parents had done so before them, but they had only lived in the house that burned down for the past five years.

Miss Lovely then told her story. She simply stated she was in a rough spot for a few years before getting an apartment with Theo and Aneta's help. Through a little backtracking, they found out Miss Lovely had been close friends with Mrs. Bloom's mother, Tapestry.

While the women caught up on the times, Aneta left some clean sheets on the cots and continued helping where she could.

Through the next few days, Theo, Aneta, and the others helped the families and owners of the buildings and houses that had been decimated by the fire. By the time Sunday came, there were twenty-three people at the hall they used as a church building. Along with everyone who normally came, the Nepenthes were there along with Advisor, plus a fireman Bold had witnessed to on Friday and an elderly couple from down the neighborhood.

While Theo spoke to the people, Faith and Courage took the little kids to the back of the room and quietly watched and played with them until service was over. Halfway through, Wonder, Candid's three year old girl, began to sob, and Courage quickly picked her up and headed out the doors. Aneta silently stood up and helped Faith with the little kids, keeping them occupied.

When Courage walked back in with Wonder, she quietly said, "Aneta! Go outside! Sorrow is across the street! I don't know what she is doing, but you better go and see..."

Aneta searched in the direction Courage was pointing, seeing the teen girl meandering along the sidewalk. Her mind raced through what to do, then screeched to a stop when she realized how awkward it would be to just walk up and talk to Sorrow.

"I don't know...I think Sorrow is fine." Aneta mentally facepalmed, knowing it was a sorry excuse.

"Aneta, you should really go talk to her. She is *not* fine."

"Yeah..." Under her breath, Aneta said, "Well, I am."

"Aneta."

"Oh, come on! Since when do *you* know what it's like? You and Faith and Bold have been born into wonderful purpose, and you three just easily float along doing your civil duty, while *I* have to fight with what to do and how to do it. Do you know how *hard* that is? Do you even *know-*" Aneta realized she had been raising her voice. She quickly lowered to a whisper again. "I don't know...I can't just..."

"Yes, you can. It's not awkward to Sorrow, whether or not it is awkward to you." Courage jabbed a finger towards Sorrow's direction. "Aneta, if you don't, we might lose this round."

"Alright, alright, I'll talk to her." Aneta folded her arms uncertainly.

Courage smiled and gave her a reassuring nod.

Aneta took a deep breath and walked outside. Sorrow just disappeared around the corner. The cold hand of urgency grabbed her, and she bolted. With a burst of energy, Aneta ran after Sorrow, skidding around the corner.

"Hey, Sorrow!" Aneta waved her hand and slowed down when she came up on Sorrow's side.

The teenager's face was unreadable. Aneta could not tell if Sorrow was happy or annoyed to see her. "Hi, Aneta." She quickly glanced behind them.

Aneta tried to slow her breathing. "So, uh, what are you up to today?" She had been so focused on catching up with Sorrow, she had no time to plan what to say.

"I don't know. Mom and Dad are...talking and...there isn't much to do. Just walking around."

Having had depression before, Aneta knew exactly how Sorrow felt about everything and anything. However, she could not tell if Sorrow wanted Aneta to ask about her day or not to mention it. Aneta remembered there had been days when she desperately wanted someone to interact with her, and other days when she wanted to steer clear of every living being.

Aneta took a chance. "Would you mind if I just walked around town with you?"

Sorrow's pause planted fear in Aneta. "Sure."

"Thanks. How is school going?"

"Good." The teen looked up at the yellow leaves delicately floating down from trees, preparing for the end of fall.

"Good. What do you do in your free time?"

"I don't know."

The anxiety melted away as Aneta realized what Sorrow wanted. "Well, I doubt you sit around." She joked. "What are your hobbies?"

"I don't know. I haven't done much lately."

"Well...what did you do before? Do you like art? Reading? Are you one of those crazy people who enjoy running as a hobby?" Aneta chuckled at herself.

A trace of amusement echoed on Sorrow's lips. "I like to paint."

"Ooh, so what kind of painting have you done?"

"I don't know."

"Is it like, abstract, nature, people, scenes?"

"I like to draw people."

"Whoa, really? Have you done any projects lately?"

"No."

"Hey, you should teach me how to paint. I've never really done that before, and painting people sounds really cool. Oh...have you eaten lunch yet?"

"Not yet."

"Do you want to go to...Lyle's Diner?"

"I didn't bring my wallet with me."

"I'm paying anyway."

"Oh. Okay, then."

The two girls walked downtown. Even though Aneta typically liked listening, not talking, she knew she had to crawl out of her shell in order to finish what she started. She talked the entire way to Lyle's Diner.

Inside the diner, the two girls sat down at the counter on the spinning bar stools. They both ordered hamburgers and waited.

From behind her, Aneta saw one demon lurking outside, suspiciously watching her and Sorrow. The demon's long black fingers clutched the threshold of the door as it watched. Despite it being faceless, Aneta could feel the demon's glare in the back of her head. It didn't try to hide the fact that it was watching them. That made Aneta slightly nervous. She wished she knew what they were planning against her.

She hoped she was able to protect Sorrow from whatever might happen. But unless the demons were actually going to attack, she did not want to start them off, especially if they were not planning to attack at all.

She turned back around, but then paused. Almost fearfully, Aneta again turned back to the doors, looking at the demon again. Next to the demon was a man in black clothes. He had spoken to the demon, and the demon immediately fled the scene. When the man looked in Aneta's direction, she froze upon seeing his brilliant green eyes. Even with the distance between them, Aneta knew the man was smiling at her in a devilish way. What did he do? What did he say?

Something rumbled, shaking the diner. Aneta spread her feet to steady herself. Trembling, she fingered the sword on her thigh. Suddenly, an ear-splitting crack of wood and glass resounded all around her. A gigantic beast crashed down on top of her, grabbed her, and charged out of the building, leaving a great din in its trail.

Frantic, she cried out, "Sorrow!" She could not see Sorrow in the rubble. Was she okay?

The beast roared and threw Aneta to the ground, leaving her without breath. When Aneta opened her eyes, she almost shrieked. Daunting stood there, fanning its forty-foot wingspan out, shaking the trees down to their roots.

"I apologize." Daunting's hot, churning whisper chilled Aneta to the bone. "I was not able to finish you off last time." It turned its head sideways and attempted to snap Aneta in half, but she flattened herself against the pavement and rolled away. As soon as she could, Aneta sprang back up, unsheathing her sword.

"*Submit yourselves therefore to God. Resist the devil, and he will flee from you.*" Aneta spoke the verse she read that morning. "I'm done with you."

"Done? We've just begun." Daunting eyed her, advancing, causing Aneta to step back. "You think you can't do this on your own. You need your Father's help...how pitiful."

Aneta stopped in her tracks, confused at what the demon just said, still gripping her sword tightly. "What do you mean? I already know I *can't* do this on my own, and I never will be able to anyway. I seek the help of my God Jesus, but I believe you are confused. I *want* His help.

And He *wants* to help me." With a smile, Aneta knew there was a fear growing inside of Daunting.

"You tried before to use your sword. You failed. Why is now any different?" he taunted.

"I may not know all I should, but I know more now than I did before. You have come to stop God's work. I cannot allow that."

Daunting sneered at Aneta. "We have no room for troublemakers like you. You will die. And I will then take care of Theo. He is a troublemaker, just like you. You can tell the coward that we will always come for him."

"*For we wrestle not against flesh and blood, but against principalities, against powers, against the rulers of the darkness of this world, against spiritual wickedness in high places.* You cannot take my life, you cannot take this town! It belongs to God and God alone." Aneta impressed herself with how she could now speak up. *Thank you Jesus, so much.* She raised her sword and stopped Daunting in its tracks.

Daunting snarled and swiped her off her feet. It then attempted to tear apart Aneta's armor. The demon did not get very far.

Aneta whipped her hand around and sliced off one of Daunting's toes. He hissed in pain as the toe deteriorated into a mist. It let go of her. She rolled and shot up again, spinning to build momentum to make her blow more powerful. She grunted as she drove Daunting back. The massive demon tried to combat her, but the glowing white rays that had begun to swirl around Aneta's feet were blinding. It desperately lashed with its tail, trying to trip her, but Aneta dodged its every attempt and hacked off the end of its tail. It gave a blood-curdling scream and shied back even more.

Aneta charged and plunged her sword into the beast's leg. It shrieked in pain. Aneta struck again. Again. Again. After a final stab to the chest, Daunting finally fell and disintegrated into red smoke, which vanished in moments.

Panting heavily, Aneta sheathed her sword and looked up. "Thank you, God. I could not have done it without You."

Even in the soaring feeling of being triumphant, Aneta's thoughts immediately launched back to Daunting's words about Theo.

Her mind flashed back to a scene from her youth...

∧ ∧ ∧ ∧
• • • •

Aneta whipped out a sword, but Coward immediately called in small scout demons to fight on his behalf. Annoyed, Aneta fended off the measly demons, but he began to meander away.

"Coward!" She called out.

This caught Coward's attention. He shot a glance over his shoulder.

Aneta stunned one demon by kicking it in the head so she could shout to him. "I know you by your trait! You won't last long!"

The battered demon slowly staggered up and continued fighting Aneta alongside the other measly demons until Coward got away. They then hurried out of her range, vanishing to the canyons.

Aneta sheathed her sword, angry. Coward was a sniveling teenager who only cared for himself. She knew this. Everyone who knew Coward knew this. Still, Aneta wanted to save him.

When Aneta found him again, he had a whip and lashed at her. She was not prepared for this, and her sword dropped from her hand as she began to bleed from her knuckles to her forearm.

Coward coiled his whip and stood over Aneta as she knelt, attempting to decrease her pain.

"Not so high and mighty now?"

Aneta looked up at him. "You are still a coward, Coward." She stood up, slightly raising herself on her tiptoes to try and meet Coward's teenage height.

As her red face flamed in anger and she began to scold him about his choices in life, Coward glared at her. He finally exhaled in disbelief and began to walk away.

"Stay away from me, Aneta. I have work to do. You are going to get hurt."

"No. You are," she replied, unfazed by his comment. She picked up her sword. "We are going to meet again, Coward. It will be sooner than you think. You can walk away now, but I train every day so when I encounter people like you, I can stop what they do. You hurt His Kingdom."

"Oh please, He doesn't exist. If He did, He would have stopped this long ago."

"If He didn't exist, you wouldn't be here."

Aneta sighed. She couldn't ignore it any longer. She had already accepted Theo. She had already determined to leave Coward behind. But did she? She felt slightly sheepish for not accepting it right away. Aneta finally realized her younger self had not wanted to see Coward ever again. Why was that? Stopping her own baffling thoughts, Aneta hurried back to the diner. Sorrow was fine, as she had not been caught in any wreckage. This relieved Aneta, but she hoped Sorrow had not been hiding anything.

Once Aneta and Sorrow received their food, Aneta asked about the fire. "So about the fire...is your family alright? Was your house affected at all? Did you have to be ready to move?"

"I don't remember. Mom and Dad were fighting all night at my house--that's what my sister said. I woke up late and missed my first period class, though."

"Oh, oops. But I am glad you are safe. And your family. God is good. No one was wounded badly in general, and that's kinda a miracle. Thank God."

"God did that?"

"Yes."

"How do you know?"

"He is the only one who does things like that. Miracles really."

"Are you sure? Dad is always blaming God for everything."

"Well, I know a lot of people do that only because they don't quite understand what happens. There are a lot of things that happen behind the scenes and we might not ever realize half of it. For example, just the other day, I was going around and I was totally mentally exhausted and...annoyed...the whole thing. Anyway, I just found out--well I did not find out, I found out a while before this, but I realized that I have to be patient. There are a lot of...forces at work behind our everyday lives. Some are good, some are bad.

"Just earlier, actually, I was-" Aneta chuckled once, "-battling something and every other time, I just could not get past it. I was...completely lost in what to do, I was unprepared, I couldn't figure out what to do or how to do it. And, and like, when I just did it again, this time, I felt prepared enough. But it turns out, over the past few days, especially after the whole fire thing, I have been able to grow in God, and we have been able to connect even more than ever."

Sorrow gave Aneta a careful look. "What do you mean by 'connect?'"

"Like...a relationship? God and I are Father and daughter."

"Oh." Sorrow's face relaxed. "So, what would you call it...when someone connects with something else?"

"What do you mean?"

"Maybe if...someone was...not *connecting*...like you. But just maybe, uh, like, connecting with...something *else*? Something creepy."

Aneta tilted her head as she thought about it. "As in...demonically? That kind?"

"Maybe." Sorrow shrugged.

"Well, so...what are you asking?"

"Do you know what it looks like when someone is connected to a bad force?"

"I don't know." Aneta tried to look oblivious to anything personal Sorrow may have been referencing. She began to wonder if Sorrow meant herself or someone she knew. "What are you asking?"

"I don't know." Sorrow shrugged and kept eating her hamburger.

Aneta did so as well, but she also noticed Ly giving them a look of either curiosity or anger. For all she knew, it was both. Something was happening, and she had to talk to Courage.

They got off that topic and finished their lunch. Aneta paid for both of them, cheerfully thanking Lyle for the hamburgers, even though all her cash was now gone. She did not get paid until next Monday. In return, Ly suspiciously gave Aneta a nod.

When they walked out, Aneta gave a side hug to Sorrow. "Hey! Thanks for eating lunch with me! See you soon?"

"Sure." Sorrow shrugged, but her small smile offered a fragment of joy.

When Aneta got back to the old town hall, the service had already ended and most people were gone but the Nepenthes, Miss Lovely, and the rest of the group.

"How'd it go?" Faith asked, leaving the group and walking over to Aneta.

Aneta slowly nodded, looking at Theo who was talking to Bold. "Good. We had some interesting conversations though." She gulped. "Has...Bold ever...told you anything about Theo, before Theo moved here?"

"No, not really." Faith gave her a weird look. "Well, what do you mean?"

"Nothing. Nevermind. Just...wondering."

|Chapter 12: The Fair|

On the way home from work, Aneta ran into Candid walking home with Rise and Wonder from the library.

From them, she found out that the Whimsicalton Fair was that evening, Friday, Saturday, and Sunday in Aphot Park.

"Oh, that's cool! How many years have they been doing a fair here?"

"Ever since I was Rise's size." Candid smiled and shrugged. "Are you going to the fair?"

"Well, it sure sounds fun. I'd like to go. I'm gonna ask the squad if they can make it. Thanks for telling me about it. Hey, how have you been doing so far?"

"With what?"

"Just...with life."

"Oh." Candid let out a loud sigh. "Not very good. Wonder is only three, but she is constantly getting on my nerves. Always asking question after question. Rise is just mischievous in her own way, but I don't ever feel like I'm a good enough mom. I hate being single. I wish I never met Devious...he was a good-looking man and he is super-sweet with kids but... he has a temper and a serious problem with..." Candid sounded like she wanted to finish her sentence, but finally decided to leave it. "He left and doesn't even send support of any kind. But I love my girls and I would never give them up. Devious just makes it hard..."

"I'm so sorry to hear that. What job do you have?"

"I work at the theater and part-time at the post office."

"Oh, that's rough. Is there anything you would like me to pray about for you?"

"Oh." Candid's face fell blank at the unexpected offer. "Um...nothing in particular."

"Alright. Sounds good." Aneta felt in her purse for a plastic bag of cookies. "Can I give Rise and Wonder cookies?"

"If you like."

"Rise, Wonder." Aneta knelt down to their level.

The two girls paused on the sidewalk.

"Do you like cookies?"

Rise did not verbally reply at first. On the other hand, Wonder hesitantly walked up to Aneta. "Can I have a 'ookie?"

Aneta grinned and handed Wonder a cookie. Rise then asked as well. After straightening up, Aneta waved goodbye and walked away.

She walked to Miss Lovely's apartment, which was below her own.

"Oh! Good afternoon!" Miss Lovely opened the door and waved Aneta inside. "I decided to use that bread mix Mrs. Nepenthe gave me." She chuckled and brought over a plate of bread. "I made banana bread this morning. Here, have some."

Aneta laughed and took a piece.

"Now, there you go again." Miss Lovely put her arms on her hips before sitting down at the table.

"What?"

"You are always laughing at something. That's a good spirit. Keep laughing. There is a lot in life to be happy about."

Aneta tried not to laugh, but ended up doing so anyway. "Alright. Well, how are you today, Miss Lovely? Ready for another Bible study?"

"I sure am. Here, I've been reading in Job. Have you read Job?"

"I have, but not for a while, and not very much."

"Oh, well, I just finished. Now I get most of it, but I don't understand why God tells Job what He does."

"Alright. Just a second. Let me turn there." Aneta flipped some pages in her Bible. "Okay, so you are asking why God corrected Job?"

"Yes. God Himself said that Job was righteous."

With a deep breath, Aneta hoped she would be able to accurately answer Miss Lovely's question. Suddenly, she did not feel very well-learned in the Bible.

"Well, I suppose it may have something to do with how Job took the whole matter. In the beginning, he was right in saying he had done nothing wrong. He knew he was righteous, and he was confident in that. Now, he seemed to be doing pretty good with what he said until his friends came around. It is odd, though; when I read Job, I am always appalled at what Job's friends say.

"I sit there and just wonder how they could not see Job was innocent. Oh! But I think they probably thought Job did something wrong because of... okay, never mind. Or..." Aneta felt like she was rabbit-trailing, but decided to finish her sentence. "Okay. So you know how the Israelites would... rebel against God, and then God would hand them over to their enemies? That would be God punishing people for what they did, or sometimes didn't, do. It is shown through the Bible as well, I think.

"See, Job's friends thought the only plausible explanation would be that Job sinned... did something wrong... and now he was being punished for that. Now, Job kept saying 'no, I am innocent,' but then Job would say something like 'I wish I was never born,' and things like that. The more Job talked about his whole matter with his friends, the more he felt like he understood what had happened, and why, less and less. Eventually, he was basically asking God why He let everything happen to him.

"And then that is where... I forgot his name. Job's other friend, the one that was younger and didn't speak up until the end."

"Elihu?"

"Yes, I think so. Elihu speaks up and reminds them all of how great God is, and how they should not speak of God in the way they had been. This is when God steps in, asking Job why he is, I guess you could almost say, complaining. So God is saying, 'I am God and you are not. Were you here when I laid the foundations of the earth?' And so God is correcting Job through that... oh..." Aneta's heart fell as she realized she was talking in circles. "Um... is this making sense?" She flipped open to the last chapters of Job.

"You're doing fine, honey."

"So, okay, right here. Chapter forty-two. After God talks to Job about how he doesn't have the right to ask God why, Job says that God was right, and these things...'things too wonderful for me, which I knew not.' So here, Job is acknowledging that no man can understand all things, and there is no use in asking God why, or being mad." Aneta mentally groaned. "I'm sorry...does that make any sense? I'm afraid one of the others in the squad would have been better to answer this question."

"Oh, Aneta, you are doing a fine job. You get along really well with the rest of your group, and you young'uns are all doing a fine job with studying the Bible and getting with God."

"Thanks, Miss Lovely." Aneta smiled, but still felt quite juvenile in her knowledge of the Bible.

"Oh!" Miss Lovely, in her frail voice, tapped her hand on the table a few times in excitement. "Aneta, I got a job at the library!"

"Oh, really?"

"Yes! I've always wanted to work at a library. I never got to do that when I was younger. I worked at a bank and married too young." She clicked her tongue at herself. "I figure that would get my rent paid here so you don't have to pay for it."

Aneta gasped in realizing wonder and hugged Miss Lovely. "Oh! This is amazing! What a blessing, Miss Lovely!"

Someone knocked on the door. Aneta stood up and opened the door. "Oh, hello, Bold."

"Hey Aneta. Miss Lovely, I have a toaster oven for you."

Miss Lovely's face shone with happiness. "Oh my, oh my. Oh my, thank you so much! You are so sweet!"

Bold grinned. "You're welcome. Let us know if you need anything else."

"Oh, you do so much for me already!"

Aneta walked into Faith's apartment where Courage was making dinner for everyone. Bold and Theo were sitting at the table when Aneta asked them about going to the fair.

"What?" With an exasperated sigh, Theo gave her a look. "Aneta. I don't have time or money to go to a fair. I've been battling things all day and everything seems horrendous right now."

"Oh." Aneta paused. "I'm sorry you've had a rough day. Um, but...wouldn't that be all the more reason to go to a fair? We all need a break, and fairs are lots of fun. We wouldn't even have to spend money, either. We can walk around and look at the animals and-"

"*No,* Aneta. Really." Theo leaned on the table. "I don't have time for that. I still need to prep my lesson for Sunday and...I have to do that tonight." He mumbled, "I really should have done that on Wednesday..."

"Theo. Come on." Aneta remained firm. "It is a fair. We are going. We need a break."

"I can't."

"Yes, you can. There is no way you can be productive in all this stress. Bold, Faith, and Courage are going. You better go too."

"*They* aren't trying to keep a church going!"

"Well. No, they are not giving the sermons, but *yes*, they are helping run the church. Our entire squad is super-stressed with all this work, and running around, and sometimes tiny meals, and sleepless nights, and giving and giving and giving, and going off of a fraction of money for everything after rent. We are *all* feeling it. Just come with us. Have a fun time. Then work on your sermon at lunch on Friday and Saturday."

Theo groaned.

Aneta laughed and threw her hands up as the wind cooled her face. "Come on, have fun! I know you want to!"

Despite trying to be melancholy, Theo eventually hinted at a smile and put one of his arms out to the side as the monstrous contraption spun them around and around. At the end of the ride, Faith jumped off her seat and grinned.

"I'm glad that group of people gave us their extra tickets. It was just enough to get us all a ride!"

Bold elbowed Theo. "Come on. Just grin, already. Wasn't that fun?"

Theo tried to hide a smile in annoyance and whacked Bold.

"Alright gang, let's go see the animals." Courage waved them on. She smiled to herself. "Not that you guys don't *act* like animals."

The entire group moved towards the tents, enjoying the cool evening at the fair. Aneta thought about Theo the entire night. When the boys left the group to seek out water bottles for the girls, Aneta took the time to talk to Faith and Courage. She got Faith up to speed on the issue of her's and Theo's previous relationship and Aneta's thoughts.

"I can't stand it! I don't know why I'm so hateful towards Theo. I mean, sometimes I'm fine, but then I just feel so...so...I don't know." Aneta looked at Faith and Courage with a pleading look.

Courage thought about it. "Well, Aneta, I can't say I've ever been in your boat before. But...maybe you're only feeling this way because you feel like you have worked so hard to change Coward...and when God finally changed him, you feel like your work was wasted? Is that where you are going?"

Sighing, Aneta nodded, slightly relieved Courage had put it into words for her. "Yes. I suppose that's how I feel. Is it wrong to feel like this?"

Courage and Faith glanced at each other. Faith shrugged. "I'm not sure I can answer that. But I do know this: God knew that was all going to happen. He can put it to whatever use He deems fit. God doesn't waste anything, Aneta. Try to focus on what God has done, not what Coward did."

Aneta tried to remember that. "Okay."

They walked through the poultry area, then watched the horses for a while. Meanwhile, Courage and Bold left to go to the bathrooms. That left Theo, Faith, and Aneta standing there watching horses by themselves.

Theo sighed. "Alright. I admit it Aneta...I'm *glad* you *made me* come tonight."

"Wow. So grudgingly too." Aneta made a face.

"Ha, ha." He gave a fake laugh. "At least I said *something*."

"Oh, really? Because you still don't sound that grateful."

"Aw...by the way, you look really cute when you're mad."

Aneta stopped. She looked at Theo and blinked. He let the comment sink in as Aneta's face slowly reddened and her eyes gradually showed embarrassed annoyance. She stood speechless.

"I can't help that you're a foot shorter than me," Theo smirked.

Aneta narrowed her eyes. "I am *five foot four,* thank you. You're only *nine* inches taller than me. And I'm not mad!"

"Alright, alright. I just...thought I would follow your advice and I am appreciating the little things in life."

"I am *not* that short!"

Theo tossed up his hands. "Hey, I'm just saying that I'm glad God makes sure we have fun. But uh, I appreciate that you thought I was talking about you."

"I will beat you."

"Can you reach?"

"I will *climb* you, towering giraffe."

"Ooh, name calling."

"Where on earth is Courage or Bold? They deserted me? They left me with you? Faith?"

Clueless, Faith put up her hands, wanting to stay out of it.

"Would you like to climb on my shoulders so you can see?" Theo offered with a grin.

"I can *see just fine, thank you.*"

"Well, if you ever need something off the top shelf, you know where I am."

"Yeah. *And I know where you live* in case I need to beat you up."

"Ah, well I thought you'd already would've done that...but I guess since you haven't, you don't hate me that much."

Before Aneta could shoot back a reply, Bold came back. "Hey, so I saw this...booth...with funnel cakes...um, what erupted here? Faith?"

Again, Faith silently threw up her hands, still clueless and not wanting to say a word.

Nevertheless, Bold's question caused Aneta to blush abruptly. Theo grinned, amused. "Oh, discussing height differences."

The rest of the evening passed with fun and conversation, including a few more shots fired between Theo and Aneta. They eventually found Candid, Rise and Wonder, and waved to them. At the end of the night, they all walked home their separate ways, Theo in a slightly better mood than Aneta.

|Chapter 13: Another Point Of View|

Advisor held his breath as his wife tearfully nodded on the phone. As she hung up, she put her head in her hands. "Free got in a car crash." She covered her face with both hands, trying to hide her reddening face full of tears. "He didn't make it."

For a while, both he and his wife cried together at the table for their son.

They did not go to the fair that Thursday night like they had planned but instead stayed home, shocked and silent. Advisor could not bear to tell anyone of what had happened, and his wife simply could not utter a word without tears springing up in her eyes.

The only thing she said the rest of the day was, "The Universe is cruel." The statement may have made sense to her, but Advisor failed to see how that was comforting. There was no possible option to overcome his grief for his only son.

That night, he could not sleep for hours. Each time he closed his eyes, horrifying images of fire and death rose up from a mangled car, black smoke billowing from the wreck and clouding the sky. His wife slept soundly, retiring to bed early and waking up late, having called for a week off of work.

In the morning, Advisor dragged himself to work early, drained and exhausted. He had not eaten dinner or breakfast, and forgot to eat lunch as he stood behind the counter of the café, staring into space. Friday inched by. When he got home, his wife had not made dinner, so he ate a sandwich in silence.

Nothing made sense. Everything was supposed to work by chance. Why, then, was his son the one in seven billion to die that day?

Faith sighed. Her legs ached from the long day. Fridays at the restaurant always exhausted her. At one point, she finally found a spare moment to go to the bathroom. When she came out, she saw Advisor there. She made a face as she remembered that he typically came on Sunday nights with his wife, Dr. A. Theist. But this was Friday...and he was there alone.

And something was very wrong.

His whole body slumped, and his countenance was so fatigued and ghost-like, with hollow, vacant eyes staring off into nothing.

Faith had to get back to the kitchen, but she wanted to ask. "Advisor?"

Advisor, who evidently knew who she was and what she wanted, but seemed too drained to react in any way, simply stopped and looked at her.

"Are you...would you like prayer?" Faith gulped.

The man stared at her. It would have been disturbing if he had not already been staring blankly at the wall. "What?"

"Would you like prayer? You seem...distraught."

"Prayer?" he repeated. "That can't do anything now."

Faith bit her lip, unsure of what had happened. "It can do miracles." She wanted to say more, but nothing else came to mind.

His countenance changed from a languid attitude to a type of fierce desperation. "I know your God does things, but He is nothing I have ever seen. If your God can do anything...if He would do something for me...please ask Him for me."

Advisor trudged in the front door around nine that night, still drained. His wife had waited up for him in bed, arms folded.

"You didn't tell me where you were," she said.

"I'm sorry. I was distracted. I ate out."

"Oh. Ready for bed?"

"More than." After hesitating, Advisor said, "Why is this so *hard*? Why should this even matter if we are nothing to the Universe?"

"What on earth are you asking?" she demanded, her confusion and annoyance tinted with sorrow. Her eyes pleaded with him not to mention it again.

"I'm sick of living with this. It has only been a day, and there is no way I could do this for the rest of my life."

"Advisor." His wife's tone of voice begged him to stop talking about it.

"I can't do it. I asked one of those young ladies to ask her God for me."

Tears sprang into her eyes. "Advisor, stop it, stop it *right now!* I can't stand the thought of Him or religion. Stop talking and go to bed."

"But I am serious. I am hoping God will help me with this."

"Are you *that* desperate?" Her eyes filled with skepticism. "Are you that desperate to ask some random fictional Being for help? Even if He exists, what makes you think He can do anything more than the Universe? Which one evolved us?"

"I'm going to church on Sunday to figure out something. That group of young people have more than we do, and I want to know *what* exactly it is. I don't know if it's their God or not. But I'm going."

His wife turned under the covers and humphed, too tired to debate about it.

In the morning, he walked to the café. Even though everything felt worthless, he still hoped one of the young men or women starting that new church could help him. His wife showed up around noon with a homemade lunch for him. She remained there until they closed, all the while gently talking to him about how they couldn't do anything about their son's accident and it was better to forget everything.

Despite his wife's careful, caressing words, which he knew were trying to calm him into thinking he did not have to go to church, Advisor still walked across the street on Sunday at noon to church.

He saw Aneta singing in front with another girl while a man played the guitar. After a few songs, Theo stood up to speak. Advisor slowly relaxed as the service continued.

He thought about sitting down near the back, but remained standing. He soon spotted Broken. However, he had heard that was no longer her name. She went by Gracefully Broken now. In awe, Advisor realized what a gentle, confident, young lady she had become. It was a vastly different image than she had presented only a few short months ago.

He watched two young women take care of a few little ones near the back, where he stood with a slight smile. It reminded him of his younger days with Free. He spotted Courage in one of the rows, intently listening to every word of Theo's. How did the five young adults have so much influence in so many peoples' lives? There were at least twenty people here, adults and children, all listening to what Theo brought forth.

Advisor stood there until the service was done. He did not know how to approach Theo, but he did not have to because Faith walked up to him, bringing Theo over.

"Hello, Advisor." Theo smiled.

Despite being over twice the young man's age, Advisor felt overwhelmed at the young man's spirit. There was something Theo possessed that he could only dream of. The way Theo carried himself, spoke of life, and walked in peace astounded him.

Theo asked, "How are you today?"

Advisor paused before replying. "My son died a few days ago." He watched as Theo's face whitened with concern.

"I am so sorry."

"I'm not quite sure what to do. I asked this young lady, Faith, to pray on my behalf, but I'm not sure what God will say." Advisor kept going, before Theo could say anything. "Why did my son die?" He threw the question out there, knowing whatever answer the young man could offer would not make sense anyway.

Theo paused. "I'm not sure. It isn't God's will that anyone dies. But men's free will exists. Every action of a person has consequences; they may be good or bad."

"My life has been a wreck, and it has only been three days. I can't live like this." All of a sudden, Advisor felt foolish for asking help from a young man like Theo.

"I don't know what you are going through, but know that you are welcome to come here whenever we have services... Wednesdays as well. The squad...Aneta, Bold, Faith, Courage...will definitely keep you in prayer. Even if we don't know what your grief is like, we understand it must be horrible to go through this."

Despite his sullen thoughts, Advisor nodded, relieved that their prayer might help, even if it was in the smallest portion. "Thank you. I might come on Wednesday."

Theo shook his hand, then Advisor left the building.

In the fifteen-second interval between the old town hall and his front door, his nightmare roared to life again as a car innocently drove by. This time, it began with the last conversation he had with his son.

"Dad, I don't want to talk about this right now." Free's frustrated voice echoed through to Advisor's side of the phone conversation.

"No, we are talking about this now. Your mother just wanted to see you for her birthday. That is the least you could do."

"I told you. I couldn't make it. I had other plans."

"Like what? Hanging out with your friends?"

"Yes! It was Sunday. What do you expect? Look, I'll come and visit you on Thursday. The fair is that day. She'll love that just as much. We used to go to that when I was little, remember? It'll be a fun surprise."

"It doesn't change the fact that you never even called your mother." Advisor humphed and hung up the phone.

Advisor shuddered. He stopped in front of the door. Instead, he backed up and walked around to the back yard, mumbling to himself. After pacing for a few moments, in a sudden burst of rage, Advisor snatched up the metal baseball bat and began whacking the trash can with all his strength. After taking his anger out on the metal canister, Advisor sank down against the side of the house, exhausted and tearful.

"Blame it on God if it will make you feel better." His wife stood next to him.

From the ground, Advisor sighed. "You don't get it!"

"Yes I do, Advisor!" His wife pointed at her chest. "He was my son, too!" Tears fell from her own cheeks. "You aren't the only one suffering! God is a cruel Being. You know it. Just admit it!"

"It's not that simple." Advisor moaned and bowed his head between his knees. "The service was quite interesting. Haven't you noticed God has a lot of followers for being 'cruel?' There is more to God than we originally thought."

Dr. A. Theist sighed and walked away. "I can't believe you."

On Wednesday evening, Advisor walked to the old town hall, earnestly wondering if God would really help him out. He arrived early and met with some other people there, a few of whom he recognized from around town. Conversing with them, Advisor slowly learned how amazing God had been to them. This put him in a curious state of mind. After carefully listening to what the young man named Bold, who taught that night, had to say, he made up his mind. When the Bible study ended, he walked up to Theo.

"I apologize for my actions towards you young people. And Broken...Gracefully Broken too. But I enjoyed the words of Bold this evening. If you could tell me more about God, it would be greatly appreciated."

"It would be a pleasure." Theo smiled.

|Chapter 14: Pain|

Even though Aneta typically did not enjoy Mondays, she was in a good mood that morning and decided to walk to the bakery to pick up some coffee before starting work. She smiled as she spoke to God, watching the sunrise unfold. After feeling her Bible in her purse, she softened and closed her eyes for a moment of peace. Upon opening them, she noticed Clinical, who worked at Chef Chava's Restaurant, was also on the sidewalk, in a more dull disposition.

"Good morning, Clinical." She gave a little wave. "How are you?"

Clinical hardly glanced up. "Morning."

Aneta paused after walking past Clinical and turned around. She furrowed her brow at the oddly plain greeting.

Please don't tell me Daunting is going to appear. Aneta looked around, hand over her sword's hilt. She hoped she did not have to fight.

A slobbering growl interrupted the beautiful morning. Almost trembling, she raised her head, looking at the roof of the building next to her. A huge demon dove off the roof and lunged at her. She yelped and dove away. She whipped her sword in front of her just in time to fend off the demon.

With a startled shock, Aneta realized it was Pain, a chief demon she had not encountered since her mother's death. She slashed a gouge into one of the demon's legs. Red mist spurted everywhere. But Pain hardly slowed down. It rushed past her. Aneta looked at Clinical, then back at Pain. She knew she had to stop Pain before it reached Clinical. Even though she still did not know what was happening, she understood why. Pain was wreaking havoc everywhere in Aphoticton.

Something likened to a panic attack seized Aneta. She realized she had to fight. Again. Defending herself was easy, perfunctory. But going out and seeking a fight was something else. Pain was not even bothered with her at the moment. She could avoid a gruesome fight.

Fight for the Kingdom, Aneta.

Aneta listened to her Father's voice and raised her sword toward Pain. "Why don't you come at me then?"

She took the first step forward and waited for Pain to give her its best shot.

Enraged, Pain wasted no time and spun around. It immediately snapped its teeth where Aneta had been standing. Aneta ducked and rolled under the legs of the colossal demon and stabbed it underneath as she went. It grunted and looked at her, twisting its neck. After Aneta jumped out of the way, Pain moved away from her again and again charged towards Clinical.

Aneta chased after Pain. "I won't allow you to remain here!"

Pain stopped and turned halfway towards her, giving her the advantage of driving her sword through its shoulder.

At the same time, Aneta heard someone say, *"The Lord is nigh unto them that are of a broken heart; and saves such as be of a contrite spirit."*

The troublesome demon fell to the concrete and began to disintegrate. Aneta and Theo stood face to face.

"What are *you* doing here?" Theo pulled his own sword from Pain's other shoulder.

Aneta took up her own sword. "I didn't know you were here, too."

"Well...usually it *is* just- *look out!"*

Aneta turned, yelled in surprise and dropped as a squirrely demon squirmed in mid air, not being able to latch onto Aneta's back like it had planned. Theo lunged forward, chopped off its head at the neck, and the pitch black demon misted away.

"Thanks. But what were you saying? Oh wait *look behind you!"* Aneta's voice rose in volume and concern.

Three more demons closed in quickly, hissing and shouting indiscernible words.

"Oh come *on!"* Aneta groaned. She lifted her sword and ground her teeth.

"Come on, it'll be fun!" Theo charged to meet the demons.

Aneta's jaw began to ache as she continued to grit her teeth. She hesitated to fight when Theo willingly threw himself into battle?

A demon with talon-like fingers attempted to rake her face but Aneta blocked it. Nonetheless, she backed up. "Yeah, have your fun. Just trying not to die here."

"Stop talking and focus." Theo, now serious again, grunted and slayed the demon, scarcely moving out of the way of the third one.

With one last ounce of effort, Aneta pummeled her demon and sighed as Theo slaughtered his. She sank down on the sidewalk, exhausted. Even so, she found it was much easier to fight when someone else was at her side. Theo stood there, equally worn out. Aneta silently observed him, now that she had time to think. She wondered if she could actually trust him. She could no longer see Coward standing there. He was too bold, too courageous, too amiable, too mature.

Physically, he still looked like the same person she had fought against years ago, minus the long hair and multiple piercings, but he'd just proven that the name she had known him by no longer fit. Coward stood before her now as Theo, a Child of the King. She closed her eyes and swallowed hard. She had no idea what to think. Only one thought stood standfast in her mind. What did Theo think of her?

Her mind traveled to the battle. She had not backed down. She used her sword. She had been able to stand against the demons, chief or non. Just as Aneta began to wonder if she could fight again with the same ambition as before, a sinking feeling slowly overwhelmed her. Even though she *had* fought demons, even though she *had* won the battle, even though she *had* been able to fight with vigor and valor, she still felt it was wasted. She knew her heart had not been in the fight.

Another thing that ferociously bothered Aneta was the fact that Theo had no problem fighting his way to victory. Much to her dismay, he reminded her of herself when she was younger.

Why did fighting demons bother her? She knew it was worth the Kingdom. She knew it was worth any sacrifice. She *knew* it.

But why did her soul hesitate and groan when she had to fight? Aneta harshly exhaled in frustration over her own feelings.

Both Aneta and Theo walked to the bakery to get coffee, since Theo had joined Aneta on the sidewalk that morning. Theo shook his head.

"I wish I knew..." He paused in mid sentence, seemingly unsure if he wanted to finish his thought or not.

Aneta gently glanced at him. With an equally gentle tone, she asked, "knew what?"

Theo waited another moment before deciding to answer. "I wish I knew if I am actually as capable as I hope I am to build a whole church."

Aneta tried to figure out what to say. She did not want to reply too terribly late, in the chance Theo might think she did not truly mean what she said. They made it to the bakery, and Theo held the door open for her.

She paused before walking in. Looking Theo in the eye, she said, "God knows you by your trait, and I know you by your trait as well."

Still holding the door open, Theo quickly glanced at the ground. It seemed everything they said had a moment's pause between them. "The last time you said that..."

"I mean it, Theo. God's grace and mercy is your trait. I see it all the time. You are daring and brave, and you are nothing like your past self. God's trait has overpowered your own." After stunning Theo with her statement, Aneta walked inside the bakery. Theo followed, silent.

They both silently grabbed coffee and doughnuts, both nodding to each other, and then both parting ways again.

Aneta realized something. She had finally come to terms with herself, and Theo. She no longer felt a barrier between them. Even as she had walked away from Theo, she had glanced behind herself and seen Theo playfully grinning as he thought no one was looking.

As she walked to the Whimsicalton Inn, Aneta skipped lightly and she could not keep a happy smile from her own face. Theo now knew she knew. At that point, it seemed silly to her she had tried to keep it a secret, or to suppress what had happened. At any rate, she was thankful for the way everything had played out, knowing it would help them immensely.

Bold glanced up from the car on which he was changing the oil and wiped his hands. "Excuse me, sir, are you looking for someone? Do you have an appointment?"

The man, who was looking around in the lobby area, fixed his brilliant green eyes on Bold as if evaluating him.

With an odd smile, he said, "Ah, hello there." He smoothly slid his hands into his jacket pockets. "Well, actually, I am just looking around. Who is that?" He motioned to Theo, who had just disappeared through the doors.

"His name is Theo. Did he help you with your car before? Do you have a question for him?"

"Ah. I *thought* I recognized him." The man smiled again. This time, his brilliant green eyes glinted. "And *your* name is?"

Bold hesitated. "Bold."

"Thank you."

Bold's hand automatically flew to his sword's hilt as a demon's laugh echoed through the building. A demon clambered up to the man and gave the man in black attire a quick note of information.

The man's countenance seemed to shift in front of Bold, revealing a dark, shadowy form lurking inside of the man. However, his brilliant green eyes remained. Both the demon and the man quickly continued on their way.

"Something else is going on," Bold mumbled as he watched the evil man leave. His hand remained over his sword, ready to unsheath it at any moment. "I don't like it. The demons did not even bother to acknowledge us. They are focused on something else."

Theo glanced in the direction Bold was staring. Scout demons were out in force, not causing havoc but watching everyone carefully, seemingly checking on the status of people. A beastly looking demon, in the form of a gigantic wolf bear, circled the area in a wide circumference, waiting for something to happen. When they spotted the man who had spoken to Bold, they seemed to know their orders, and many of them dispersed while others hurried up to him.

"I don't like it." Bold scowled. "Not one bit."

Aneta received a text from Candid around nine-thirty p.m. She seemed eager to talk. Even though she was tired, Aneta sat up in her bed to chat.

<yes, I'm doing well ;) How is Rise and Wonder doing?> - Aneta

<good. Have you ever come up against something that you don't know how to deal with? That you're afraid of it?> -Candid

<uh, I'm not sure. I have come against difficult issues that scared me, but I'm not sure we deal with the same things> - Aneta

<I really need guidance in what to do. I was even too nervous to go to the park today with the girls> -Candid

<Oh, really? What or who have you been seeing or..? Could you give me something a little more detailed?> -Aneta

<I saw Devious at the store today. He didn't see me I don't think, that is. I don't know what he is going to do if he sees me. I don't want him to hurt Rise or Wonder> -Candid

<The squad will pray for you on this. Why do you think he is in Aphoticton? You said he moved away a while ago right?> - Aneta

<I don't know! I thought he was long gone. I really hope he doesn't find me.> -Candid

<Do you have a pic of him? We can watch out for him and see where he goes, maybe> -Aneta

<I deleted all my pictures of him> -Candid

<Okay, thanks, we will do our best. I can ask Helpful if anyone has come in by the name of Devious. She might know someone who knows Devious. I'll let you know.> -Aneta

In the morning, Aneta asked Helpful about Devious. "Hey. Is there a man here under the name Devious?"

Helpful glanced through her files. "No. Not here. You could check the motel if you are looking for someone."

"Alright, thanks."

Aneta spotted a large demon pacing back and forth around the inn's entrance. When it spotted Aneta, it let out a pleased growl and lumbered away, allowing her to enter.

Jesus, please show me what to do. I'm clueless.

After making sure no other demons were visible in the entryway, she quietly moved further inside. Two demons, suddenly appearing at the far end of the hall, spotted her and screeched a shrill battle cry.

Aneta gasped. She spun around and bolted. If she could go fast enough, she would not have to fight. The idea of fighting seemed tiring.

"Pull yourself together!" She quietly hissed at herself. "You just finished a battle. You need to stop this!"

Still running, she glanced quickly behind her, but she could tell she would not be able to outrun the hench demons. As one leapt to jump on top of her, Aneta turned and whacked it away with her shield. Nevertheless, that slowed her down and let the other one catch up. She blocked that demon as well and backed up as fast as she could, trying to get away.

The two scout demons were quite weak and not skilled enough to put up a big fight. She made quick work of them simply by using her foot to kick them away, but their calls alerted other demons that she was on the move. She ran faster, trying to get away, just away…until a demon stepped out in front of her..

Aneta stopped, snarled and reached for her sword.

It wasn't there.

What? Aneta glanced at her empty scabbard, then snapped her head around. Her mind whirled. Her eyes raced.

A nearby demon screeched in glee, holding her sword. Had she been that careless? Aneta stomped her foot in anger and tightly gripped her shield. "God, I'm sorry. Please show me a way out."

The demon chortled mirthlessly and advanced towards her. It widened its mouth, but Aneta dropped at the last second and rolled

144

under the demon. She popped up behind it, but could not get very far before another demon showed up. Fear.

Aneta's heart recoiled. What was *Fear* doing here? It barked sharply, and a messenger demon appeared.

"Tell Lost that I will join him in a moment," Fear sneered. "I have to deal with an old friend." The messenger laughed and sped away.

With a fierce glare, Aneta raised her shield, ready to fight, although she wished she had her sword. The demon holding it did not seem concerned with running off with it; it was too busy taunting Aneta, just beyond her reach.

"I'm done with you, Fear. You should have figured that out a while ago."

"Ah, but you aren't. You say you are, but you are afraid right now, aren't you?" It's brilliant green eyes illuminated brightly, contrasting it's dark skin.

Aneta's breath shortened. She had seen those eyes before. *God, I need someone or something right now.* "Maybe I am. But that doesn't matter, because God is still on my side."

The Spirit of Authority appeared in a brilliant flash at Aneta's side, holding his flaming sword, ready to defend Aneta. *"For God hath not given us the spirit of fear..."*

As he began to speak, Fear let out a shaking shudder and reared to attack them.

Aneta remained where she stood, refusing to back down from Fear as the Spirit of Authority continued to speak: *"...but of power, and of love, and of a sound mind."*

Fear's jaws met Spirit of Authority's sword. The Spirit of Authority reached out and grabbed the demon which was holding Aneta's sword by the neck. Aneta snatched up her sword as Fear lost confidence and scurried away, leaving Spirit of Authority there. He gave a respectful nod, then vanished.

With determination, Aneta gripped her sword and moved through the halls. The demon that had tried to get at her earlier with Fear burst through the wall, knocking her down.

Aneta let out a shocked yelp and raised her shield over her face. In the tulmult, she gripped her sword again, determined to keep it by her side. With a large amount of effort, Aneta escaped the drooling mouth of the demon and chopped off a leg. The demon screeched as it began to mist away. Other demons began racing towards Aneta. She assumed a fighting stance and tried to figure out what to do in the two seconds she had before they were close enough to claw and bite. She fended off the demon on her left with her shield and slit the demon on her right.

On top of multiple attacks, the demons began filling the air with their screeching whispers full of discouraging thoughts. Attempting to combat that as well, she began to talk to herself.

"For verily, when we were with you, we told you before that we should suffer tribulation; even as it came to pass, and ye know. For this cause, when I could no longer forbear, I sent to know your faith, lest by some means the tempter have tempted you, and our labor be in vain." She slowly grew weary. *"And let us not be wearing in well doing: for in due season we shall reap, if we faint not."*

By the time Aneta sliced the last demon, she tasted blood in her mouth, her right hand was covered in scratches, and her arms ached. She leaned against the wall, exhausted.

"Praying always with all prayer and supplication in the Spirit, and watching thereunto with all perseverance and supplication for all saints..." Aneta sighed, gathered her strength and hurried down the hall, through the lobby and glancing around in every direction.

A roar behind her made Aneta jump. She spun around as another large, ugly demon lurched into the lobby. It was Angst.

"You have *got* to be kidding me!" Aneta groaned and lifted her sword again, ready to combat the miscreation.

"In need of assistance, milady?" Theo waltzed up next to her, armor donned and sword and shield in hand.

"Oh, please." Aneta rolled her eyes, tired but amused. The pawing demon charged at them. "But hey, at least you showed up."

Both of them grunted at the beastly demon's impacting blow. Together, they hacked the demon to nothing but red mist.

Aneta looked at Theo as he sheathed his sword. She had tried to be annoyed with him, but she could not bring herself to despite Theo. Not any longer.

"One more thing." The man in black attire asked Helpful at the front desk of the inn. His brilliant green eyes shone in pleasure. "I am looking for a man named Advisor; do you know him?"

At the same time, Aneta walked up to Helpful to ask her about a room she was cleaning.

Helpful nodded. "Well, Mr. Devious, he owns Gray's Cafe down the street."

"Thank you. I will probably find him there." The man of black attire, Devious, walked away.

Aneta stood off to the side until the man was done. Her jaw laxed. Her breath shortened again. Forgetting about her question for Helpful, Aneta grabbed her phone and texted Candid.

<I found Devious! He was just at the inn. Are you home right now?> -Aneta

<Yes> -Candid

<Don't worry about him. God will take care of you. Just be careful and trust Him> -Aneta

Aneta then sent the information to group chat. Even though she did not have a photo of Devious, she gave them a description of what he looked like. Much to her horrified astonishment, everyone had seen him before, all telling of his odd nature. Because of the recent happenings, the girls decided to go to Gray's Cafe the next day on Wednesday.

|Chapter 15: Devious|

During her lunch break on Wednesday, Aneta met up with the girls to head over to Gray's Cafe. When they walked in, Dr. A. Theist cheerfully greeted them, her eyes still on the countertop she was wiping down. Upon looking up, her smile disappeared.

Courage walked up to the counter, "Hello. How are you doing today?"

Faith and Aneta stood behind Courage.

"Fine." Dr. A. Theist's reply sounded flat. "What do you want?"

"Well, we all might get the special today."

"No. What do you *want?*"

"Oh. Sorry. We are also wondering about Advisor. We met up with a man who wanted to see-"

"He isn't here."

Aneta hesitated. "The man, or Advisor?"

"Both. They went somewhere for lunch." She did not sound thrilled about that.

Aneta glanced around the place. The pictures on the wall still hung in their places, the rug on the floor still collected water and dirt, the menu was still the same, but the eerie shadows and haunting black fog were gone. Demons still hissed at them from the differing booths, but the stifling sea of smoke that had always seeped through the floors and wafted through the air was absent.

"I have to say, I am not happy with you girls." Dr. A. Theist poured them glasses of water while they waited for their food. Aneta expected her to tell them to get out, but she did not. "--or with Advisor as a matter-of-fact--for visiting your little get-together on Sunday for lunch. But now...he has been on my nerves so often, it's almost sickening. First, he tore up the contract, and then regular customers have stopped coming in, all because of-"

"What contract?" Faith interrupted.

Dr. A. Theist showed no emotion in her face. "Listen here. You and your group of do-gooders know more than you let on. You know *exactly* what contract I'm talking about. And I suppose that is who that man is. Advisor told me he had never seen that man before, but claimed he knew who he was and what he was here for. As soon as he comes back, I am-"

"Where did they go to lunch?" Faith interrupted again.

"The Sandwich Shop. Advisor did not want me to hear their conversation. But we all know I'm going to know every word anyway." Her attitude told the girls she was more bothered by her husband at that point than the young women.

Aneta unsheathed her sword and immediately stood up, looking around. The demons in the cafe continually hissed and chafed at her, but none moved from their spots. With an annoyed exhalation, she knew Devious was planning something against Advisor. Aneta bounded off to the sandwich shop, leaving Faith and Courage behind.

When she was about halfway to The Sandwich Shop, she noticed a small crowd of demons in a tight cluster. Not knowing if it was Devious and Advisor, Aneta decided to go and see the commotion anyway. She half-expected Theo to be in the midst of them, fending and fighting, but he was not. Only two people were in the midst of the demons. Fear and Advisor.

Devious spoke with sly, cunning words, keeping his hands in his pockets. He and Advisor strode in the park, talking business. However, only Devious spoke while Advisor quietly listened.

The chief demon Pain and two other demons tore at Advisor's soul, shredding his form away piece by piece. Aneta shouted and ran at them, sword raised.

"Be not overcome of evil, but overcome evil with good."

When she spoke of course, Fear, Pain, and the other two demons gnashing at Advisor immediately noticed her. She hacked away at the three towering demons standing guard on the outside but kept her focus on protecting Advisor.

To her horror, when Fear whipped its head around, casting a seething glare at her with its brilliant green eyes, Aneta immeidately recognized the obvious. With an unearthly roar, Fear transformed into its human form.

"Girl. You need to stand back." Devious growled.

Per Devious' hand motion, none of the demons attacked her yet.

"I will give you exactly one chance to walk away now." Devious' brilliant green eyes flashed in rage and burned in anger.

Advisor stood motionless. Aneta could not read his face. Was he terrified? Annoyed? Was Advisor in danger at all?

She gripped her sword a little tighter. She breathed a little faster. She prayed a little harder. She was in for a fight. "I'm not the one who needs to stand back."

Engulfed in fury, Devious morphed into a wolf bear of a beast. In seconds, she found herself frantically trying to keep herself out of the jaws and claws of Fear, and at the same time trying to keep the other demons from gnawing at Advisor.

"God," Aneta panted, on the verge of crying. "Please help. I can't do this. I'm not strong enough." Tears finally spilled from her eyes as she found herself overwhelmed. Her vision blurred. She tried to wipe her eyes, but that let Pain through to Advisor.

Pain suddenly recoiled and screeched as it disintegrated into black vapor. That caught Fear's attention. Theo grinned at Aneta, sword and shield in hand. Aneta managed a small, weak smile back and sniffled. Together, they fought off the other demon that plagued Advisor as well as keeping Fear at bay.

"When did Fear get here?" Theo grunted.

"That-" Aneta paused as she ducked, "would be Devious."

Theo gaped. "Wha--" He never finished his thought. He too, had seen Devious' signature eyes, and knew of Fear's terrorizing tactics, but with Aneta's help, he had paired those characteristics to one being.

Demons kept getting up and fighting to get at Advisor. Fear made Aneta and Theo's job harder. It was a master of deceit, constantly morphing from Fear to Devious and back, doing anything and everything to keep Theo and Aneta from winning. At the same time, Fear kept dragging further and further from the city and closer and closer to the rows and rows of houses.

Every time Theo or Aneta would knock one down, more demons would come and lunge at the Gray's Cafe barista. Much to Aneta and Theo's dismay, Pain would break through more often than not, ripping at Advisor. Nevertheless, Fear made it difficult to get anywhere. The chief demon stopped Advisor from doing anything to help Aneta and Theo.

Aneta subtly texted the boys while they finished talking to Dr. A. Theist, requesting prayer for her, Clinical, and Advisor. The three girls then left the cafe as their lunch hour was almost over.

Nevertheless, Devious and Advisor seemed in no hurry to get back to the cafe, but rather began to walk down the street, after finishing at the Sandwich Shop, away from Gray's Cafe.

Aneta could barely lift her arms by one o'clock. Theo told her to rest for a moment while he defended Advisor. Aneta did not want to allow him to do that, but she realized her arms had already made the decision. She plopped down on the sidewalk, exhausted. Painfully, she watched as Theo struggled to keep the demons away.

Out of nowhere, Bold burst onto the scene, taking out a demon that had flown past Theo's sight. This calmed Aneta down so she could take a few normal breaths before getting up again. When she sprang up, Theo rested, then took up his sword again. Soon, white wisps of angelic threads wafted close by. That greatly aided Bold, Aneta, and Theo. However, after a while, Aneta noticed Fear had a designation in mind near the neighborhoods.

"Leave my daughter out of this." Advisor said again, partly nervous, partly protective. "She has enough on her plate, working two jobs and Free. And now this. She has nothing to do with anything. This is her only day off in the entire week. Please don't ruin it."

"We had a contract, Advisor," Devious warned. "I am at least going to talk to her. I don't seem to be getting through to you."

They soon stopped at a house, and Advisor sighed and walked in. "Clinical? Honey, someone is here to talk to you."

Aneta shoved a rasping demon through the wall of the house, and glanced up to find Clinical standing there on the porch.

Devious was now his human-looking self, seeing the group of young people were getting weary of fighting. Was that a smile on his face? The glorious white cloud wisps were slowly fading.

"Clinical, would you like to walk with us?" Devious asked, not giving her a choice.

She gave her dad a questioning look, then pulled on her shoes to walk outside. The prolonged fight began to make Aneta exhausted again. She had never had to go on for such a long time. Her heart almost failed her when she saw that demons were tearing at Clinical's soul as well. However, they did not get very far.

Courage charged through and sliced the demons in half. Faith bolted out of Clinical's house as another chief demon, Angst, shot out of the doorway.

Seeing that Courage and Faith had joined the fight, Devious grew agitated again, and ripped into his demon body. Fear growled before them.

Both Courage and Faith were shocked to see Devious had been Fear the whole time. Bearing the brunt of Fear's vicious outrage, Theo got whacked to the side. His grunt stopped short when his back hit a building wall. With gritting teeth to handle the pain, Theo slowly stood up, adjusting his helmet.

And the fight raged on.

"Nothing is working." Aneta sank down on the sidewalk next to a store around three p.m.

The rest of the squad was fighting, but she had nothing left. She trembled all over, overwhelmed, exhausted, wondering how they would end the day. She could not go on forever.

She sat, head in her hands, ready to cry again.

Aneta finished work at three. She had been praying periodically throughout the day for Advisor and his family, but it had been hard to work and pray at the same time. On her way home, she was not quite surprised when she soon found Clinical with Devious and Advisor walking on the sidewalks.

"Hey, Clinical! Hello Advisor."

Devious' brilliant green eyes focused on her. "Oh, good afternoon, young lady. Aneta, correct? I remember you from earlier." He seemed to be choosing his words carefully through closed teeth.

She smiled. "Correct. I remember you too. Hey, Clinical, I just wanted you to know that you are totally welcome to come to church tonight with your dad. I had to tell you before I forgot. I don't have your phone number."

"Oh, I apologize." Devious intervened. "We are a little bit busy this evening. We have a lot to do."

Advisor did not say a word.

Aneta kept smiling, which seemed to warn Devious of something he did not like. "Oh, I am sure there is not much going on this evening for them. But Advisor, if you want, you're welcome to ask Dr. A. Theist along as well. Clinical? We meet at the old town hall if you want to come at seven."

More forcefully, Devious said, "We are busy."

Looking him in the eye, Aneta straightened. "Not anymore. You need to leave. Now."

"Submit yourselves therefore to God. Resist the devil, and he will flee from you. Devious, you need to leave. Now. You know you can't win." Aneta had her sword raised.

She took on Fear with the last ounces of her strength. She pleaded to her Father for more. Fear seemed to lose strength as she gained hers.

Fear stumbled and she forcefully struck the troublesome demon with her gleeming sword.

Devious, however strong he had begun when he transformed into Fear, was now battered with strikes and blows. He had finally sustained too much damage. With brilliant green eyes, Devious glared at Aneta and Theo, then fled the scene, trailing a large red trail of mist. The other demons immediately departed as well.

Devious jolted backwards. "I actually have more work to do." He immediately turned around and hastily walked away from Aneta, Advisor, and Clinical.

"Hi, Clinical!" Aneta hurried up to her after the Bible Study that night. "I'm so glad you could come!" She turned to Clinical's parents, "I'm glad you could come too."

Dr. A. Theist sighed. "Well...I suppose I am too."

Bold and Theo came over to talk to them, so Aneta pulled Clinical aside. "How have you been doing?"

"I'm doing good."

"I see. Are you okay? Really?"

This seemed to break open a fissure. "Oh, well..." Tears sprang up in Clinical's eyes. "I just...yeah, I'm fine." She wiped the tears, trying not to cry in a room half-full of people. "I just..." Her voice trembled and her hands shook. "I...just lost my brother. He..." She choked out a few sobs before wiping her eyes again. "My brother...Free...was going to come here for Mom's birthday. He missed it, but he was going to come last Thursday, the day of the Whimsicalton Fair. Because..." Her voice still cracked and wavered, but Clinical pressed on. "Mom loved to take us to the fair, and he thought it would be a good surprise. But he got in a car wreck. And he died. And we can't bear to tell Mom he was on his way to the fair because that would just..." She began to weep, "that would just *wreck her*, you know? I'm just not sure what to do.

"We were never bonded and close, but he was my brother, and we had some good memories growing up, and...he was always sweet to Mom. And he remembered my birthdays... but now my rent is due on Monday, and there is no way I am asking Mom and Dad for money right now. The cafe is not doing very well, and their best staff just quit, and...everything since Free died has gone so horribly. And I didn't think I could lose another sibling, but everything happened so fast. Oh, gosh I am so sorry. I didn't mean to tell you all that."

"Oh, it's alright." Aneta quickly spoke up. "I will keep praying for you."

"You've...already been praying for me?"

"Yes. I've... been fighting for you. Our entire squad has."

Clinical teared up again, and opened her arms for a hug. "Thank you." Her teary voice choked up.

Aneta sighed in relief. They were fulfilling what God had told them to do. Better yet, Aneta knew she was in God's will. She was fighting for the Kingdom and lost souls. She was *fighting*. And she was winning.

|Chapter 16: Too Much|

The group had long ago planned to get together that next morning, and following the recent events, they decided to meet at Gray's Cafe instead of Lyle's Diner.

During breakfast on that Thursday morning, they discussed different things. Aneta announced that she had enough money to rent an apartment. While everyone figured out how to get Aneta settled in, Theo got a phone call and walked away to answer it. When he came back, he sat down and sighed.

"Guys...they are closing down the old town hall. It's too old to be used and there is insurance policy stuff involved." Theo groaned. "We have to move church to somewhere else."

"How are we supposed to get past this?" Aneta closed her eyes and laid her head back, mentally exhausted.

Bold and Faith pulled out their phones at the same time, saying, "I'll look for another building."

"When does it close, exactly?" Courage asked.

"We only have one more Sunday. Then we have to be out." Theo groaned again. Almost promptly following, his phone rang. He exhaled and flipped it open. "Hello?"

As Theo talked on the phone again, the rest of the squad conversed.

"Alright, so where are we going to have church now?"

"I'm still looking for available places. There isn't much church material."

"We might be able to ask if we can have church at someone's house."

"Possibly."

"Maybe someone will offer their house when we tell them that we have to move."

"Oh, I don't like this."

"God already has a place set aside for us, don't worry."

"Easier said than done."

"We need a nice place. Something that has plenty of room. The attendance is always unpredictable, and sometimes people come and sometimes they don't. It's almost impossible to know when someone is going to come or not. We have to keep that in mind."

"What about a school?"

"We need Sundays too. I doubt they would let a church in there two times a week anyways."

"Theo's off the phone." Aneta glanced up as Theo again walked back to their table.

With little emotion, Theo said, "okay, so the Nepenthes are moving and they are looking for help. Mr. Nepenthe was just offered a really good job about an hour away, and their last service here is this Sunday as well."

As Bold, Faith, and Courage began to see how many people they could round up to help the Nepenthes move, Aneta noticed the light fade from Theo's eyes. He looked empty and exhausted. His face spoke of nothing but silent, hopeless agony.

She thought about how to ask him if he was doing okay, but decided against it.

Aneta knew there was something about Theo's past that bothered him off and on, but she did not know that it was such a brick wall. She had been able to bypass his past. He couldn't? Aneta caught her thoughts before they fluttered too far. Theo's problems and dealings were a lot different than her own. Even though she had no clue as to what specific thing he was battling, Aneta quickly asked her Father to give her wisdom on what to say.

"Theo?"

"Hm?" Theo had one hand on one of his temples. He had not been very engaged at all.

"Just so you know, I think that we are going to do great. It's really getting difficult to keep going, even when it feels like nothing we do is noticed or makes a difference, but I think you are doing an awesome job with leading this whole church plant, and I'm glad God chose you, and not anyone else."

The others chimed in, giving their quick affirmations.

"Not right now, please." Theo said, "I think we might have to stop having services. There is no way I can keep doing this."

Aneta looked at Theo. She knew something was going on. Did he have something to fight that she did not know about? "Theo? It probably doesn't feel like it, but you are doing great. It's going to feel like everything is pulling you down, but you are the only one who can build a church here." She hoped her second word of encouragement would help.

Theo grabbed his coat, "Alright. I'm heading out. See you later."

Slipping on her jacket and ear warmer, Aneta hurried outside after him, bracing against the chilly breeze. "Theo. Theo! Really, you are doing an amazing job!"

Aneta realized what had been happening. Hordes of demons were attacking Theo. Mistake and Fear were the only chief demons though. And they had begun to tear at Theo's armor. His sword was out of reach. Feeling a deep draw of emotion, Aneta felt a tear fall to her cheek. In his vicious rage, Fear snapped a look at Aneta, his brilliant green eyes glinting at her. Her own watery eyes equally glinted at the eyes of Devious, her own eyes, however, full of determination and courage.

"Theo, please don't give up. No one cares about what you did before." Aneta struggled to keep up with Theo's fast walk. He did not turn his head to her as she talked. "That isn't held against you. Please listen." She tried to keep her tears at bay, but they trickled down in a near-continuous stream. "Please, just keep fighting. Our past will only keep coming back. We have to fight it every time. If we let our past win now, we may never get back up. Please don't give up. I don't know about everything you did, or what you *didn't* do, but Father doesn't care. He knew what you did, and He wanted to use you here anyway. Don't give up, Theo." Aneta pleaded, thinking of Sorrow and Gracefully Broken, Diligent and Fair, Rise and Wonder, Candid and Clinical, Dr. A. Theist and Advisor, Miss Lovely and Helpful. She could not imagine what would happen if the only church in Aphoction ceased to exist.

Theo stopped his brisk pace and looked at her. She tried to stop crying, but silent tears kept coming.

Aneta turned her attention to Theo and stared at him, hoping that he would reach for his sword and keep fighting. She knew he felt like Coward that moment, but to her, he was still Theo. And Theo was a Child of God.

Aneta watched as Theo hesitated, breathing hard. In a moment, he kicked his feet up, pushing through the demons, reaching for and swinging up his sword, decapitating multiple demons in one mighty blow.

Aneta held her breath, waiting for Theo to answer her.

Catching her off guard, Theo hugged her, holding her for a moment in the freezing air. "Alright. I will keep going."

On Sunday, church started at noon as usual, and Diligent played the guitar as Gracefully Broken and Fair led the congregation in song. Bold then jumped up after the first song and walked up to the front.

"I have a quick announcement. In case you were not contacted, this is the last Sunday service here." Bold slightly paused as the audience acknowledged his statement. "They are closing down this hall, and we have to find another location to have service. We have not found a place yet, but we are considering all options. Also, today is the Nepenthe's last service, since they are moving. Thank you to all who came to help throughout the week; it has been an enormous help. And now, Mr. Nepenthe will come up and say a few things."

Mr. Nepenthe and Bold shook hands as they passed. "Thank you. Well, before I get to it, I would like to say how much Bold,

Courage, Aneta, Faith, and Theo have touched our lives. They have been simply incredible and outstanding for such young adults. I have been to church my entire life, and this service is missing something, and I believe everyone here can make this happen. I would like to take up today's tithes and offerings. God tells us to tithe and give without holding back, so today, let us obey Him. Send in your tithes today, and maybe, if God puts it on your heart, offer a little bit of what you have to these amazing, God-chasing young people who have put this all together. Thank you."

The two oldest Nepenthe boys walked up and passed two plates down the rows.

Theo sat there in shock, staring at the wall in front. Faith and Courage happily gave Bold a thumbs up, soon revealing to Aneta that they allowed Mr. Nepenthe to stand up and take offering. They began to sing the next song, and Courage took the offering plates and went to the back.

Right before Theo walked up to give his sermon, Aneta gave him a reassuring nod and smile.

Theo started off well. He began to talk about Jesus feeding the five thousand, but he lost his train of thought, and had to pause for longer than he liked. He finally remembered what he was saying and quickly resumed, but not before giving out the wrong verse and stuttering. Theo had no idea as to why he was suddenly nervous, but as soon as he began to think about that, he lost his place in his notes and had to pause again to find out where he left off.

In the end, Theo wanted to get away from the little podium stand and rush home before anyone could talk to him. However, the Nepenthes pulled him and the rest of the squad aside and gave the group of young people a little gift basket of thanks. They then hurried home to finish preparations for their move. After they left, Theo still could not escape his embarrassment because Marvel and Chava came up to him, remarking that his sermon was incredible.

Much to his annoyance, after talking with Marvel and Chava, Fair and Diligent invited the squad over for dinner. After cleaning up, they left for their house, piling into Fair and Diligent's cars. When they arrived, Diligent, Bold and Theo sat down and talked while the five women bustled around in the kitchen. Fair and Gracefully Broken mainly set up everything, but the others helped out here and there, being careful not to overcrowd the kitchen.

During dinner, the door of the house opened and Not walked inside. Fair jumped up to get him a plate of food, but Not held up his hand.

"Thank you. I'm not hungry yet." He leaned forward and whispered something in Fair's ear. She whispered back. Not glanced at the table. "Theo, come over here. Lemme talk to you for a second."

Theo stood up, completely clueless as to what Gracefully Broken's big brother wanted. They walked into the hallway, out of sight, then stopped.

Not folded his thick arms. "Theo, I have something to say. Gracefully is my little sister, and I hate anything that poses a threat to her."

Theo gulped.

"Mom and Dad adopted Gracefully when she was two; I was seventeen and Seem was fifteen. We were never close to her. We were already off on our own. But after Mom and Dad died, it got harder because we did not know how to care for her. She knows she is adopted, and she knew that our parents loved her more than anything. She loves us, but the three of us don't know how to be siblings. I'm thirty-five and she is eighteen. How am I supposed to compensate? Well, she had been off the deep end for a while now, but with you and Aneta, she has come back. I had thought she was completely lost a year ago. Thanks for being here. Fair and Diligent tell me you have been a huge blessing. I talked with Fair just a little bit ago, and she said you were having service in the old town hall, but that is now closed down. I talked with Seem." He pulled out an envelope. "Use this for your church. For rent, for savings, for whatever you might need."

Theo absent-mindedly let the envelope fall into his hands. "Mr. Not, I...I don't know how—how can—how could I accept this?"

"You gave Gracefully a new name and a new life. You can't buy that. But this might be a nice tip. Keep working. I don't know how much God cares about me or others in Whimsicalton, but He cares about something, so it has to count. Maybe He'll come up my alley." Not nodded and walked upstairs.

Theo dared to peek inside the envelope, but he quickly folded the top over again, his eyes suddenly wide. He had only glimpsed at it, but he knew there was a large sum in there.

He sat back down at the dinner table, shaky with anticipation. "I...guys, I think God found a place for us to have church."

An explosion of questions erupted.

He shrugged, "I don't know *where,* but I know He has a place. And I trust that God's got us covered."

|Chapter 17: Old Enemies And New Friends|

Just when Aneta was about to fully wake up, her phone shocked her eyes open, angrily vibrating on the wooden nightstand. She groaned and picked up the phone, answering it.

"Hey."

"Sorry it's so early. But I just counted how much we have in our church bank account." Courage sounded excited on the other side of the phone.

"It's Monday morning at...too early. Can it wait?"

"We have $5,305!"

Aneta shot straight up in bed. "What?"

"We have $1,305 from offering and tithes, and then Mr. Not gave us $3,500! Plus that other $500 that Theo found in the P.O. box! God is so amazing! We haven't found a place yet, but I think God has a place in mind for us! Keep an eye open for any opportunities, because I have a feeling one is going to show up soon."

"That...is amazing news to wake up to." Aneta laughed. "Although you *could* have texted me. Or knocked on my door."

"Oh, how was your first night in your new apartment?"

"Pretty good. But since we don't have a place for church, we should probably cancel Wednesday night service until we have a place."

"Sounds good. Bye."

"Bye."

Aneta hung up, then started her Monday. Between bits of breakfast and her shower, she texted everyone to let them know there was no Wednesday night service. The only person she could not get a hold of was Sorrow, but she assumed that someone would see her and tell her.

On Tuesday, Faith told everyone that Miss Lovely was teaching her first Bible study to one of her old friends, and that

Gracefully Broken had found Sorrow and brought her to the cafe to give her a Bible study. Throughout the day, Gracefully Broken had texted questions to Aneta about different themes and statements in the Bible. Aneta made sure she found time to answer them quickly, knowing half of them were probably Sorrow's questions.

Her mind filled with wonder. During lunch break, Aneta marveled at what had been accomplished. After recounting her first thoughts about building a church, she smiled. She had wondered many times when they first started, and even before then, if they could really pull off building a church in Aphoticton. Nevertheless, God had His way and sent people to populate the church. Light was beginning to shine. Love was beginning to spread. Hope was beginning to fill.

By Saturday, they had not been able to find a good place to hold services yet. To Aneta and Theo's shock, Advisor contacted them and offered his house for church, since he and his wife lived right across the street from the church's old location.

Aneta was slightly uncomfortable about it, but Theo walked with her to Advisor's and Dr. A. Theist's front door, so she would not end up there on her own.

Nevertheless, Aneta immediately felt comfortable in Advisor's house, which was odd to her. Dr. A. Theist offered them coffee when they slipped off their shoes. Dr. A. Theist had her own cup of coffee, and sat down across the table of Theo and Aneta.

No one else was there yet. They had time to talk.

"To be perfectly honest, I was not sure if I wanted church here," Dr. A. Theist began. "Advisor suggested it, and I was slightly surprised, but not very. Of course, I first said no, but the more I thought about it, the more it appealed to me. So we will see how today goes."

Aneta gratefully smiled. "Thank you, Dr. A. Theist, for opening your house for our service. I appreciate it very much."

"Oh, call me Affection. I am not a doctor here."

Even without looking, Aneta caught a glimpse out of the corner of her eye. Theo smiled.

Sorrow soon came with a boy around her own age. Aneta at first thought it was her boyfriend, but then Affection introduced them.

"This is Valor. He knew our family, and he also knows Sorrow. We have been good friends for a while, and since he knew Sorrow and knew us, he decided to come today. He lives out of town, but his parents are moving to the area soon, so he is spending the weekend here."

"Nice to meet you!" Aneta beamed and shook his hand.

Theo greeted him and talked to Sorrow and Valor until the service started.

When they did start, the front of the "stage" was in the kitchen, while the "sanctuary" was in the living room. It was not overly crowded, with the Nepenthe family no longer attending, but Aneta did notice two new faces she had not seen before.

After service, an older couple approached Theo and Aneta. "We enjoyed your service today. Advisor tells me you were originally meeting in the old town hall? Are you the young people who started it?"

"That is correct." Theo answered. "My name is Theo, this is Aneta. We started this with three other people as well."

"My name is Noble. This is my wife Constance. We have a meeting to attend, but could you call me around five?" He handed Theo a slip of paper with a phone number.

"Of course."

"Thank you." The couple turned and left.

"Well, that's odd. Sorta." Theo shrugged. "Do you know who they are?"

"No." Aneta shook her head. "I have no idea. I'll ask around. Don't forget to call them though. I think we are having dinner at Gracefully Broken's house again at five."

When Theo found a spare moment, he stepped out of the dining room at 5:15 and called the number Noble had given him.

"Hello? This is Theo."

"Oh, good evening. Thank you for calling. Now, today was the first day Constance and I were able to visit, but we had heard about your church from a friend. Advisor, actually. He was not so excited about it then. Tell me, why did you decide to build a church in Aphoticton?"

Theo leaned against the wall in the entryway. "Well, the first reason is God wanted me to build a church. That's all the reason I'll ever need."

"Do you know of any other churches in Aphoticton?"

"Yes, I do know of one. But I do know there used to be more churches around the area, but from what I heard, they are no longer up and running."

"So what makes you think your church will take root?"

Theo paused, wondering if he had just dug himself a hole. "Well, for one, we are still young. The enemy may be against us..." He tried to organize the words he was attempting to get out. "But I just know we are an authentic church. We have already run into many obstacles. I mean... I didn't even want to do this at first. There have been a lot of bumps, but God sent us here, and He is going to have his plan fulfilled one way or another. God is gonna keep the church, not me." Theo quietly smacked his forehead in embarrassment.

"That is an amazing answer, young man. How old are you?"

"I am twenty-four."

"And the others?"

"They're all in their twenties, too."

"I am amazed, Theo; that God is using such young folks to bring about His plans are extraordinary! I would like to meet you on the corner of World Boulevard and Beet Avenue. When are you available?"

"Oh, um, I don't think tonight would work. How about Thursday?"

"Yes, any time."

"Okay, let's shoot for eleven a.m.?"

"Very good. See you there, Theo. World and Beet. Goodbye."

"Bye." Theo ended the call. With a thoughtful face, he shrugged and headed back to the table to eat.

In the midst of laughing and eating, Theo's mood shifted. Aneta, sitting close by, noticed the change.

. With a snarl, a demon rushed out of the concealment of shadows and pummeled Theo. It was Fear with his brilliant green eyes raging in anger. Theo slipped out of its clutches just in time and drew his sword.

"I thought I was done with you," Theo growled, gripping his shield.

"I am not done with you, though," Fear scoffed. "You still have a debt. You agreed. You cannot break your contract!"

Theo swung, but missed. "There is no use telling me that! I already know the contract vanished as God took me back. His grace set me free already."

Chains appeared beside him. "They all tell you that." Its sympathetic voice droned in Theo's ears. "It's hard to know if God really meant it. Or if that grace vanished the moment you slipped up. You just... never know."

"You good, Theo?" Aneta asked.

Theo nodded. "Yes, why?"

"Just...wondering." She kept eating her dinner; however, Bold was almost successful in making her spit it out with his next joke.

With a grunt, Theo blocked Fear, Chains, and other pesky demons that tried to attack him. His helmet served him well, keeping him safe from many blows he could not block in time. He was slowly backed up, being pushed away from Gracefully Broken's house, and ending up in town. Their fight ranged all over the place, from the roofs to the sidewalks, then around the stores. The demons refused to let up, but

Theo held strong, refusing to give in to defeat. Nevertheless, his arms began to tire.

The squad thanked Fair and Diligent for another delicious meal, and went on their way. When Aneta, Faith, and Courage went their separate ways to walk home from the boys, she paused for a moment to look at Theo. He seemed extremely distracted. She knew something was up, but she could not figure out what. Instead, she prayed for him.

Theo gasped in pain as a claw ripped across the front of his left leg. He crumpled for a moment, then regained his balance. His feet felt like lead.

"Father...Jesus," he panted, "Please. I can't."

He sliced a demon that jumped at him, and gasped, tilting his head back in exhaustion. At that moment, he felt something. He looked around, seeing curly waves of white light gently billowing through the streets, coming and swirling around him. Though he had seen them before, Theo did not know where they came from, or if they were simply gifts from God. Sometimes, when he fought, thosewhite wisps would come around and strengthen him, though he did not know by what means. At any rate, they helped him, and hindered the demons, their bright white glare distracting them as the sun does. So he went on.

On Monday, Aneta set to work, but something was bothering her. She felt like Theo was up against something, so she prayed for him throughout the day. On Tuesday and Wednesday, something was still bothering Theo. When she texted him, he replied, but was not in a chatting mood. Even on Wednesday, at Advisor and Affection's house, where they met for service again, he was still in a bad mood. Aneta began to wonder if he was fighting his past again, and to what extent. She nodded to herself and kept praying for him.

After the service, as they headed home, it began to snow for the first time. Aneta laughed in delight as the gentle flakes floated and flittered to the ground.

With a groan, Theo watched as the snow began to cover the ground. It came down in large, thick flakes, making the sidewalks hard to fight on. He wiped his face. As he pulled away his hand, it was covered in blood. He had no idea where exactly he was bleeding from, but he just tried to keep it from getting in his eyes. With an irritated grunt, he slipped, landing on the cold, wet sidewalk.

A demon took the opportunity to jump on him and scratch at him with a vicious snicker. With effort, Theo yelled in defiance and flipped over, crushing the demon. He laid there for a moment. He would have fallen asleep if it were not for the freezing snow melting on him and soaking through his clothes, the immense pain that plagued him, and the gentle, wispy clouds of light that steadily swirled around him.

Part of his body screamed at him to get up, not liking the cold, but other bruises and swellings welcomed the sidewalk as an ice pack. Reluctantly, Theo stood, holding his sword again.

In the still night air, as his breath fogged in front of him, muffled sounds of metal scraping against snow-covered asphalt told Theo that Chains was back. Every time the demon's feet touched the ground, it sounded as if there were chains everywhere, being dragged behind. But no chains were visible. The only thing he could see was the chief demon, walking towards him with a cold eye, hard as steel.

"You just don't give up, do you?" Chains asked, tilting its head.

Theo breathed in and out a few times before answering. "No. Apparently you don't, either. But it looks like I still have more stamina. God has my back. As long as I can stand, then you will not."

With an angry growl, Chains leapt forward, sweeping its paw out, knocking Theo off his feet. Theo groaned, then stood up again.

"You can do better than that."

"Oh, I can," Chains replied.

Theo grinned. "Actually, I was talking to myself." With the white, wisping fog swirling at his feet, he stepped forward, spinning his sword and moving with quick, specific movements. His aching arms, complaining ribs, and rubbery legs were now beginning to feel numb. As he moved faster, the pain faded for a moment. He was soon sweating in the early winter night, pressing his attack, causing Chains to back up.

"My past is done. There is nothing you demons can do to bring it back. I don't want it and I don't need it. I am no longer a coward. In Jesus' Name, let me go!"

Fear, who had just leapt towards him as he began to speak, suddenly screeched and stopped in mid-air. Chains spun around and high-tailed out of town. Fear followed suit.

Left in peace, Theo slowly lowered himself to the ground, sitting on the snow in the middle of the road. Worn out, Theo laid down right where he sat, letting the snow cover him. His burning wounds slowly flamed up as his pulse slowed down to normal. Everything hurt, but he could hardly move from exhaustion.

The battle had lasted from Sunday evening to Wednesday night. It was finally over.

Theo woke up on Thursday morning in relief. He did not work until noon. He spent the morning with God, then walked to the corner of World and Beet. Noble was waiting in his car there. When Theo approached, Noble got out and welcomed him.

"This," Noble took out a set of keys and indicated the building behind him, "is my son's church. I started it decades ago. He took it over about twenty years ago. It has almost died out completely. Only a few members left. He is close to retirement. Come inside. I will show you around."

Noble showed Theo the little church that stood on the east side of town. To the north were farms and fields, and to the south was the town limits. To the west was the rest of town. It was in an ideal location, for the most part. It had beautiful stained-glass windows and lots of character. The basement was mostly unused, and it only had one bathroom.

"So, how do you like it?" Noble asked Theo.

"It is an amazing little church."

"Yes, it is. I am getting old. It's getting hard on me and my wife to clean. My son's wife helps us, but there is hardly anyone to help. If you would like, under agreements, you would be welcome to use this building for your church services at eleven. We get done around ten, so it would not be a problem."

Theo gawked. "I don't think...maybe I should talk to...Mr. Noble, I think that would work."

With a grin on both of their faces, the two men shook hands. Theo had a place for church services.

|Chapter 18: God Does Amazing Things|

"Oh, for goodness sake," Aneta complained as she beheaded another pesky demon.

She had been walking along when she found herself unexpectedly in the midst of several small, obnoxious demons. They had been conversing and hissing when she had stumbled upon them. Naturally, she had whipped out her sword as they flung themselves at her. They were not really suited for battles and Aneta easily dispatched them, one by one. However, after they had been slaughtered or run off, she began to wonder what they had been doing.

Aneta held her hands more firmly in her pockets in the cool weather. That Saturday morning, before she had to work, Aneta had decided to go for a walk around the neighborhood, praying as she went. She had not meant to walk as far as the poorest sections of the neighborhood, for it was in the farthest corner of Aphoticton, well away from everything else. It would take a while to walk back. She glanced at the house where she had seen the short scout demons gathering; a weathered, run-down little place with peeling paint and a snow-dusted lawn overgrown with stubborn weeds. It matched a lot of other houses in the vicinity. After a moment, she began to hear agitated voices rising inside. Feeling like she was loitering or eavesdropping, Aneta hastily moved along. Before she could walk far, she heard a door open and close in the most gentle and quiet way.

Overcome with curiosity, Aneta slowly turned her head. A girl sat on the doorstep, head in her hands. Aneta took a deep breath, wondering if she should do anything. As the girl raised her head, Aneta pulled in a surprised breath.

It was Sorrow.

Aneta frowned at the sight of two more slithering demons lurking near the house. One of them slipped through the roof, probably intending to wreak more havoc, and the other waited dangerously close to Sorrow as she sat on the steps. Without waiting another minute, Aneta hastened out her sword and advanced on the demon.

Aneta walked up to Sorrow. "Hi!"

Sorrow glanced up and quickly, but casually, wiped her face. "Hi. Aneta, right?"

"Yep. Enjoying the sunshine? It's rather chilly today. Where is your coat?"

"Inside. I just...wanted to be in the fresh air."

At that point, Aneta realized she had no clue what to say next.

Aneta's sword had barely passed through the hapless demon when three more erupted out of the house to take the place of their fallen comrade.

"Fool!" one scolded her.

Another spat, "You think you can prevail against *us?* "

"You will pay for that mistake!" the third shrieked.

Still defensive, wanting to protect Sorrow, Aneta kept her sword pointed at the demons. They did not seem eager to attack her or Sorrow yet.

They warily watched the tip of her sword, but still stood in front of the door.

"Is he done yet?" one demon asked.

"Go in and check." Another piped up. "Fear doesn't take long. Tell him he has another minor problem...if you can call it that."

Aneta gulped. Before anything else could happen, a demon phased through the house door and promptly came back out with Devious.

Before Aneta could think of something to say, she spotted a man walking down the sidewalk towards them. Sorrow saw him, and immediately jumped up and ran to meet him. Aneta froze in horror as she realized it was Candid's ex-husband.

173

Devious.

Down the sidewalk, Sorrow flung herself into Devious' arms, embraced him, then continued to walk with him. They stopped in front of Sorrow's house where Aneta stood.

"Good morning," Devious cheerfully greeted her.

"Good morning." Aneta gulped.

Devious was in his human form, not his demonic form as she assumed. She stood there dumbly.

His brilliant green eyes flashed at her. He frowned in annoyance. "A minor problem indeed. Very well, let's get this over with."

As he spoke, Devious snapped out a black, smoky whip that emitted shadowy rays of dark mist. Without hesitating, he twitched his arm and let the whip curl around Aneta's back and legs. She gasped in pain as she was caught unprepared again. Searing agony racked her body, and she staggered as Devious brought the whip back again. Frantically, she attempted to get out of the whip's range as she tried to fend off the other demons joining in the fight.

As she turned around to run, Mistake stood there, about to slice her in half with its talons. It raised its paw, but a crack of the whip from behind her sent the monstrous demon lumbering away.

"Yes. Well, thank you. You helped me greatly. The meeting with Advisor...went well." Devious smiled.

Aneta almost shuddered. Devious hid his actual agenda well, and it scared her. What else was he doing today? "I see. Well, what brings you here today?"

"Ah, yes. I am visiting Sorrow's parents. I hear they have not been doing well lately, so I am here as a counselor. But I'm afraid it really is a private matter. You see, it is technically rude to ask-" Devious' expression remained polite, but his tone warned her to leave. "-but I will let it slip this time. It was good to see you again, Aneta." With a devilish glance, he ascended the steps of the house.

Aneta ducked, then glanced behind her.

Devious coiled his whip. "My apologies. I did not mean to catch you in my whip the first time. Demons are obnoxious, no? Mistake lives up to his name. He isn't supposed to be here."

Aneta tried her best to hide her baffled expression. He made it sound like he was now on her side. He had not meant to catch her in his whip? What was that supposed to mean? Why did he subtly drive off Mistake?

"You have no place here," Aneta firmly stated, attempting to ignore her confusion.

"That is correct. I do not always know why the chief demons are here. I thought they did not work in cities or towns. But what do I know? Maybe their orders were changed. But I do wish someone would tell me these things. It interferes with my working schedule. Now, Aneta, let me tell you something. I am not here to wreck anyone's life. You do understand that, right?"

Aneta gave him a weird look. "Devious, you convinced me otherwise a long time ago. I *know* why you are here. The squad and I are here to protect everyone in Aphoticton, including Rise and Wonder."

To her shock, Devious inhaled in genuine alarm and his brilliant green eyes shone in curious pleasure. "How are they? Ever since I lost connection with Candid, I have no information on my little girls. Are they doing okay? Do you know? Have you seen them?"

This caught Aneta off guard. "Oh. Yes, they are doing fine." She stood poised and wary. What was Devious doing?

"Oh, good. Would you do me a favor? Could you go and check on them? I do not know where they live, but I would give anything to know their current health. I know Candid, and I left her on a rough note, and I understand if she never wants to see me, but I would love to see pictures of the girls. Do... do you have any?"

Aneta's cold answer quickly came. "No."

"Could you...go and get some? I might be called out of town for another business meeting, and I have no idea when I might come back."

Aneta swallowed and stood motionless. How was she supposed to react to that?

"See you later, Aneta." Sorrow waved as she and Devious walked inside her house.

Aneta remained glued in place. Confused, she finally walked away, wondering what happened. As she made her way back into town, she replayed the scene in her mind again and again. What had gone wrong? Something bothered her. She remembered seeing Sorrow's face as she sat on the doorstep. She had looked so sad and angry. Aneta had seen that look before. Where? *Where?* Where had she seen that same pain and anguish?

Clouds rolled in with the chilling wind. In dismay, she began to remember. That was what Gracefully Broken used to look like. Without permission, tears began to spill out, trickling to her chin and down her neck. Aneta let out a short cry and tried to stifle her emotions, but they poured out anyway. Eventually, she stopped in the middle of the sidewalk and covered her face with her gloved hands, crying her eyes out.

She had let Sorrow go. She had let Devious go. She had let her guard down. How could she listen to Devious' voice? Had his name not reminded her to be careful? As she cried on the sidewalk, her phone began to ring.

She fumbled to pull off a glove and opened her phone. "Hello?" she sniffled.

"Hi, Aneta." It was Courage. *"Hey...are you okay?"*

"Yeah, why?" Aneta moved her feet and kept walking.

"Are you sure? It sounds like you were crying."

Aneta burst into tears again. How did Courage know? "Yeah. I'm not okay. I met up with Sorrow, and Devious came up. He won. And I did not even try. I hate him. I hate him!" She moaned her loss, still sobbing.

"Oh, Aneta. Aneta. *Aneta.*" The third time was more stern. "Just...tell me what happened. Just slow down and tell me what happened."

Theo glanced up from the garage floor, hearing the door chime as he was sweeping leaves out before closing up. He set

176

down the broom and hurried out front. His attitude changed when he spotted Devious.

"Anything I can help you with?"

"I just happened to be walking by, and I decided to come in person to ask how much it costs to get an oil change. Your name is Theo, right?"

"Yes."

"Right. Well, I was walking past Sorrow's house, and I happened to see Sorrow talking to Aneta and...oh. Well, I suppose I really shouldn't say much."

"What did they say?"

"I don't quite remember. I shouldn't say this...but you didn't get it from me. I'm sorry the church isn't doing well."

"What? Where did you hear *that?*"

"Oh..." Devious shifted nervously. "I'm sorry. I guess...I thought you...Aneta says you aren't doing a very good job with the church. I'm sorry. You didn't get it from me."

"Wait, wait, wait. What?" Theo made a face. "I don't think that's right. That doesn't sound right. That's not Aneta."

"I'm pretty sure it was Aneta. It wasn't Courage, I know that. Sorrow said Aneta's name a few times. But I would be careful. I don't think Aneta trusts you...but that is just what I heard. Well...good evening."

On Sunday, Aneta and Bold were at Noble's church building around ten-thirty. Noble was still there with his wife Constance to hear the first service. People began arriving soon after that, and Noble looked like he was so relieved to see the pews fill up again. However, Theo entered the church building five minutes before the service started and stayed afterwards long enough to talk to Noble and Constance, then promptly left. Aneta wanted to tell Theo about Devious, and to ask him about his opinion on what she had planned for the Bible study on Wednesday night, so she hurried out the door to catch up.

She glanced up at the cloudy sky as her breath fogged her vision for a second. They needed to buy a car sooner than later.

Winter would make walking through town a tedious chore. "Theo!"

Theo turned around, evidently annoyed. "What?"

"So, for Wednesday night...are you okay?"

"What do you need?"

Aneta did not know what was wrong, so she decided to give him a quick warning about Devious so he could be on his way. "Okay, never mind. On Saturday morning, I was talking with Sorrow and-"

"I already know. There is no need to point it out."

Aneta stopped, gulped, and blinked. Had Courage already told him? "You don't need to be so rude," she whispered as he walked away. Aneta walked back inside, and went straight to Courage. "Courage, did you tell Theo about Saturday and Devious?"

"No. Why?"

"Oh. Okay." Aneta told her friend of how Theo was acting.

"Maybe he has a lot on his—oh. Aneta." She paused. "If Devious went after you, he may have already gone after Theo."

Aneta widened her eyes, realizing what Courage had just suggested. "Oh..."

"I don't know what he might have said to him, but if Theo is mad and won't talk to you, then maybe you need to clear something up? Maybe you should ask him about Devious?"

"I don't know...I'm not sure what to do."

"Ask Bold. He might know."

Aneta hesitated and finally nodded. "Alright."

When Aneta inquired about Theo to Bold, he suggested that it could be something completely different. She would not know until she asked. Bold then confessed he had limited advice on the subject because it was different between two men than a man and a woman.

Aneta sighed and thanked him. She began to wonder what to do. She felt angry that something was held against her, but she had no idea what she did. She also felt annoyed because Devious had gotten in between the squad, and there was nothing she could do. After asking Father about it, she exhaled and sat on her bed, clueless.

Monday drifted by and nothing happened. On Tuesday, she brought the boys' suits to the inn after they were dry-cleaned, as she always did.

Theo put on an annoyed expression and opened the door to the Whimsicalton Inn. Even though he never spotted Aneta when he picked up his suits from the washroom, he still wanted to leave quickly as possible. He did not feel like taking that chance. Helpful called him over as he was on his way out.

The secretary had just been talking to a man at the counter about something else. When Theo walked up, she grinned.

"This is for you. Aneta left it to me to give to you." Helpful stood up, addressing the other man. "One moment, Mr. Seem. The files are in the other room."

When she left the desk, before Theo could continue on his way, he realized that Mr. Seem, Gracefully Broken's other brother whom he had never actually met face to face before, had been watching him in a confused manner.

"You are Theo?"

Theo nodded, assuming that Not and Gracefully Broken had mentioned him before.

"But...I know *who* you are." Seem said.

Theo stood, slightly nervous. "Excuse me?" It was not the response he was expecting.

"You *are* Theo, aren't you?"

Theo slowly nodded.

"Yes. I know you. You are the young man who led people astray for years." Seem's voice remained steady and low, but his voice relayed agitation and disgust.

"We will always find you. We told you that." Devious' jet-black misting figure slowly circled Theo.

Theo gulped. The words of Devious jogged his memory. The day God rescued him from his own mistakes, Lost had told him that even though he was under protection of royalty, they would still chase him down.

Theo glanced around, expecting Devious to be nearby. It seemed like the green-eyed man had been busy lately.

"I doubt you remember me. But I remember you." Seem gave a slight nod to himself. "You told me that I would be safe in that place. It has wrought pain-" With every phrase, Seem's voice rose in anger, but still remained under control. "It has rained terror on me. I can't escape because I was forced to pledge allegiance to them. I hope you know what it has done to me."

Theo gulped. "I-I'm sorry." He licked his lips, and backed away. "I'm...I'm..."

"What I want to know is...you are the Theo that has saved my sister, brought peace to my elder brother, and has impacted this city... so why are you still the Coward that led others astray? You led others to their destruction." Seem shook his head, confused and depressed. His voice still rang out clear and low, and it shook Theo to the core. "I don't know what happened. But you ruined my life. How could you live the life you lead in peace? *How?*"

Theo could not answer. Doubt crept closer to him. Even though Theo acknowledged the demon, he did not react. Then, looking at Devious, Theo ignored Seem for a moment.

"You make it sound like you have found a way to enslave me again." Theo tried to sound confident in his position, but his voice gave him away.

"Oh. No," Devious purred. "Unfortunately, we are still unable to avenge ourselves. But. With your permission, we *will* run you over. Are you okay with that?" His voice slithered through the air.

Theo shivered as all his memories of Coward flooded into his mind. He had always been certain that he would never think of his old life again. Devious proved him wrong with Seem's help.

Devious leaned in close to Theo's face. "I am not allowed to kill you. But with all. My. Power. I will make sure you suffer until you join us again. And your 'squad' will then join you." He straightened his lean figure and smiled. "Thank you for understanding."

Without another word, Devious vanished.

Theo stood, nearly trembling with anxious thoughts. He scarcely nodded to Seem, and immediately left.

The cold wind chilled Theo immediately as he left the inn. He ran his hand through his hair with ragged breaths. Tears threatened to emerge if he did not hurry. He made his way down the sidewalk, walking hastily to get to his apartment.

He swallowed nervously and raced along in his mind, retracing his mental steps. He did not know what to do. When he closed the door to his room, tears pushed their way to the open air and dropped. He shook as he sank against his bed, sitting on the floor, leaving his neatly pressed suits on the ground in a heap. Two more tears made their way out. His body trembled again. What had gone wrong? He then remembered his white knuckles were still grasping a note from Aneta.

Knowing it could not get any worse, Theo opened the note.

Theo—
I apologize if I offended you. It was never my intention. I still think you can strongly lead our squad and our church into greatness. I love your passion for lost souls. Keep going. God has your back. We have your back too.
—Aneta

Theo read the note over and over. Then he read it again.

Aneta lay in bed, hoping her note was sufficient. She felt like it might have been too simple, not explaining anything about Devious, but it had already been delivered. There was nothing she could do.

For hours, Theo sat against his bed, staring at the note. Finally, he realized that God had still looked out for him. Like Aneta said, God had his back.

"Fool! Coward!" Devious burst into Theo's room, whip in hand.

Theo's head jerked up, answering to his old name.

"You believe those lies? Aneta hates every part of you. You have lied!" He thrashed his whip. Theo barely had enough time to grab his sword to defend himself. "You have cheated!" Devious shouted again, his brilliant green eyes shining in rage.

"No!" Theo refuted Devious' words.

"You have cheapened everything! You have lost God's approval!"

"*No!*" Theo held out his arm to catch the whip's end. "You lie!"

"Have I? Or have *you?*"

Theo's legs began to shake. He tried to remain firm. *God, help me.*

With a groan, Aneta woke up. It was almost one in the morning. She closed her eyes, wanting to go back to bed, but sleep ran off, leaving her wide awake. She finally sat up and sighed. "Alright. What do You want?"

After a moment, Aneta decided to pray for Theo.

Devious retracted his whip, yanking Theo forward. After a brief struggle, Theo freed himself and poised for battle. He felt in no shape to fight. *God, I feel like a worthless wretch right now.* Theo's eyes ached.

In the moment of standstill between Theo and Devious, both waiting for the other to make the first move, white clouds of mist gently rolled in. They materialized around Theo.

Devious saw the miraculous sight and, with another enraged yell, charged forward.

Strengthened by the white stuff, Theo stepped forward and slashed the whip out of Devious' hand. It vaporized to nothing. Devious yanked out a twisted dagger and clashed with Theo, puffing angrily.

"You won't win Aphoticton while I'm here."

"Not with that attitude." He raised his sword, and brought it down in full strength.

Devious somehow mostly blocked it with his twisted dagger, but he was not ready for Theo's shield flying at him like a disk. Devious shouted in pain, then vanished.

Theo stopped, and sighed in relief.

Theo stood up, and shook his head in wonder. He glanced at the clock. It was one a.m. He had sat there for that long? Theo looked at his Bible on the nightstand. He gently laid his hand on it before slipping into bed.

On Wednesday, Theo got to the church early, and as he expected, Aneta was there. She was alone. When he had walked inside, she looked back over her shoulder.

Theo tried not to smile, and held up his hand in a single wave of greeting. "Hi, Aneta. Thanks. For the note."

Aneta smiled. "Of course. How are you doing? I was praying for you last night."

"Oh, really?" Theo chuckled. "What time?"

"Like...in the middle of the night. God woke me up."

"Okay, but...what *time?*"

"I don't know. Maybe around one?"

Theo let out a single laugh and rubbed the back of his neck. "Wow."

"What?"

He smiled. "Just remember, God does amazing things."

|Chapter 19: Aneta's Struggles|

"I'm not sure how to handle it." Affection wiped her eyes with her arm as she cut up a tomato. "It's been--it's been almost...almost a month since--since--since...Free. An-and I'm not sure how to carry on. I want to ask God for help, but I feel like I could never ask for anything from Him." Affection's voice wavered as she attempted to hold her emotions. "I have left Him out of my life for so long, and I'm not even sure He wants my leftovers." Affection rapidly blinked her eyes.

Aneta swallowed hard, not knowing what to do. She kept grating cheese at the kitchen counter, as she was helping Affection prepare dinner. How was she supposed to answer?

"To be honest, I was a little jealous when...when Advisor started coming to you young people for help. You see," Affection sniffed and wiped her face with her arm again, "I had been a Christian when I met Advisor. And I liked his life better, so I left God when Advisor convinced me that I didn't need Him. And we have stood against God for years. And...and when *he* began to go to you, I felt deserted." She held a lighthearted scornful disposition. "I remember crying when he went to that town hall for the first time. I thought I had completely wasted all of...everything."

Surprising herself, Aneta felt like she understood what Affection meant. "I see how that can be frustrating. It was like you gave up something precious for him, and then he goes and says he wants that same thing back. Was he raised in the church as well?"

Affection smiled and sniffed again. "Well, I don't quite remember. I think his dad took him to church, but his mom did not. He hated church and he hated God. I don't know why, but it seems you and your group have made such a big impact that he willingly went to church. You are all so precious in the Father's sight." She began to tear up again, and this time she began to weep. "I know God is a God of second chances, but for some reason I can't help but believe God is done with me. I know He accepted me again, but how could I possibly ask Him for anything?" Strain wrestled with agony in Affection's voice.

Aneta struggled with what to say. She had never been in a situation like this before.She kept her eyes on the cheese and silently prayed for wisdom.

"Well, God created us to need Him. It says in 1 Corinthians 13 that God is love... no. I'm sorry. Not Corinthians. I... think it's First Peter? Or Second Peter?" Aneta's throat tightened. Her ears burned as her face flushed in embarrassment. "Anyway, God is love, and..." Aneta froze as she realized she forgot where she was going with that phrase. "And...we need love. Everyone needs love." She focused harder on grating the cheese rather than thinking about her lack of terminology. What did love have to do with feeling unwanted? Nothing was going as planned. Theo made it look so easy to console and counsel people.

Aneta took a breath and blinked. "And since we all need love, it would make sense to go to the people who love us. It makes even more sense to have a God who *is* love. And...as a God of love, Jesus also loves to give us grace and mercy. You already repented. He has put your sin away, as far as the east is from the west. It's gone." Aneta kept her voice level as she explained God's love. It made her fall in love with Him all over again. "He still loves you, no matter what your past looks like. God really wants you to know that He loves you."

Sniffing again, Affection nodded and wiped her face multiple times. "Thank you so much for understanding, Aneta. It's no wonder you are called to build a church."

Aneta's mind fixated on that last sentence. As they set out the condiments for tacos and sat down for dinner with Advisor, Clinical, Valor, Gracefully Broken, and Sorrow, Aneta began to wonder. Did Affection really think she was actually suitable to help build a church? She thought that Aneta was mature enough to lead?

Someone chuckled, "No. Of course not. One person's opinion doesn't matter."

Aneta's heartbeat sounded within her chest. She knew that voice all too well. It was her own voice. It had been her own voice that chuckled and her own voice Aneta knew would soon begin to spew foul philosophy and twisted truth. When she had turned around, Aneta saw Voice standing nearby, occasionally moving about in a wide circle. Upon seeing Voice, Aneta scowled. She had had debates with Voice before. Even though she had not argued with Voice lately, she used to battle numerous debate rounds when she was younger, a lot of them actually happening because of Coward and his questions.

Nevertheless, Voice knew her too well, and used that to an advantage. Aneta's vigor fled. Before, she had been slowly conquered by Voice. Voice had been there the day she fell into the canyon. She had not successfully conquered Voice in the past. How could she conquer Voice now?

Annoyed, Aneta unsheathed her sword and held out it. "Come one step closer."

Voice rolled her eyes. "Oh, please. No need to bring about the formalities. Don't worry. I won't be long. But… " She held up her hands as Aneta brought the sword's tip closer to her face. "Well, aren't *we* pushy today? You didn't do this last time. What's your problem?"

"You're talking."

Scoffing, Voice lowered her hands. "Oh, please. Like that's a bad thing. After all…I'm you."

"Yes. Stop talking. I have other things to do."

"Aneta. Listen to me. You are not mature enough to lead anything. You are only twenty-two, and, if I may add, you're the youngest in the entire squad. Seriously? Why did God pick *you* to help Theo? He should've picked Faith or Courage or someone else. It could have been literally anyone else older than you, child."

"Stop it. Stop it or else." Anetacound not find her confidence, but she refused to lower her sword. She could not let Voice win this time.

"*What* else? What are you going to do to me? To yourself? Not much. You're stuck, Aneta. And unless you remove yourself, you're going to get trampled. You know…while Faith and Courage are here...you may as well back out because...well, let's just say someone can still take your place now. If you wait much longer, it's gonna be super awkward to just leave because I know you will want-"

"Shut up! Just shut up!" Aneta shoved her sword closer to Voice's neck even though she could barely hold up her sword. "I'm completely *done* with you! Stop talking to me and leave me *alone!*"

"I'm trying to help you!"

"Well, you're doing a terrible job!"

"Complimenting yourself now? Just give up, Aneta! You're too *young*. You're too *inexperienced*. You're too *weak*." Voice spat out each word, fiercely bringing forth Aneta's thoughts she had not yet dared to form. "You don't know God as you *should*. There is absolutely no reason for you to continue."

Aneta began walking forward, forcing Voice backwards. "You are absolutely right. I am too young. And I don't know God as I should. But...no one knows God as they should. He is too good and too amazing for us. But if I did not know God...there *would* be no reason to continue. You are completely right about everything. One person's opinion really does not matter. Especially yours."

Gracefully Broken laughed between bites of a taco. "Okay, here's another one." She scrolled up on her phone and then showed it to Sorrow who was sitting next to her. "Look at it! Isn't it adorable? I should paint kittens in my bedroom too." She gasped. "Sorrow! You should totally come over to paint!"

Sorrow's face lit up, but soon faded again. In a quiet voice, she said, "I'd...have to ask. I'm not sure if Mom can get me painting supplies or not."

Waving her hand, Gracefully Broken laughed. "Don't worry about that! I'll make sure I have supplies for you. Just text me if you can come at some time, and I'll send you my address. Actually, let me do that now. What's your number?"

As the two girls exchanged phone numbers, Aneta smiled.

On Saturday morning, as Aneta started work, Courage came up to her, saying, "Hey. Theo got super sick last night and doesn't think he'll be well enough to do the sermon, and then Bold got sick this morning. He was going to preach in Theo's place, but now, he's trying to figure out who's gonna do it. I told him I thought I could do it."

"Oh, you'd be great! But I can't believe that Theo and Bold got sick! Hopefully they feel better soon. Oh, it's just going to be you and me on Sunday, because Faith gets back on Sunday night, right?"

"Yes. Hey, since everyone else is gone, can you go to Sign's store and pick up stuff for Sunday lunch? Faith usually does that."

"Sure."

"What?!" Aneta whispered to Courage on the phone a half hour before service started. "What do you *mean* you are busy?! Church starts in a half hour and *you're* giving the sermon! Who else is going to give the sermon?"

"*Someone who is trying to jump off the bridge! I can't let him win again! I have to help him. You were there when I was looking at Theo's notes. Just glance over them and do a quick sermon! You'll be fine!*"

Aneta stared at her phone after Courage hung up. *She* had to give the sermon? She stood in the middle of the church. It was just her, out of the whole squad. Only her.

She would have broken down crying if not for Affection, who walked up to her to ask a quick question. Aneta nodded and sat down in the back pew, grabbing the notes that had passed through Theo, Bold, Courage, and now rested with her.

As the song service ended, Aneta slowly walked up to the platform, shaking and sweating. Her stomach twisted, and she could hardly breathe. Her hands fumbled and her ears reddened. Her voice shook as she greeted everyone and explained that she was giving the sermon. As she finished saying that, she realized it had not been necessary.

Gulping again, she dropped a paper and accidently banged the microphone. Following that embarrassment, she stumbled through the sermon and blundered her way to the end. She ended seventeen minutes early and made the ending prayer too short as well.

Throughout the whole thirteen-minute sermon, Aneta had kept looking down or closing her eyes to keep the tears from escaping. It had been thirteen minutes of embarrassment, stuttering, and humiliation.

As soon as she could step off the stage, she retreated and locked herself in the bathroom. She cried for a few minutes and then washed her face. After waiting a little longer, she finally composed herself and exited the bathroom.

Aneta casually greeted a few people, and then hastily left. She sniffled the whole time as she walked back to her apartment in the cold afternoon. She shivered and soon reached her apartment. One of the other tenants happened to be walking in at that time and kindly held the door open for Aneta.

Not glancing up for very long, Aneta smiled in thanks and hurried inside the building, stopping in front of her door. She felt in her pocket for her keys. Not in there. She felt her other pocket. Not in there either. With a shaky sigh of annoyance, she reached inside her purse for a moment before remembering she had left her keys, wallet, and phone on the pew.

She broke down crying and sat down in front of her door. She was hungry. She was embarrassed. She was sobbing. Aneta wanted to be behind closed doors, not locked out.

Aneta day by her door for a while. No one had come or gone through the hallway, and for that she had been thankful. However, it did not take away her embarrassment of the entire day.

After about a half hour, Affection walked inside the apartment building, holding her things. Aneta was still tearful and quietly thanked her.

They both walked into the apartment, and Aneta sat down.

Aneta had not necessarily asked for the prolonged company of Affection, but it happened, in spite of her feelings.

Even then, Aneta refused to start the conversation. She sat down on the couch. Affection sat down as well, quiet and reflective. A moment passed. Nothing was said. Aneta stood up to grab a tissue.

Forgetting her previous thoughts, Aneta scowled. "Don't you dare tell me I did a good job today."

"No. That was..." Affection stared at the wall to avoid eye contact. "I've never heard a sermon that short, that...unprepared."

Aneta began to bawl.

"Yeah." Affection nodded. "You did...terrible. But I think everyone enjoyed it."

"It...was *only* thirteen minutes long." Aneta managed to finish her sentence before breaking down again. However, she still attempted to state her resolutions. "I *hate* this. I hate doing this. I'm not doing it anymore."

"You won't quit, will you?" Affection's motherly tone, a mix of scolding and astonishment, shocked Aneta.

Wiping her face with her sleeve, Aneta dumbly stared at her in annoyance and disbelief. Pointing with her outstretched arm in no general direction, Aneta said, "If you think I'm going to waltz back there on Wednesday, you're a hundred percent *wrong!* I hate *all* of this! Theo and Bold had to get sick *at the same time?* Faith abandoned me going off to visit relatives, and Courage stuck the excuse of saving someone from suicide on the board!" Tears jumped to her eyes again.

"Aneta!" Affection chastised her.

Aneta halted her complaints. She knew it was too far to add Courage's situation to everything of which she had grumbled, but it was too late to take it back anyway.

"I'm the youngest in the whole squad. I can't do *anything* they can do." Mumbling to herself, Aneta said, "I can't believe I didn't quit before."

Affection sighed and stood up. "I'm not sure how to help you." She sounded slightly frustrated with herself. "But...promise you will ask *someone* for help? Call Courage or Faith? Or someone?"

Aneta nodded.

With a deep, worried sigh, Affection left Aneta's apartment.

Aneta threw down her sword in anger and flung her shield away, letting it slide beneath the damp leaves on the forest floor. With a trembling chin and watery eyes, she fumbled to take off the shoes God had given her, along with the belt that held her sheath. All her other armor fell to the ground. She snatched off her crown and threw it behind her, not daring to look at it.

"I *hate* it! I hate it *all!*" Aneta shouted as she threw off everything God had given her. "I hate fighting. I hate it with a passion. I made a complete fool of myself." The last sentence Aneta spoke quietly, almost afraid that God would appear right then and there to discipline her. With a gulp, she shook her head and held her arms. "I told You. I didn't want to fight. You gave me too much. It was *too much*. I thought You would understand, I thought You would care, but then again...maybe You don't."

She walked off, leaving her apparel strewn about on the ground.

She did not get far when Affection ran up to her. "What happened?"

Feeling indifferent, Aneta shrugged. "God gave me too much. I quit."

"You can't just quit."

"Yes I can. Leave me alone." Aneta kept walking.

Affection hesitated, then caught up with her again. "Why are you quitting? What about Theo? And Courage and the squad? They need your help to-"

"They really don't. I'm the youngest of them all. What on earth am I going to do to help out? Shine their shoes or fetch a glass of water?" Sarcasm filled her voice.

"What about today?"

"What about it?"

Affection's eyes pleaded with Aneta to stop and rethink her decision. "They asked you to cover for them! You were the only one who could do it! No one else could..."

"And guess what? No one else seems to know I hate fighting. I hate it. I *hate* it. They all leave me the dirty work and run off doing who knows what. And I failed. I *failed* and miserably embarrassed myself." Aneta scowled. "So excuse me if I seem a little cross."

"What will everyone else say?"

"They'll find out sooner or later."

Affection sighed and stopped trying to keep up with Aneta as she briskly walked ahead of her. She refrained from trying to convince Aneta to stay. Aneta wasn't listening.

"Okay. Fine." Affection's voice was quiet. "But...why do you hate fighting?"

When Aneta turned to face Affection, her face displayed a wild expression of fierce passion. Aneta's outburst made it sound like she had been waiting to tell someone for ages.

"It does *nothing!* I fought for years! I fought for as long as I could hold a sword! And it went for *nothing!* I even fought a boy named Coward! He was cheating souls for who knows how long, and I went to stop him. That's what God had asked me to do. And I failed *that* too!"

Aneta paused for a moment, then decided to go on.

"But guess *what?* Do you know who Coward is?! He is now known as *Theo!* I can't *believe* he has the nerve to assume I'll just *up* and *forgive* him! He tormented souls for a long time, and now, I can hardly bear to use my sword because of him. So *yes!* I'm upset! I'm annoyed! I'm *completely* done! Theo is so high and mighty, so he is completely welcome to carry on without me! *I don't care!*"

Affection pursed her lips. She could not find any words to say.

From behind them, something chortled and chuckled. Both Affection and Aneta spun around, spying a miscreation that had been eavesdropping. The scout demon soon began to laugh, running off in a gleeful mood.

Affection gasped. "You are going to cause more damage than you think! Aneta!" She called her name when it looked like Aneta was not paying attention. "Aneta! What do you think you're doing?"

"God messed up! Okay?"

"You don't even care for the trouble that you're about to put Theo through?"

"Why do *I* need to care?" She shouted at God. "You messed up, okay? I'm not the person You really want!" She looked back at Affection, daringly defiant.

"That's not all of it." It was Affection's turn to scowl. "God doesn't give us more temptation than we can handle. However, whatever trouble we run into, God will guide us out of it. But we have to listen to Him. I'm sorry that you don't like to fight, but...well... I don't have anything. I...just can't understand why you would want to escape God. I've fought *against* Him my whole life. But now, I have Him again. And...it's the most *amazing* thing I've ever experienced. And I fight any time He wants me to. But you...you have so much time to walk with God. You have years and years ahead of you. And I can't figure out why you'd want to throw that time away."

Aneta teared up. Her arms and shoulders sagged. "I...can't do this anymore." Tears spilled out, and she stood there sobbing. "Everything is too hard."

Pulling her in for a hug, Affection sighed. "I know. I know, sweetie. Can you do me a favor? Ask Courage, or Faith, or someone for advice. *Talk* to *someone*. I so, *so* want to help you. But I think someone else would be more able to help you. That's... one of the repercussions of being outside of God. I don't know as much as I would like. But...please promise me you will ask someone and tell someone tonight. *Tonight*."

Aneta shivered and nodded, still hugging Affection. "I promise."

She left Affection's side and kept walking by herself.

Her face wet with tears, Aneta stumbled along the forest path, trying to keep her hair out of her eyes and her sight. She finally stopped and leaned against a tree.

"I'm sorry, God. I can't. I can't do...anything anymore."

193

"It's not like I said you could in the first place." Voice folded her arms and leaned against the tree as well. "But hey, I'm glad you see it my way."

"Can you *ever* leave me alone?" Aneta began to feel a slight déjà vu.

"No."

Aneta sighed and slowly blinked, feeling exhausted. After a moment, her head shot up and she whirled around. "No...no, no, no." She muttered to herself. "How did they find me? Why are they looking for me?"

Voice glanced around. "Who?"

Before Aneta could answer, a demon appeared. "Just me." It smiled at her.

"Lost?"

"Yes. I figured you could use my company in the forest."

Aneta looked around again, and suddenly she felt that the demon had a point. It made no sense, but then again, nothing else did right now, either.

Seeing her confused expression, Lost smiled charmingly. "Don't worry, Aneta. I'm not here to harm you. Since you're neutral now, I have nothing against you."

Aneta warily nodded, not knowing what else to do. She folded her arms and wandered the forest with Voice and Lost in tow. They talked to each other a lot, but rarely spoke to her.

Eventually, Aneta had to stop. It was getting dark out, and she could no longer see very well. She began to cry again. "I have no idea what to do."

Voice piped up, "Hey. You could ask God. He's helped you out before."

Lost whacked Voice's arm and gave her a look.

Aneta sighed. "There's no way I could do that. I...not now. A person would be nice."

"Um, hello?" Voice held up her hands.

"Not you, obviously." Lost rolled its eyes. "Leave the poor girl alone. Now, Aneta, listen. So, actually, when we…"

Aneta shut out Lost's voice. Everything seemed horrible. This was just a repeat of her previous years. How had she jumped back and forth so many times? She was sick and tired of trying to balance in the middle. It was utterly exhausting. It was draining. Couldn't she just pick one side? Had she actually left God's side? She could not figure anything out. She desperately wanted to talk to someone. She desperately wanted to have someone understand her.

Voice and Lost soon made a fire and sat by the flames, talking long into the night. Aneta laid down next to the fire, but it gave her no warmth. She woke up before dawn as rain began to fall, chilling her and making her miserable. She slowly stood up and meandered around, trying to keep her blood moving. The rain increased until it steadily pattered onto the leaves of the trees.

Lost and Voice came along beside her, not minding the rain, cheerfully chatting again. Their endless chatter soon became white noise.

"I...just want to talk to a person." Aneta whispered so quietly to herself that her own ears could hardly pick up the words.

As Aneta kept walking, her feet weighed more and more. Why did it seem worse than before? Had she really gone back to her old lifestyle, like the time she lived among the crags in the canyons? God had done so much for her. What was wrong with her? Why did she refuse to ask Him?

Aneta wished she knew the answer to at least one of her questions.

When she was about to ask God for help, she remembered she had left her crown somewhere on the forest floor. What would God say when He arrived, when He saw that she wasn't wearing the crown He gave her? It would be too embarrassing. She decided against it. *Anyone but God.*

She kept trudging along, wondering if she would ever find her way out of the forest. She found a river and began to walk along the edge of it. The rain continued to fall. She was soaked to the bone by now, causing her to shiver. She took two more steps and the ground sank beneath her. The bank collapsed. Aneta was sent sprawling into the water. She sputtered and sat up, muddy and soaking wet. As she raised her head, she looked up and saw Theo standing there.

Theo hid a smile and helped her out of the water. Aneta's face fell. She folded her arms and looked at the ground. He obviously saw that she had given up.

"Aneta?"

She had already been on the verge of tears. When she said that she wanted anyone else but God, she did not mean *Theo!* Anyone but God or Theo! Tears sprang to her eyes, but they were hidden in the rain. Aneta flung her dripping hair out of her face.

"What?" Her question came out exasperated and harsh.

"I...am sorry. I told you, a long time ago, that fighting wasn't worth it. Do you remember?"

Aneta slowly nodded. "Yes. I remember."

"So…" Theo looked forward again. "So. You actually quit?"

Aneta wanted to negate his question, but she found it to be true. Was there a way to reverse it? "Yes. I did."

"I see."

They both kept walking. Aneta could find nothing to say. She finally bit her lip. "I'm sorry, Theo. I...I'm afraid I can't come back. I know it wouldn't matter now, but...I can't stand fighting."

"So you were serious, huh?"

"Yes! I hate it."

"But..." Theo looked at the ground. "You were so *good* at it."

Aneta gave him a look.

Nodding, Theo kept his eyes down. "Yeah. I was...uh, always jealous of you. I made a whip because...maybe it would stop your sword. I mean, it worked the first few times, but then...you could beat me again."

"I never beat you."

Theo laughed, but it turned to slight embarrassment. "Well, if I never called for backup, you would've beat me every time. I never counted my victories as victories. I'm still not sure why you hate your sword."

"I'm not so sure, either." Aneta quietly replied as she turned away. "Goodbye, Theodore. I...hope you guys can keep at it."

Theo could not find words to reply.

Aneta blinked to keep the tears away. She refused to look behind her as she left Theo standing by the riverside. It would be better to leave before he could call after her.

Before long, she heard a shout. Heart racing, Aneta rushed back to the river where she had left Theo. He was being attacked by multiple demons. She hesitated, then moved forward, wanting to help him.

Lost stepped in her way. "Slow down there, Aneta. This is our battle. You are neutral now. You can't intervene. You have no authority to do so."

Aneta's face hardened. "We'll see about that!"

"No!" Lost grabbed her arm.

"You can't touch me!" Aneta refuted. "Remember?"

Lost scowled and let her go. "The moment you put that crown on, you're dead, you know that?"

"Again. We'll *see*." Aneta bolted.

She tripped and stumbled through the wet forest, desperately trying to remember where she had left her belongings. "God..." A single tear escaped. She wiped it away, done with crying. "Please show me where I-" She halted.

She saw her shield sitting on the ground a few feet away.

She lunged towards it and soon found the rest of her armor. She pulled it on, and fingered the leaves until her hands touched gold. She picked up her crown from the leaves. It still shone brightly. With a deep breath, she put it back on.

"God, forgive me. I don't ever want to leave you again."

Shrill screeches and muffled shrieks filled the air. They were coming for her too. Aneta frantically searched the brush and dead leaves for her sword. Where was it? A demon flew at her, but she deflected it with her shield.

More were coming. Her hand brushed over something metal. She picked up her sword and swung it in a full circle, slaughtering a demon that came dangerously close to her head. Tossing the sword up and catching it again, she readjusted her grip and tightly held her shield.

She charged through the forest again, knocking down every measly demon that contended with her. With a running leap, she barreled into the group of demons on top of Theo.

They all tumbled into the water, surprised and furious. Lost, who had been watching from afar, straightened and growled at her in annoyance. She adjusted her crown, still staring at him, and then helped up Theo as Lost, Voice and the other demons grudgingly retreated.

Theo grinned at her, although he was bruised on his cheek and bleeding from a cut on his arm.

"Nice look." He nodded at Aneta's crown.

"Thanks. I plan on keeping it."

|Chapter 20: More Problems With Devious|

Aneta scoffed good-naturedly. "Yeah. I was...definitely nervous on Sunday. I'm sorry I didn't stay very long, though. It would've been nice to chat with you."

Aneta had found Sorrow in a grocery store and they were now both walking together as they shopped. Sorrow gave a small smile. "I didn't know you ever got nervous."

"Of course I do!" Aneta chuckled. "I get nervous...all the time." She smiled again, but refrained from telling Sorrow she was nervous right then and there. She had just spotted Devious in the store. He and Aneta had locked eyes for a second. He saw that she was skittish around him and they both knew it.

Aneta and Sorrow kept strolling along. Aneta wished she could grab Sorrow's hand and pull her away, but she could not do much of anything. She could not see Devious now, but Aneta knew he was probably following them.

Sorrow looked down. "Aneta. I...see Gracefully Broken a lot. We are in the same classes. And...she is...a lot different. Is it because of church, or you girls?"

Aneta laughed. "Well, it *isn't* because of me. But, yes, you could say it's because she is in church. But, it's not specifically church. She realized that God loved her. And she accepted His love. When she realized that God could be like her...spiritual Father, she allowed Him to-"

"Is God's love what changed her?"

That question stood out in Aneta's mind. Her own heart warmed up at the thought of God's love. She had never quite thought about it in that specific way, of God's love being the reason for change in a person's life, but she nevertheless realized it was true.

"Yes. Yes, it is. God loves us...way more than I can imagine. I'm not sure how good your imagination is, but...I don't think anyone can imagine how *much* He loves us."

Sorrow was quiet for a moment. "I...I've already heard about repenting and...accepting God into my heart. I heard Courage talk about it. I...think I want to-"

"Ah, good evening, ladies." Devious smiled at both of them, intercepting them from a side aisle.

Aneta glanced at Sorrow's face, but it was unreadable. Was Sorrow happy or annoyed to see Devious?

"Hello, Devious." Aneta gave him a smile.

"Are you feeling better now, Aneta?"

"Excuse me?" She remained overly polite.

"I hope you're feeling better now, after Sunday. Sometimes, it can feel like you're lost in the woods, am I right?"

Chills ran down Aneta's spine and through her bones.

"And how are you doing, Sorrow?" Devious turned to her.

"I am doing well, thank you."

"So what are you ladies here for?"

Aneta spoke up. "Just grabbing a few things. But it's getting late, and we need to be going."

Devious smiled again, making Aneta nervous. "Well, I will see you around, then. Pleasure talking to you."

Sorrow and Aneta headed for the check-out. As they bagged their items, Aneta fumed with irritation. Sorrow had come so close, but Devious *had* to interrupt them.

Aneta gulped as they exited the building. That was where they had to part ways. "Sorrow? Did you...want to-"

"See you later, Aneta."

Aneta nodded mutely as Sorrow turned around and walked toward her house. Aneta fought back tears and turned to go to her own apartment.

All sadness disappeared and was replaced with anger when Devious appeared beside her on the sidewalk.

"Hello again, Aneta. Fancy meeting you here. It's a bit cold out. Would you like me to carry your bags?"

Aneta stopped and glared at him. "I can carry my own bags. Leave me and Sorrow alone."

Devious stepped closer.

Angry, Aneta unsheathed her sword. "I said: Leave. Me. Alone."

"I see your fancy crown has given you some gumption."

Immediately, Aneta shot back, "I also see your throne of lies has been lying to you."

"What do you mean?" Devious' tone was the only thing showing slight disturbance. He kept his face unchanged.

"This crown alone has not given me courage. You know as well as anyone that anyone can display a crown. I thought you *were* there, but maybe you were just bluffing. Because *my* God gives me sustenance. He is the one who protects and guides me. He gives me my gumption. Where does yours come from?"

Enraged, Devious snatched a whip from his belt as quick as lightning and slashed it across her sword arm. Aneta yelped and struggled for a moment to back away.

"That. Never happened, Aneta." Devious rasped and grinned. "That little event in the forest? It never happened. That was all Voice. You aren't wearing a crown. You aren't God's daughter." He recoiled and lashed out again.

Aneta held up her shield and gave her wounded arm a break. She gasped for breath, trying to not listen to him. "Devious! Your name gives you away. There is nothing you say that I need to heed. I am bought with the blood of Jesus. Let me *go!*"

Aneta raised her shield and struck Devious in the head with it, stunning him. She took that opportunity to escape. She wanted to fight, but she feared she would not be able to win. Aneta hurried away.

"Aneta?" Aneta looked up as Faith ran to her. "Are you okay?"

She nodded. "I'm fine. But...Devious is after me again. I don't know how to win this battle." Aneta teared up.

Faith gave her a quick hug. "I can help you, don't worry. But remember, it's not us. God is the One who fights and wins our battles."

Wanting to give up, Aneta sighed. "That's so hard to remember."

Three demons and Chains, a chief demon, charged towards them, no doubt sent by Devious. Aneta gathered her strength and sliced one, then spun around and speared the other. The thuggish demon leapt on top of her, knocking her down. She cried out and tried to free her sword arm, but the demon pinned it down firmly and snapped at her with razor-sharp teeth.

Aneta avoided the drooling jaws by shoving her shield in front of her face. She tried to roll over, but the demon was too heavy. She jabbed it with her knee, and then freed her right arm. She thumped its neck and chin with her shield and then stabbed it twice.

"Oh, Aneta?"

Spinning as she stood, Aneta froze. Devious stood there patiently, holding Faith with his whip wrapped around her neck.

"Aneta, you young people...are getting very tiring to deal with."

Faith's dangerous predicament added to Aneta's labored breathing. "You are, too. I suggest you leave."

Devious laughed and tightened the whip. Faith wheezed and her eyes widened. "Actually, it would be easier for you to leave. You and your so-called 'squad.' Although it might only be four of you leaving."

Aneta could not bring herself to move.

"I'm waiting." Devious' voice was ice.

Faith's face was turning an ugly shade of purple.

Aneta looked down. Devious wanted her to surrender. To leave town and end the church. She could not do that, could she?

But Faith...

Aneta's eyes softened when she saw the white wisps begin to appear and slowly sweep around her feet. Aneta remembered from years ago when the prayers of someone would help her in the heat of battle.

She looked up to see fear in Devious' eyes. He, too, knew what it was. Aneta gripped her sword with renewed courage and charged for Devious.

To her surprise, Devious punched Faith hard, knocking her unconscious. He caught her limp body as it sagged, then drew her close again. The prayer clouds faded.

Devious gave her an evil grin as Aneta realized what he had done.

Turning into his monstrous demonic form, Devious began to carry Faith away.

"To be honest," Devious snarled, "I did not think that you would cause this much trouble. Theo surprises me too. But I'll deal with him when I'm done with you."

Aneta's anger flared. Was Faith alright? Could she get to Devious' fearsome form without wasting too much time? *Come on, sword. Just like old times.*

With a fierce swing, Aneta started the battle. Devious maneuvered around her blows and pounded her multiple times, without releasing his grip on Faith. In moments, other smaller demons came and distracted Aneta. Devious began to lumber away with Faith in his grasp. Struggling to keep up, Aneta swiftly secured her shield on her back again, and used both hands on her sword's hilt. She wanted to focus all her strength on her sword. And her shield sat waiting patiently.

Aneta finished off the last little demon and charged again after Devious who still clutched Faith. Even then, she began to cry as her arms weakened. "God. Please help." Her plea sounded pitiful, and Devious wasted no time in pointing that out. Aneta tried to ignore him, but she could not focus.

No help came. No one was praying for her. What was she supposed to do? She could not focus enough to pray for herself, and she could not go on without backup.

"Please, God." Aneta's plea sounded again.

Apparently, Devious now had gotten quite annoyed at Aneta's efforts, and was beginning to drive her back. Aneta switched to defense. That seemed to drive her back further. "I...need help. Please."

Still nothing.

"Look at that." Devious paused his attacks to circle her. Faith barely let out a moan on Devious' shoulder. "Your God has forsaken you. To be honest, you should have seen that coming."

"God will never leave me. He will never forsake me. I *will* beat you, Devious."

Devious laughed, and gave a signal, like the click of a tongue. When Lost rushed out from behind a building and jumped at Aneta, Devious laughed again. He continued on his way.

Lost speedily approached Aneta, and she took a fighting stance. Her legs began to tremble as her arms sagged. A threatening thought of losing the battle crossed her mind.

Intending to quickly finish its job, Lost widened its snarling mouth, ready to engulf Aneta. To her surprise, Lost's dull eyes widened and it scrambled to skid to a stop. Aneta looked behind her in time to see a fierce being charged past her. With a swipe of a fiery sword, Lost was dematerialized.

The angel turned to her. "Aneta. Go. You have an appointment with Devious."

Trembling, Aneta nodded to the angel, touched her crown, and sprinted in the direction of Devious.

With Lost vanquished for that battle, she could move easily as long as another demon did not find her again. Aneta found Devious. Before she could call him out as she ran towards him, Devious spotted her. He was in his human form again, still hauling Faith over his shoulder.

Oddly, he blinked and staggered backwards, as if he was blinded. Aneta took this as an opportunity to attack at once. Devious dropped Faith to defend himself. He barely blocked her flurry of swings. She fought more and more fiercely, soon noticing that her sword was becoming red hot. It burned through Devious' whip and scarred him on the shoulder where her sword had broken through.

Devious fled.

Exhausted, Aneta checked how Faith was doing. She did not look injured at all. Aneta laid down, nearly collapsing in the process, next to her friend. Exhausted, she closed her eyes, amazed that God had enabled her to win that battle.

"Thank you, God. I could not have done it without You."

After a few minutes, Faith stirred. "Aneta?" Her voice sounded groggy and strained.

Aneta held up a hand, not opening her eyes. "Yeah, I'm fine. Just tired. You good?"

"Yes. Aneta?"

Aneta opened her eyes.

"Thanks." Faith smiled at her and helped her up.

"My pleasure, but thank *you* for praying for me."

Faith sighed as they both slowly made their way down the road. "Devious was smart. Was anyone else praying for you?"

Aneta shrugged. "To be honest, I don't know what happened. I asked God for prayer, but no one prayed. So He sent an angel instead."

Both beginning to smile and chuckle, Faith and Aneta kept walking, helping each other stand.

Tuesday morning, Aneta did not feel like getting up. She wanted more sleep, but she had an early shift. She glanced at her phone and immediately perked up. Sorrow had texted her around midnight that night, saying she still wanted to accept God. Her heart leapt when Sorrow asked to meet her. Aneta told her to meet at three-thirty at the March Coffee café.

Aneta remained in high spirits during work...until she got another text from Sorrow, saying she was unable to make it. Even though Sorrow had never told her dad what she was doing, her dad had forbidden Sorrow to go anywhere. He did not give any reason.

Frustrated, Aneta threw the dirty towels into the hamper as she cleaned out the room. She thought about asking for a raise. It had been a while since she started her job at the inn, and she knew it as well as Courage. As her mind raced back and forth, thinking about her current job, keeping a church going, and maintaining her own life, Aneta began to wonder if she could actually accomplish anything she was supposed to.

Aneta felt tired and worn out. It seemed like work just to keep breathing, like waves crashed against her as she struggled to keep her head above the raging water. One part of her began to wonder if it was worth the effort, but the more optimistic side of her felt confident God would light her way.

With one last glance, Aneta double-checked the room. Satisfied, she wheeled the cart to the laundry area to put the sheets into a hamper. She found herself getting annoyed as seconds ticked by. Everything she tried to do seemed to be shot down. She had come so close with Sorrow, but Devious burst in and ruined it. Who knew if Sorrow would still want to become a Christian?

The squad had planned to get together for lunch at Bold's apartment, so Aneta finished her shift, which ended at noon, and hurried to his apartment. When she got there, Bold opened the door for her, but he was still talking to Theo and Courage.

"No, it's probably more serious than that," Bold said, his head turned away from Aneta.

"What are you all talking about?" Aneta asked.

"Faith isn't here yet," Bold explained. "Faith is *always* on time. She said she would be here at noon sharp, and it's almost twelve-thirty. Your sandwich is on your plate, by the way."

"Thanks."

"So anyway, we are trying to figure out why she is late. We're playing 'Maybe They.' Courage suggested that she had to work into her lunch shift. I don't think she feels like playing. I doubt that. *Theo* thinks that she forgot. Which is... possible...? But do you have an idea? For Maybe They?"

"I'm not tired!" Courage protested. "I was being literal."

Aneta sat on the counter, since the tiny table Bold had in his kitchen was full. She hoped Faith was not in trouble. "Well, maybe there is a tornado."

Bold gave her a look. "Absolutely." There was a slight twinkle in his eye.

"A tornado?" Theo gave them a look.

Aneta and Bold stared at him.

After a pause, Theo stated, "It would take more than a tornado to make Faith late. Most likely it was a hurricane."

"Here? A hurricane?" Courage looked doubtful. "Oh, please. It was probably a tornado that caused an earthquake."

"Or! Maybe she decided to travel to a mountainside instead." Aneta threw out another idea.

206

Courage countered her. "Nope, she wouldn't have enough time to drive there. She probably went someplace closer. She could be kayaking in the river."

"Why would she go kayaking? It's the middle of winter," Theo said.

"Uh, to get a breath of fresh air? I don't know! Ask Faith! Not me. I'm not the one going kayaking in winter. Besides, she hasn't texted us, so her phone probably fell in the water."

"Well, to be honest, it *would* make sense, especially if the roads were closed off because of the damage from the tornado and earthquake...and a kayak would be her only way of transport." Bold nodded.

Someone knocked on the door fifteen minutes later. Bold jumped up and flung the door open. "Faith!" He paused as he realized there was another person standing next to her. He was equally pleased, although he showed more restraint. "Hello, Pastor Kindly. Come in! Would you like lunch?"

The middle-aged man stepped into the suddenly crowded kitchen and smiled. "Well, if it's already out, I wouldn't mind. But don't go to any trouble on my part."

Bold immediately made him a sandwich and brought out a soda. "Oh, not at all."

"This is our former pastor, Pastor Brave Kindly." Faith began introductions. "Pastor Kindly, this is Theo and Aneta, and Courage."

"Nice to meet you all." Pastor Kindly shook their hands before sitting down. "Theo, I hear you are doing a good job."

When Aneta glanced in Theo's direction, the blood had drained from his face. When color returned, it came accompanied with reddened ears. "Thanks, Pastor Kindly."

"So, Faith did tell me, but what are your ages one more time?"

"I'm twenty-nine," Courage answered. "Theo and Faith are twenty-four, and Bold is... twenty-six? And Aneta is twenty-two."

"Extraordinary! And I say this with all sincerity, I am immensely impressed with everything Faith has told me."

"Is that why you were late, Faith?"

Faith nodded, then grinned. "But why *else* was I late?"

"Well," Courage explained, "we eventually decided that a tornado touched down and you had to go around, but because of the tornado, there was an earthquake. Because the roads were closed down, you had to get a kayak from Sign's Store, and you had to paddle until you got around the back of the farms, and then you walked through the fields to get to here."

Faith nodded again after everything. "Solid. A very solid Maybe They."

"'Maybe They' is a game we were playing to explain why Faith was late to lunch. She's never late," Bold explained to Pastor Kindly.

"Ah, I see."

"Pastor Kindly, which church did you pastor before you retired?" Aneta asked, trying to spark conversation.

"Ah. Well, my church was one of the churches that was run out of Aphoticton. It was called New Beginnings. It was a fairly good-sized church, and we were getting ready to move into another building, but then the town mayor changed his mind, and he wanted all of us out. We were the last church to go, but when we got a bombing threat, I closed the church. I am relieved that God is sending more people to start a church again."

Aneta's heart lifted up as Pastor Kindly began to talk. She listened the best she could as Sorrow began to text her, asking questions about God's love or what to do when she had no idea what to do, as well as how to pray. Aneta replied, then flipped her phone over, hanging onto Pastor Kindly's words. Everything about Pastor Kindly encouraged her, and she was reluctant to leave when her co-worker asked if she could cover a two hour shift. She had to get back to work. Faith and Courage had already left, but Bold and Theo were planning to stay longer.

In high spirits, Aneta braced for the cold and hurried down the street, not necessarily wanted to cover a shift, but she had nothing else to do.

"Well. We meet again."

Aneta jumped as she recognized the chilling voice behind her. She spun on her heel and locked eyes with Devious.

"Time for round two," Devious said, marching briskly toward Aneta, a new whip in hand and a wicked glint in his eyes. "We both know how this will end."

Aneta took one step back, then another.

"I am coming to get you, Aneta. I may have a scar from you... but after today, there will be *nothing left* of you. As soon as I'm done with you..."

As Devious spoke, Aneta carefully unsheathed her sword. She pointed her blade at Devious and backed away as he continued his approach. Aneta waited for him to move first, even though she trembled with confusion and fear and her heart hammered in her chest. Would his words be true?

Could she beat him?

If not, then she would die.

"...I will be chopping off one member of your group at a time. But right now, you are the worst of my problems."

Aneta steadied herself. She forced herself to stop moving backwards. "You fool yourself." Why did Devious not strike? What was he waiting for? And why was *she* the biggest target in her group?

"Oh. *No*. I do believe you are mistaken."

Aneta held back a shiver. She hated Devious' sleek, unwavering voice. She found it hard to beat his dominating tone.

His brilliant green eyes flashed in controlled rage. "But no matter, your opinion of me means nothing. Although, it is a pity. You would have been a marvelous warrior for us. You were so close too, all those years in the canyons. You had so much time to decide... but you never did."

Devious stopped in front of Aneta, only a few feet away, and stared into her eyes. "Well, I suppose I should ask one last time.

Would you rather die or help us? You would never have to fight your friends, of course. You would only deal with strangers. People you don't know. People you don't care about. It wouldn't bother you too much."

Aneta kept her sword ready. The words *marvelous warrior* stuck out in her mind. "You made one mistake, Devious."

His face showed genuine confusion.

"I decided a long time ago."

Seeing that she had no intention of turning, Devious let out a growl, and the whip snapped in the air with a vicious crack. "You are nothing! You have no purpose! Nothing! *Nothing!*"

Then he turned the whip on her.

Aneta found it difficult to keep up with him. She could block his attacks, but she could not think of any way to force him to retreat.

Nevertheless, his statements began to penetrate her mind, sounding more and more like truth. A demon ran up to Aneta and latched onto her back, trying to rip off her shield from her back. She immediately dropped, crushing the demon underneath her. However, she was now on her back and Devious had an advantage. Aneta scolded herself. She had not grabbed her shield, and now it would be nearly impossible to grab it without further endangering herself.

She blocked his whip again; however, she had to use her own arm since she had not been able to react with her sword, or shield, fast enough. Her arm stung until it slowly grew numb. She could still move it, but it became increasingly difficult. More pesky demons began swarming her as she fought with Devious. If she was nothing, how could she hope to accomplish anything for God?

Aneta immediately corrected herself. "Devious. You made a mistake." She could not help but smile, because Devious had inadvertently given her the key to victory. "If I am nothing, if I don't matter, and if my contribution to my friends, my church, and my God are useless, then why do you attack me first and foremost? It seems to me you know God is on my side."

Devious' eyes widened as she spoke.

Staring at him, Aneta said, "My God fights for me. And you *know* you can't win."

Enraged that Aneta uprooted his work, Devious ravenously lashed out at her. His anger-fueled speed and renewed savagery surprised Aneta, but she recovered and eventually drove him back. She then speedily snatched her shield from her back. She kept striking.

Aneta noticed that her sword began to heat up again, slowly turning a red color. Devious also recognized what was happening and moved in quickly for the kill.

Now able to focus, With her shield in her left hand, Aneta blocked his blow and let it wrap around her shield. She pulled back, making the whip's tail taut. In one swift swipe, she sliced his whip. Again. He was defenseless.

Devious backed away now. "I will be back."

Aneta shook her head. "You might be, but that would put you in danger. You know you can't win, Devious. You can't beat God. I am covered in Jesus' name and Jesus' blood, and there is nothing you can do about it. You better put that in your report. Maybe your boss can transfer you."

Devious snarled and vanished.

Right before Aneta opened the doors to the inn, she got another text. It was from Sorrow. She had decided to pray to God in her bedroom, and she became a Christian.

As Aneta walked into the inn, looking at her phone, she involuntarily let out a squeal of delight.

|Chapter 21: A Friend in Need|

Aneta walked into the book store. After Sorrow expressed her desire for a Bible, Aneta invited Sorrow to meet her there to pick one out. She waited near the front when she arrived and messaged Sorrow that she was there.

After a moment, someone behind her exclaimed her name. As Aneta turned around, she had just enough time to brace for Sorrow's hug.

"It's so amazing!" Sorrow gushed. "I can't believe I didn't do this sooner. God is so... well, *amazing!*"

With a grin, Aneta nodded. "Absolutely. He is incredible. It only gets better from here. Come on! Let's go find a Bible!"

As Sorrow peppered Aneta with questions about God, Aneta could not help but smile the whole time. God *was* good. She marveled at how He worked and how He put things into motion. Aneta loved every single question Sorrow brought up, whether or not she could confidently answer it.

Even though money was tight, she insisted upon paying for Sorrow's Bible, and writing in the date she received it.

"Now I have a Bible for tonight!" Sorrow beamed as they walked out of the bookstore.

It was clear that day, and the light reflecting off the snow was brilliant, almost blinding. The bright sun gently warmed the chilly winter day.

Neither of them had a car, and Aneta decided to walk Sorrow home before heading to her own apartment for dinner. Since it was Wednesday night, she had to fix her meal early to get to church on time.

"Now you can follow along," Aneta said. "And really, having a paper Bible is so nice. Electronic Bibles just don't cut it. And I'm actually kinda impressed you wanted a King James Version."

"This is so elegant! Even the first chapter in the whole thing is amazing. Doesn't it just put your imagination to work?" Sorrow held up the Bible to Aneta, showing her the first chapter of Genesis. "How do I study this? There is so much in here."

"Well, there are lots of ways people study the Bible. Some people might stay in a certain passage for a week or so, or however long it takes for them to satisfy their mind with how much they take in. Anyway, you could start in the New Testament and go from there. Maybe Acts and First Timothy and Second Timothy after the Gospels? You can read through them, maybe a chapter a day. And write down anything you like. Maybe write down the places where the people are, good points they say that you really like, interesting statements. It's chock full of everything. People who have studied the Bible their whole life can still always find more new revelations."

"What do you mean by a revelation?"

"Sometimes, you can read a verse every day and nothing changes. But then, maybe one day, you might be having a rough time with something, and when you look at that verse again, you might see it in another perspective, or God might show you something that the verse says that you have never realized before. God gives us revelations about His Word to encourage us. A lot of times, that is what a pastor shares at church."

"How do you study every day? Personally?"

"Well, I change it up every now and again. Sometimes, I pick a book of the Bible and I slowly read through that book, writing down everything that interests me, anything God reminds me of, and I might look a certain word up in a concordance-"

"What is a concordance?"

Aneta paused, trying to figure out how to define it. "It's...a book that has a lot of main words from the Bible. They are in alphabetical order, and it kinda tells you about the word. Like... the last word I looked up was 'alabaster.' And you go to the concordance and it tells you about alabaster and such. Anyway, it helps with research."

"Why would you need to research something?"

"A lot of times, when you come across something in the Bible, you might not know why people did certain things, or how things worked. I mean, I'm not an expert on the culture back in Israel or anything, and if I wonder why they did X thing, then I research it. A lot of times, researching can give us more understanding and even appreciation for what people did in the Bible."

"But how would I know what to research?"

"Well... anything that interests you. Look, open to Genesis 1 again. You can research why God uses third person to refer to Himself while creating the world. He says things like... here, let me see it. Like, in verse twenty-six. *'And God said, Let us make man in our image, after our likeness...'* See, He says *'us'* and *'our'*. This one is fun to find. I'll give you a hint, though. Look up royal decrees. Let me know if you can't figure it out, and I'll help you out."

Sorrow brought out a pen. She glanced at Aneta. "Is...is it okay to underline in the Bible?"

"Of course! My Bible is *full* of highlights, notes, question marks, circlings, everything. You can look up stuff about culture too. Like, if you read about Esther, you can research Persian culture and such. A lot of times, if you do that, you can find out why they did X thing that way. My favorite part about researching stuff in the Bible is that it brings things to my attention that I never noticed before."

Sorrow jumped a few times in excitement. "I heard about Esther before! Wasn't she a queen?"

"Yes! Her story is super amazing. There are not a lot of women in the Bible who have their own books, but there are still a bunch who did important things. I know there was a time when Israel did not have a king, and they had people who acted like judges instead--in the book of Judges--and there is a woman who is a judge and she is *super* cool. That might be one of my favorite stories. I...oh boy, I *think* her name is Deborah, but I can't remember." Aneta laughed.

Sorrow simply smiled at her. "You know *so* much about God and the Bible. I am never going to catch up." Her face fell.

"Oh, don't worry about that! Really, someone will *always* know more about the Bible than you. I mean, there are sixty-six books. I probably understand only...well, I probably don't understand any of them all the way. But you don't need to catch up at all. God is perfectly content with you going at your own passionate pace. You can go at the pace you want, but don't try to speed through anything."

"Oh, alright."

The girls were coming up on Sorrow's house.

"But hey," Aneta said, "if you ever need help, or you want some ideas on what to study, or you would like to study with someone, or you just have more questions, then you can always text me, or Courage, or Faith."

"Thanks, Aneta!" Sorrow embraced her again and, clutching her Bible with glee, hurried up her steps into her house.

Aneta hurried away, knowing that she had to get ready for church that evening.

Aneta unlocked the church door and walked in, sighing in relief. She scarcely got the lights on and the furnace turned up, when Gracefully Broken texted her and asked if she could come to church early to talk with her. Aneta said it was fine and, to her surprise, Gracefully Broken entered the door only moments later.

The girl hastily sat down on a pew. Not knowing what else to do, Aneta sat next to her, waiting for Gracefully Broken to speak.

When she did not say anything, Aneta went first. "Is something bothering you?"

Gracefully Broken flashed her a look. "Yes!" Irritation put an edge to her voice. "I am *so* annoyed. And confused. I feel...worthless. Like no one understands me right now. That...the girl I was doing Bible studies with at school asked not to do them anymore, and I'm wondering how else God can use me. I feel like I'm a complete waste of space. What am I supposed to do? I spend my days after school wondering if there is anything to do, and even when there is something to do I don't feel like doing it."

Aneta opened her mouth to say something, but Gracefully Broken kept going.

"And, I'm annoyed because I feel like everyone around me has a purpose and *I don't!*" Tears sprang into her eyes. "I'm so jealous of you, Aneta. You have purpose, and Theo has purpose, and Faith and Bold and Courage have purpose, and everyone else does too. Me? I can't even figure out if I have it, and if I will ever be able to find it. And...with all my depression..." Her voice finally softened, and it grew hollow and vacant. "I don't want to go back."

Aneta put an arm around Gracefully Broken and squeezed gently. "I did not know you felt like that."

Gracefully Broken began to cry. "How are you so good at being...you?" Tears spilled down her face. "You are always so calm and collected and beautiful, and I can't figure out how to be any of those."

"Well... would you like me to listen to you, or would you like some advice?"

After a few shaky breaths, Gracefully Broken said, "I just need help. I don't want to go back."

Aneta straightened again and sat back. "Well, I'm not completely sure how to help you if you think I am always calm and collected. I hardly ever feel calm and collected for more than a day."

"Really?"

"Oh, yes. Really. You are seventeen, right? Getting to eighteen?"

"In July, yes."

"Yeah, yeah. Remember, I'm really not much different than you. I'm only twenty-two. I don't know about you, but I really don't feel that old. A lot of the time, I still feel like a teen. So I have to say...I'm not an expert on this subject. I don't know everything. I know that God calls us to be who He needs us to be. I mean, I suppose that some people's calling is amazing and majestic, but for the most part, I don't think the first thing that comes to mind when you say 'my calling' makes you think of glory and such. Usually, His calling for us gets us in deeper than we can handle. That's when we have to call on Him."

Gracefully Broken didn't say anything.

Aneta swallowed. She did not know if her words were reaching the troubled girl at all. She felt like she was failing. She desperately prayed for wisdom on what to say. "Gracefully Broken, what is it that you want to know?"

"Does God have a purpose for me?" Gracefully Broken had almost stopped crying, but her voice cracked with desperation. "Am I worth *anything?*"

"He does. Even when we feel like nothing is happening, we are still full of greatness in the quiet places in life. Gracefully Broken, you are worth *so much.* Your soul is priceless, and it is absolutely full of beauty and grace. You have a special love for people. Don't think that is nothing."

Gracefully Broken hugged Aneta. "To be honest, I...you didn't say what I wanted you to say, but everything you said was just right."

When Bold walked in, Aneta turned around, expecting Theo to be there as well. Not this time. Odd. The boys typically came at the same time.

"Hey," she asked, "where is Theo?"

Bold shook his head. "Theo got super sick right before dinner. He threw up and everything. I'm doing the lesson tonight."

"You're... did you have any time to prepare?"

Bold glanced at his watch. "An hour. Maybe."

Aneta's eyes widened. "Oh, wow. Okay, well, I'm sure you'll do great. And I hope Theo feels better. That's a bummer, though. Pastor Kindly was coming tonight."

Courage arrived a little bit later and practiced the song for that evening. As she was doing that, Pastor Kindly showed up and chatted with Aneta, Gracefully Broken, and Bold while more people slowly trickled into the church.

Watching Bold closely, Aneta wondered if he was nervous. He did not seem to be in the least, but then again, it was hard to tell. After a song, Bold went up and, using Theo's notes, taught the lesson. As Bold began to wrap up, Aneta realized that Bold did a much better job than herself to substitute for Theo. A *much* better job. He was clear and clever, adding in his own humor along the way. She would have never known that Bold had only had an hour to prepare.

With a deep breath, Aneta reminded herself that she had done her best, and God had not been disappointed. As she cleared her head, Aneta remembered there was no reason to be jealous. It was better to rejoice that Bold had been able to relieve Theo by taking care of the lesson.

Pastor Kindly approached Bold after the service, saying that he greatly enjoyed Theo's lesson, even though Bold presented it. "Bold, be sure to tell Theo that I am impressed with what he is able to do. Tell him I am planning on making it on Sunday as well." After a few more words of encouragement, he left.

After most of the people left, the squad was closing things up and turning things off. Aneta was grabbing her things from the pew. Faith and Courage left the sanctuary.

"Well, actually, I think I know why Theo was sick," Bold admitted as he flipped off the lights.

"Really?" Aneta waited for him to walk out of the sanctuary.

"I think he was nervous."

"As in, he got so nervous he threw up?"

"Yes. To be honest, I don't know what to say to him to help him out. I mean, Pastor Kindly has no regard if you mess up. He just loves on people. But there is no way for me to tell Theo that. I mean, Theo is super nervous and I heard part of what he has planned for Sunday, and there is no way I can cover for him. It would be wrong of me *not* to tell Theo that Pastor Kindly is coming on Sunday as well...so...maybe you should talk to Theo."

Aneta looked at Bold, but his face showed no sign of joking around. She began to laugh, but changed to a serious tone. "*I should talk to him?*"

"Why not? You probably know him best, other than me."

Even though she knew Bold was right, it still made Aneta slightly nervous. "Okay. I'll see what I can come up with."

"Well, do it sooner rather than later. I'll probably tell him tomorrow about Pastor Kindly."

Aneta nodded and exhaled. "Oh."

Bold began to walk towards the door to leave.

"Bold!" She slung her purse over her shoulder and hurried up behind him. "Don't tell him you told me..."

"Oh, yeah. Obviously."

On Saturday, Aneta had a day off from work. But she still ended up cleaning because the church had to be ready for Sunday. When she got there, she got a text from Gracefully Broken, asking if she could call Aneta.

Aneta said yes, and her phone immediately rang. "Hello, Gracefully Broken. How are you doing this week?"

She had been hoping it would be good news, but everything Gracefully Broken shared was bad. Aneta sighed in despair as she listened to Gracefully Broken talk about her horrible week.

Aneta sprinted toward the pack of demons, shouting as she drove them away from Gracefully Broken, who hid in a crumpled ball on the ground. The petty demons scurried away but called over bigger beasts to help.

Aneta stood her ground as Fear and Faint lunged at her and Gracefully Broken. Keeping an eye on reinforcements trying to get past her, Aneta fended off the two chief demons as she attempted to protect her friend. Angst attacked Aneta, pulling her down.

"Jesus!"

Aneta could hardly cry out His name before crashing to the ground. She kicked off Angst, a wiry yet powerful chiefdemon, and was instantly swarmed by half a dozen more. She desperately needed help. She needed someone to pray for her. She gasped in shock as Pain reached Gracefully Broken. Aneta stood up, trying to get away from the little demons clawing at her. One pulled her leg and she fell. She lost her breath as she landed on her chin. It stung at first, then began to warm up as blood dripped to the ground. She stuck her leg out and hooked Faint's ankle, tripping it before it could get to Gracefully Broken. But Chains had arrived and was already on top of the girl.

With a screech, Chains toppled over and scrambled away, streaming red smoke from a gaping wound. Aneta looked up and saw Theo there with his sword in hand. Right at that time, the now-familiar white clouds began to flow towards them. Most of the demons fled.

"Oh, thank you, Jesus." Aneta was able to stand. She grinned at him. "Thanks, Theo."

Theo smiled at Aneta and winked. "I had nothing better to do." He cut down one bold demon which attempted to engage him as its remaining companions closed in. "Hey, we got those... that fog again. Clouds."

"What?" Aneta looked at Theo after she ran off Faint and the last demons turned in retreat.

Theo pointed at the clouds swirling around their feet.

"Oh, those are prayer clouds! At least, that's what I call them. You know someone is praying for you when they come."

Theo's face lit up in awe. "Really? I never knew what they were."

"Well, now you do." Aneta found herself laughing as she sheathed her sword.

Between the two of them, they were able to help Gracefully Broken to her feet and lead her to safety.

Aneta hung up the phone. "I hope Gracefully Broken feels better. Thanks for lending me your Bible, Theo. I really could not remember those verses."

When Gracefully Broken had first called, Aneta had put her phone on speaker as she began to clean the mirror in the foyer.

When she had been trying to remember a verse to reference to Gracefully Broken, Theo had walked out of the sanctuary and gave her his Bible to look them up.

Theo smiled half-heartedly.

"Are you nervous?"

"About what?"

"About tomorrow."

Theo's facial expression gave everything away.

Aneta leaned against the wall. "So...were you here talking to God?"

Theo nodded. "Yeah. I forgot you were cleaning today."

"I can come back later, after lunch, if you like."

"Oh, no, you're fine."

Aneta glanced down. "Well, Theo...if you would like, I can listen as I clean. If you need...to talk to a person. I know sometimes talking to a human being helps too."

Theo shot Aneta a look. "I don't need your pity, and I sure don't need your advice."

With a sincere face, Aneta made sure Theo knew she understood. "I know. I have never been in your position before, and I don't know what it's like. I did not offer my advice. Just a listening ear."

"Sorry," Theo mumbled.

Aneta nodded and walked down the stairs to clean the bathrooms. She had finished almost the entire church, and had just started on the kitchen, when Theo walked in and put his hands in his pockets.

There, as Aneta wiped down the sink and counters, he told Aneta about the pressure he had been dealing with.

"And I don't want to disappoint anyone..."

Aneta nodded. "I totally get that." She used the dustpan to finish sweeping the floor. "But I think I'll leave you with one little tidbit. You don't give God enough credit for how well He has equipped you for this. I have absolutely no doubt that you can do this with excellence, and I hope you know and realize this too. God doesn't give just anyone an opportunity to build a church."

Aneta held a glowing smile as Theo stepped to the pulpit on Sunday morning. He fumbled once with his notes, but worked forward after that, communicating his sermon clearly.

As Aneta talked with Gracefully Broken and Affection after service, Pastor Kindly approached Theo and spoke with him. Long after Aneta finished talking to Gracefully Broken, Theo conversed with the other pastor.

Bold eyed Aneta as he turned off the computers in the sound booth. Finally, when Pastor Kindly left, Theo saw Aneta and beamed.

Happy for him, Aneta smiled back, although she did not really know why he had grinned at her specifically.

|Chapter 22: Memories Of The Past|

"I can't believe it." Aneta slumped at the table in Affection's kitchen. "I feel like it was so random...but I suppose I can't do much. I feel like I totally failed."

Affection was sitting across from Aneta. She nodded. "So did Gracefully specifically text you that she was not coming anymore?"

Aneta brought out her phone and showed Affection their texting thread. "Right there."

"Well...I don't mean to sound like this," Affection began, "but I should have known that she would do that. I've known her her entire life, and she has become so...how do I put this? Ever since my sister died, Gracefully Broken has had trust issues. But even though Not and Seem have been distant, Seem *is* closer to Gracefully. He may have said something that made her doubtful about Jesus. It could have been just about anything, and it snowballed into this."

Aneta had multiple questions about what Affection said, but one rose above them all. "Wait, wait. *Your* sister?"

"Yes, Gracefully Broken's mom. She is my niece...you did not know?"

"No!" Aneta chuckled in disbelief. "I suppose it makes complete sense. But no, Gracefully Broken never told me you were her aunt." Aneta rested her head on her hands. "This is so stressful."

"I know you were mentoring her, but if *she* walks away, you don't have to stress about whether or not you were *good enough*. It was her decision."

Aneta nodded. "Oh, yes, well...that, but I'm also stressed about...Theo. I told you before that he used to be Coward?"

"I remember you mentioning that. Could you please refresh my memory?"

"So..." Aneta ran her hand through her hair. "I grew up in the church, and I...well, people *said* I was on fire for God, if you want it in their words. I was in a program that was a competition for memorizing Bible verses and such, and...I was pretty much *that* Christian girl. But...I grew up with a mom and no dad, and she worked two jobs and she wasn't around much. I spent a lot of time doing my own things. One of them was...my, uh, excuse for 'missionary dating.'" At this point, Aneta fidgeted with her hands. Her face slowly shaded over red and she avoided eye contact. "To be honest, I have no clue if she even knew I was dating Coward. I kinda started seeing him at thirteen. He was fifteen. You know, I thought he was cute, he thought I was cute, so we dated.

"And...well, I was a Christian and he wasn't. He was actually *against* Jesus and the church and everything. We dated--if you could call it that--for three years though. We both knew we could not live with the other, but we both wanted to get married eventually. During that time when we were dating, he and I had...*so* many fights. I don't mean a *fight* fight, but an argument...a debate. But every. Single. Fight was about what I believed. But I was..." Aneta spitefully chuckled. "I was determined to make him a Christian. But we usually debated back and forth about my beliefs, and I suppose he did way more convincing than me, because the day after we broke up, I...fell." Aneta closed her eyes. Her arms raised goosebumps and her cheeks burned. She tried her best to keep her tears at bay. "I left God. I was sixteen...and I think he was eighteen. And I still loved Coward, but at *that* point I never wanted to have any kind of debate ever again. I never wanted to talk to people with the mindset that I was going to turn them to God. And...to be honest, this is all kinda...nerve-wracking. Building a church...with Theo."

Affection held up a hand to interrupt. "So... how has it been working with Theo?"

With a frustrated sigh, Aneta looked away. "I don't know.The other day, I was going to go up to someone I saw in the library and chat with them, because I have seen them around town, but I lost my nerve. It reminded me of the time when I did that before, and Theo--Coward--he didn't get *mad* at me, but he was really critical. And when Gracefully Broken first began to ask questions, I think I began to get slightly...I don't know. Flustered? As her questions got more and more complex and deeper, they began to sound like Coward's questions. He would come up with the most ridiculous questions to try and stump me. He did not stump me often, but he never really accepted my explanations, either. And I feel super stressed out about Gracefully Broken and Theo."

Affection nodded. "So, you feel like you weren't able to put up a fight for Gracefully? Kinda like how you felt with Coward?"

"Yes." Aneta sighed in relief as Affection connected the dots for her.

"I see how that can be difficult. I had...a similar experience with Advisor. But it sounds like to me you should deal with this. If you think you might have anything against Theo, it would be best to take care of it sooner than later."

"I know. I know." Aneta sighed, exhausted. "I'm not even sure if I have anything *against* Theo. I don't know." She glanced at the time and groaned. "Ugh, I have to go. It's almost ten, and I have to work tomorrow."

Affection stood up. "I'll drive you home."

With a tired sigh, Aneta poured herself a cup of coffee at the cafeteria at work. "Oh, it's too early to be conscious," she mumbled to herself.

"Aneta?"

Aneta turned around. She blinked. "Yes, Mr. Not?"

Not poured himself a cup as well. "I heard...Gracefully talking to Fair."

Between her mind still being half-asleep and the events of the previous evening, Aneta was not sure if she was too worn out to be anxious about talking to Not, or whether she was truly not nervous at all. She decided it was probably the former.

Not continued. "She said that this whole 'Jesus thing' has gotten confusing. She did not know I was there. I was just in the office area working, since I am getting my apartment redone."

When he paused, Aneta gulped. "Okay." She carefully worded her next question, not knowing what Not was trying to say. "So, what would you like to know? Did you have a question?"

"Well, I'm not going to go into the topic now, about Gracefully. I'm sure you already know enough. But she did have one question that Fair could not answer well enough for my satisfaction."

Aneta nodded for him to continue, hoping she could answer whatever he asked.

"How do we know that God accepts people like her...or me? She was Broken. And she changed her name to Gracefully Broken. Did God ever accept her? I know Christians have a lot of criteria for becoming one of God's children, but...does God *love* Gracefully? What about Immoral? He was my friend in college. We still work together in business. Would God accept him? Even with who he is?"

Dumbfounded, Aneta stood blinking. How could she answer that? She had never changed her name. She had no experience in this.

When she didn't reply, Not nodded. "I thought so." He began to turn away.

"Mr. Not?"

"Yes?"

"I don't know how well I can answer your question. I'm not sure how much sense I would make, to be perfectly honest. But... I know Theo can answer it."

"Theo? What does he know about this?" Not looked slightly agitated. "What does *any* Christian know about this? Do any Christians ever come from a regular background full of what you might call sin? Do any of you ever have to restart from the beginning? Are there any true Christians that aren't raised in the church?"

Aneta gulped again. Her stomach tumbled and twisted into knots. "I'm sorry, Mr. Not, if you are confused. I really want to answer you right now. But I think Theo would do better. He has a lot of experience in the area of your questions. Do you have his phone number? I'm sure you can call him when he's done at work. I think he finishes at six"

Not thought about her offer. "I think I'm good. Thanks, though." He turned and walked away.

Aneta nodded mutely and stared wide-eyed at the floor, trembling in dismay.

During her lunch break, Aneta knew it would be best to tell Theo that Not might call, although she had no idea if he actually would. She called him a few minutes into her lunch, but then realized he probably would not pick up if he was busy. She was about to hang up when Theo answered.

"Hello?"

"Oh, you picked up. Are you on lunch break right now?"

"Actually, I'm home right now. Why?"

Aneta paused. "Why are you not at work? Aren't you working today?"

"I was. Didn't you see the group chat? I burned myself pretty good on my hand, so I went home for the day."

"Oh. No, I never saw the chat, sorry. I was working. I didn't bother to look before I called. But I talked to Mr. Not this morning--Gracefully Broken's brother? And...he had a question...that I could have answered I think, but...I told him to ask you."

"What was the question?"

Aneta licked her lips. "Well, he said that Gracefully Broken asked this while talking to Fair, and he was not satisfied with the answer given. So...I don't remember it word for word. He is asking if God actually accepts people like Gracefully Broken, or like his friend from college, Immoral. He was asking about people changing their own names, and about what God accepts and such."

227

Theo did not respond at first. "*I see. And you directed him to me because...*" His voice trailed off. There was no question in his tone of voice, only a reluctance to finish his own sentence.

"Yes. Theo? For the record, I'm...not holding anything against you."

Theo's quiet scoff carried through the speaker. "*I can't believe I was so dumb.*"

"Don't say that. I know it's been...a little odd...but I think you are doing a great job building a church."

"*Are you being serious?*"

"Yes! I don't think anyone could actually accomplish what you're doing right now. But Theo..." Aneta hesitated. The pause grew long and awkward. "Theo? Are you still there?"

"*Yes.*"

"Are you okay?"

"*What do you mean?*"

"I guess...nothing. Forget it."

"*You can say it if you want.*"

"Say what?"

"*You know. Don't play around, Aneta. You always acted clueless to give me more credit. You still do. Say it.*"

"I forgive you."

Silence took over Theo's side of the phone. After a moment, he quietly said, "*That's not what I expected you to say.*"

"I know. But I forgive you, Theo."

"*For what?*"

"The day after...you broke up with me, I..." Aneta held her breath, trying not to let any tears escape. She had been successful so far, but she didn't know if it would last. "I fell. And...I blamed it on you."

"*What do you mean?*"

Her voice was a broken whisper. "I walked away from God."

Theo grew quiet again. "*What?*"

"I haven't been a Christian all my life, Theo."

Another lengthy, uncomfortable pause.

Theo finally found his voice again. *"When did you come back?"*

"When I was about twenty-one."

"But...you're only twenty-two."

"Yes."

Theo was quiet for a long time. *"Oh. I...didn't know. I am sorry that I was so brash back then. I was so sure that no one would want me, and I was mostly skeptical that a...beautiful girl would choose me. I was so rude, just to make sure you really meant it. I'm...so sorry I turned you away."*

Aneta looked around the cafeteria where she had been taking her lunch break. She hastily dumped her trash in the nearest can and hurried into the janitor's closet as Theo spoke. His last sentence rang in her ears. Her eyes filled with tears in the cover of the closet, and she blindly pressed the mute button. In the clear, she burst into tears, covering her mouth with one hand.

The door opened to the closet. Old Mr. Sweet, the head janitor, stood there, looking quite uncomfortable that he had interrupted Aneta's crying session. Without a word, he slowly grabbed the mop right inside the door and closed it again.

After a moment, Theo spoke again. *"Aneta? Are you okay?"*

With a quiet gasp, Aneta realized she had missed the mute button, and Theo could still hear her. She gave a single, half-hearted laugh. "I thought I put myself on mute. I'm...fine. I just...miss our younger days. We had a lot of fun back then."

"That's for sure. Theme parks. Ice cream shops. The...dreaded church services you brought me to." Theo laughed.

"And the sledding hills."

"And the parades."

Aneta let a laugh flutter out. "Yes."

"Aneta? So...you aren't mad or annoyed or irritated with me?"

"No."

"*Oh, thank God.*" Theo paused. "*I totally never deserved you.*"

"And we don't deserve God's love. Just remember to tell Mr. Not that. If he calls you. I don't know if he will. See you on Sunday?"

"*Yes. Thanks, Aneta.*"

"And thank you. Buh-bye."

"*Bye.*"

With a flutter in her heart, Aneta smiled.

As it neared noon on Sunday at church, more people filtered inside the building. Aneta beamed and shook hands with Advisor, then hugged Affection. "It's a nice day out for February!"

Affection wholeheartedly agreed.

"Aneta?" Someone called her name.

She turned around, greatly surprised to see Not there in a decent pair of jeans, a button-down shirt, and wearing his shiny black dress shoes.

"Have you seen Theo?" Not inquired.

She bobbed her head. "Yes. Yes, he is in the sanctuary. Nice to see you here."

Not gave a single nod as he walked by, thanking her.

Aneta turned to Fair and Diligent, who had followed Not in. She raised her eyebrows in astonishment, jerking a thumb toward Not. With the same unspoken excitement, they replied with vigorous nods of agreement.

|Chapter 23: More Stress|

"Hey Aneta!" Faith grinned as she walked into church on Wednesday night. She hugged Aneta. "How are you?"

"I'm doing good."

"Hey, don't know if we are actually doing anything, but just to put a little bug in your ear. So Bold and I are thinking about camping sometime soon...we don't know if it will happen yet, but just keep that in mind."

Aneta absent mindedly nodded, not specifically paying attention. Sorrow and her sister Agony had just walked into the doors.

"Yeah, yeah sure. Just a sec, see you after church Faith. I gotta talk to Sorrow."

Faith nodded as Aneta smiled at the two girls. "Hi! Good to see you again, Sorrow. Is...your name Agony, right?"

Sorrow's sister nodded, quiet.

"Nice to meet you." Aneta pleasantly smiled at her. However, Agony's attire disturbed her. Typically, she did not have any problems with clothing, but Agony's shirt and shorts revealed a lot. "Hey, church is starting soon, but I would love to chat with you after church!"

While in the middle of service, Bold had texted her, asking her about Agony. Aneta pursed her lips. She needed to make sure Agony would not wear anything like that again, but she felt uncomfortable doing anything about it. Would she just go and tell Agony to put on a trench coat? Aneta knew there was a high chance of Sorrow's sister not coming back if Aneta even mentioned Agony's clothing. For the rest of the service, Aneta tried to think of what to say that would be subtle, and not too offensive. Nevertheless, she could not imagine any scenario working out for her.

To her surprise, Aneta's stomach began to twist up as service ended, knowing she set herself up for a talk already. If she could, she would want to get out of it, but she also remembered there were many men at church.

Gulping, Aneta smiled and sat down on the pew in front of Sorrow and Agony, turning sideways to talk.

"How did you like the Bible study?" Aneta wondered how to work her way into a modesty topic.

"It was good." Both sisters replied at the same time.

Aneta nodded. "That's good. It's good to see you Agony. I think you have been to one other service here before, right?"

"Yes, a few Wednesdays ago." Agony's quiet voice answered.

Aneta struggled to hear her since there were many other conversations happening in the sanctuary as well. "Oh, that's right. Well, how has life been? It's finally getting warm out. It's really nice."

Agony simply nodded. Sorrow gave a one word response. Mentally sighing, Aneta realized keeping a conversation going would be harder than she thought.

"So, are you girls doing anything after church? Or just heading home again?"

"We just wanted to get out of the house. That's all."

Aneta nodded. She burned with curiosity, but she held back her numerous questions, only sticking with the polite ones. "Well, it is super nice out. I think it's supposed to rain tomorrow though. Do you girls have lots of homework to do, or not really?"

Sorrow shrugged. Agony did not reply in general.

"What grades are you in?"

"I'm a sophomore, and Sorrow is a freshman. Are you a senior?"

Aneta paused for a moment. "In college?"

"How old are you?" Sorrow made a face.

"I'm twenty-two years old."

"Oh."

Aneta laughed. "How old did you think I was?"

Agony finally spoke up. "I thought you were seventeen or eighteen."

"Oh goodness." Aneta sat amused. "Well, no, I'm not in college either. I'm just working two jobs right now. At the inn, and here."

"What do you mean here?" Sorrow asked.

"Well, that man is Theo. He is twenty-four. You obviously saw him do the study. We actually trade off and on. I do one week, and he does the other. Anyway, he preaches on Sundays. That technically makes him pastor, and that is part of his second job as well. He works at the dealership right now. For me, I work here as a..." Aneta's voice trailed off. She did not know what her job title would be called. "Well, I work to keep things going here. Bold does a lot for sound and media for slides and such. Courage actually works with the money, the bank, and she is basically like a secretary. Faith takes charge of the ministries here, like nursery for toddlers and such. I kinda just help everywhere, and when someone has questions, I answer them. It's a lot like a second job."

"Do you get paid for it?" Agony questioned.

Aneta hesitated, wondering how to answer. "Well, typically, in a church, the people give tithes-"

"What are tithes?"

"Tithes is another word for tenth. In the Bible, God asks us to give ten percent of what we have to Him, through the church, to keep the church running. That is our tithe. Through tithe, and offering as well, the church is able to pay bills, and such. And of course, in bigger churches, it would be kinda crazy for the pastor to work as a pastor *and* a...I dunno, an accountant. A pastor is paid to be a pastor. I mean, it's a full time job. But there is not enough income here yet for Theo to make it a sole full time job, so he technically works two jobs."

Sorrow frowned. "Wow. That's a lot of work. Agony and I work only part time at the diner...and that is a lot with school. I could not imagine working two full time jobs."

"Well, when you're passionate about something, it really helps. Theo, Bold, Faith, Courage, and I all are super passionate about helping people here. We love the people here, and we want to make sure they know that they are loved."

Again, Agony paused in thought. "What does loving people have to do with church?"

"Oh. Well, a whole lot. We are here to show people that God loves them too. A life without love is rough. It doesn't matter who they are; everyone deserves to be loved. It's human nature to want to be loved. And God really loves us because He created us. We are just here to let everyone know."

"Oh. I see. I mean...which title does your God go by? Is it Allah?"

Aneta stood confused. "Sorry, come again?"

"My friend is Islamic. She told me there is only one god, and he just has lots of titles. Like, she calls god Allah. But her other friend calls him. But I do have another question. I know a Catholic girl who says her God is the only God, but when she tried to explain it, I thought your names for god was lame."

Aneta held off her multiple questions and single answer for a moment. "What did she say His name was?"

"Father, Son, and Holy Ghost...or Spirit. Whatever that means. Those sound like titles more than names."

"Oh. Well, actually, those are titles we use for God. But...I will let you know. Here, we believe there is only One God, and He is not Brahman or Allah, or anything else."

"How do you know? I mean, does He actually have a name? Trust could not explain it very well at all."

"Oh. Well, God's name is Jesus."

"What about the titles and such?"

"Well, in the Old Testament, the people did not actually know Jesus' name. They only had titles. A main one was I Am. And it was fitting because God was everything His people needed. In the New Testament, He comes to earth as a man, and His name was Jesus."

For a moment, Agony thought about her explanation. "Okay. I can see how that can make sense."

Aneta smiled. "Well, I think you might know more about other religions than me. To be honest, I have never had anyone ask any kind of thing like that before."

"Well, my mom is super spiritual. She is always having to buy new candles and everything. But she says her religion is all of them. I know a lot because we pick and choose from each one. That makes it super easy. But...Mom never liked Christianity. I think if she knew me and Sorrow were here, she would get mad. But, I wanted to know how you Christians get your credibility. How do you even know the Bible is true?"

"Actually, it's very credible. One thing I love about the Bible is all the prophecies. I mean, you know a prophet is a real prophet if his or her prophecies actually come true. And in the Bible, the prophecies happened exactly the way they were supposed to happen. Some of them are not actually fulfilled yet, but every single one that has happened has been 100% accurate. Does that make sense? That is one reason to believe the Bible. Another-"

"Can you give me an example?"

Aneta was about to answer, when she realized the entire sanctuary was almost empty, and Bold and Faith were getting ready to lock up. "Of course! But I haven't been keeping track of time. Hey...are you girls busy on Thursday? Tomorrow night?"

"I'm working that night." Sorrow said. "The only day we both have off is Monday night."

"Okay. You know, we can do Bible studies if you want. We can chat, and you can ask all the questions you want. I would love to answer them! I can't promise that I can answer them all right away, but I will do my best." Aneta laughed again as she stood up.

Sorrow glanced at Agony. Agony looked back at Aneta. "I think that would be good. We can probably do that."

Aneta waved as Agony and Sorrow began to walk home.

Bold stood next to Aneta in the parking lot. "Did you get to talk to her about her...uh, attire?"

With a sigh, Aneta shook her head. "No...but I think we might get to that soon. Their family is...very religious and spiritual...but not in a good way. We are going to have a study on Monday. Hopefully, I can talk about it then."

"How are you doing today?" Aneta held the phone with her cheek against her shoulder as she folded laundry on her bed.

Miss Lovely said, *"I'm doing pretty good. I never got a chance to talk to Theo last night after church. Tell him I enjoyed the study."*

"I'll do that."

"Oh, I am reminded every day of my age. Oh. I can't imagine life without a good bed and pillow. You know, I just met up with someone the other day in the store. I bought their groceries for them. She is homeless off and on...and she asked me why I was so cheerful. You know Aneta, ever since I knew her, she is always sullen. She seemed annoyed that I was cheerful, but I told her about everything. She was skeptical, but nodded and thanked me and left the store."

"That's good, Miss Lovely. That was very generous of you to buy her groceries. Do you see her often?"

"That depends. I sometimes see her four times in a week; other times I don't see her for a month. But we have been talking all about me. What about you? Where are you in the Bible right now?"

"Well...right now I just finished Esther. Usually, lots of things will pop out at me. I will always see many different things in what I study, but...Esther felt dry to me. Only one thing stuck out to me. I was just wondering how Esther fasted for three days and nights. I doubt I could ever do that." Aneta laughed. "That's...that's just a little insane."

"Oh, don't say that!" Miss Lovely's scolding tone came across as motherly and humorous. *"You young people can do much more than you think. Now me...I don't know if I could. I have never fasted before this year. And it might take me a little*

bit to get up there. But Aneta, you could do it. When are you--do you fast this week?"

With a quiet sigh, Aneta paused. She had not fasted in a while. When she was younger, she used to fast every month. She had fasted in the past year, but nothing recent. Aneta's face tingled with embarrassment. "I haven't...done much fasting lately. Actually."

Miss Lovely did not seem put off one bit. *"I've actually gotten in touch with an old friend lately."* With a petite laugh, the elder woman explained. *"We knew each other decades ago. She lives hours from here, but she called me up and we talked for several hours. Together, we decided to fast on specific days of the month. Is there anything I can pray for you about?"*

"Well..." Aneta let out a long breath. "I'm not sure. Maybe just for me in general. I feel really stressed out about Gracefully Broken...I'm not sure what to do. I've prayed about it...but I feel like I'm in a rut right now. I haven't actually fasted in a while."

"Well, I would encourage you to fast about it."

"Yeah, I figured you would say that. It's been on my mind for awhile. Do...you think I did something wrong?"

"About what, Honey?"

"About...helping Gracefully Broken?"

"What makes you think you did something wrong?"

"I don't know..."

"Aneta. Pray about it. Fast. Don't focus on Gracefully's actions."

Aneta put a stack of clean towels in her apartment bathroom. "That is so hard. Not keeps coming up and I can't help but think that he's...nevermind. On Sunday, Not talked with Theo, and Theo said he and Not were going to talk more. I think Not just has questions. I can't believe that Theo is taking this so normally. It is stressing me out way too much." When Miss Lovely did not reply, Aneta kept going. "Well...I only work until 5 on Thursday. I can probably fast then."

"Oh, I'm so glad you are deciding to fast. I always love you young people."

Aneta appreciated the comment, but she was still slightly curious about why Miss Lovely said that. "Thanks! Any...specific reason why?"

"You are all so encouraging! You have no idea how refreshing it is to see young people care so much about others. You are all in your twenties and you have decided to build a church and you have decided that God is your absolute goal in life. Now that is something to look forward to every week. You five make church alive!"

"Oh-" Aneta had not expected that answer. She attempted to say something, but her sentences fumbled. "Well, I know-- seeing people and...I mean Courage is almost thirty, and I am pretty much--I mean, with all the work...and-"

Miss Lovely laughed. *"Aneta, accept a compliment! You work so hard and everyone appreciates it. I don't think anyone cares how badly the service goes. We notice, but we don't mind. You do an amazing job, and all you need to do is say thank you."*

With a defeated half sigh, Aneta nodded. "Thanks."

"There. See? Now, I have someone else calling me. Talk to you later sweetie."

"You too. Bye."

After hanging up, Aneta rose to her feet and sat on her bed. She closed her eyes, slowly inhaled, and then exhaled. She eventually sighed and slightly slouched. Answering Sorrow's and Agony's questions were hard on Wednesday, and she had a difficult time mentally preparing for Monday when she would see them again. It had been good to talk to Miss Lovely, but the thought of fasting overwhelmed her. She did not have time! Between work and church, she had hardly any time to herself.

"God doesn't *care!*" Candid burst out, almost in tears.

Aneta opened her mouth to ask what had happened, but Candid kept going.

"He just forgets people and it doesn't matter to Him! He just tosses them aside! I have cancer! What am I supposed to do

238

about Rise and Wonder? If Devious gets his hands on them, I don't know what I'd do." At this point, Candid wiped her eyes, fretting about her girls. "I don't have enough money to do anything. I can't afford my cancer, and there is no way I could possibly afford child care. What happens when my little girls don't have a mom? And their maniac father wants them? How does this happen to people who consider following God? I was thinking about coming to church more often, but now I don't want anything to do with Him."

On Saturday morning, Aneta had bumped into Candid in the library's bathroom. The second Aneta asked Candid how she was doing, Candid exploded.

Aneta embraced the upset woman. "I'm so sorry."

Candid, already upset and teary eyed, pulled back, but then fell into the hug. She began to bawl as Aneta tearfully held onto her.

Choosing her words with consideration, Aneta said, "I'm not sure what will happen. And I'm not sure about much right now, but God makes everything seem okay. Life is going to be hectic, but if we give it to Him, He will make sure you are taken care of."

"How does giving it to God help?"

Aneta stood lost at Candid's question. She stumbled in her answer, and Candid left feeling slightly better, but Aneta was not satisfied with her own answer.

She grabbed her books and rested her eyes as she leaned against the wall. After a moment, Aneta left. She gave her books a slight swing as she walked to her apartment. It was Gracefully Broken, then Sorrow and Agony came along, and Miss Lovely challenged her to fast, and then on top of that, Candid was having a rough time. Aneta shook her head. The cool breeze cheerfully curtsied to the sunshine and brushed through Aneta's hair. A tear brimmed her eye, but she blinked it away. There was no reason to cry. She closed her eyes again, still walking on the sidewalk, attempting to calm herself. She wanted to put everything on pause.

Aneta halted a demon trying to attack Candid. However, she had tripped in the process, and another demon had rushed past. Worn out, Aneta threw the clawing demon off of her friend. She eyed the area. She could not spot Gracefully Broken anymore. Who knew where she was? Sorrow and Agony were a few yards away, sitting on the grass, almost oblivious to the war-like zone around them. Relieved the fight was over for a moment, Aneta relaxed and sank to the ground, leaning against a tree. She held one knee to her torso, and stretched out her other leg. With a long sigh, she closed her eyes, exhausted.

Struggling for breath, Aneta gasped as she found a demon trying to strangle her. How had she fallen asleep? She reached for her sword, but the demon had already shoved it out of reach. She whacked its face with her elbow, and tried to kick it with her knee, but it would not release her.

She threw herself to the ground, trying to wrestle with the pesky demon, but two others lept on top of her. Losing her balance, Aneta toppled. In a moment, someone's shield catapulted one demon away, and smacked another.

Fumbling for her purse, Aneta quietly sniffed and answered her phone. "Hello?"

Slightly shaking from lack of oxygen, and the sudden scare, Aneta straightened up. "Thank you, Miss Lovely."

The elderly woman, clad with sturdy yet lightweight armor, smiled as she hugged Aneta. "How are you doing, Sweetie?" She bobbed her head as she inspected Aneta. "You look like you had a rough time."

Aneta examined herself. She was bruised in many places, and bloody in others. "I suppose."

"You never called for help?"

"Well," Aneta's cheeks turned rosy and her ears reddened. "I suppose...I forgot. I've been super overwhelmed lately."

"And...I can't believe that building a chuch could be so hard." Aneta shook her head as she talked with Miss Lovely over the phone. "I knew it was going to be hard, but I hadn't figured it would be *this* hard. At least not in this way."

"*Aneta, you need a break. Working yourself overtime does not do any good. You have two full time jobs between your work and church. Take a day or two off to rest and refill.*"

"I don't have time for that!"

"*Make time!*" Miss Lovely clicked her tongue. "*My husband would work way too much. He never took time off until he was too stressed. When you are too stressed you are not much worth to whatever job you have. Aneta. Listen, take a day off. Soon.*"

As Aneta walked home, she listened to Miss Lovely and chatted some more.

|Chapter 24: Complaining|

On Sunday, Aneta was delighted to see Not walk in the church doors again, dressed semi-casually, hands in his pockets, with a slight look of interest on his face.

She looked around the church sanctuary as Not sat down, seeing it slowly fill up with the small congregation. Candid was not there, and that slightly bothered Aneta, but she tried to focus on everyone who was present. She spotted Chava, Faith's boss, and Marvel, Chava's husband, sitting in their pew in the back, furthest to the left. They sat there every time. Advisor and Affection were present, sitting right in front of Valor and Clinical. Agony was not there. Miss Lovely was, and had been since Bold had arrived that morning to unlock the church. She had been waiting on the front step. She never missed a service. Fair and Diligent usually sat by Miss Lovely on the front row.

Seeing the various couples and people from around town, Aneta gently inhaled and exhaled, wondering how she ever got to this point. A year ago, she had never dreamed of planting a church, much less being successful in any way while doing so.

Right before Courage, Fair, and Faith walked up to the stage to sing the opening song, Aneta's phone buzzed. When she looked at the text message, her face shifted to shock.

It was Gracefully Broken. And she had a question.

She looked at her phone, then clicked off the screen. She could not focus on that. She wanted to be focused on the sermon. When they sat down, Aneta's phone buzzed again. Almost reluctantly, she looked at the messages. Gracefully Broken had asked three other questions.

Slightly intrigued, although annoyed, Aneta exhaled silently and began to answer Gracefully Broken. As she sent a paragraph explaining one question, another question would show up.

As Gracefully Broken kept texting her, Aneta grew more and more agitated. She wanted to listen to the sermon, not answer complex questions about God! Aneta rolled her eyes as the text conversation stretched on. She couldn't stop herself from mentally complaining about it. Gracefully Broken *knew* Aneta was in church. Why did the teenager insist on keeping Aneta's attention?

"Did you enjoy the sermon, Aneta?" Theo smiled as he walked up to her after church service.

Aneta let out a small groan. "No. I mean, well...yes, it was good. But Gracefully Broken texted me question after question and I could not focus on taking notes at all. Sorry."

"Gracefully Broken?"

"Yes! All of a sudden, apparently, she has an interest in God again, and don't get me wrong, I *love* to answer her questions, but I *wish* she could have asked them after church."

"Why didn't you just... answer the questions *after* church?"

Aneta paused. She thought about Theo's suggestion. After coming up with no good explanation, she sighed in defeat. "I don't know. I thought Gracefully Broken might do something if I didn't answer her questions. I don't know...I'm sorry. I'm really stressed out."

"Are you going on the camping trip with us? It'd be a good place to unwind."

"What camping trip?" Aneta had no clue what he was talking about.

Interrupting Theo's answer to her question, Faith came up to them, hastily apologizing for interrupting but not caring in the least. "Hey, Aneta. Are you going to go camping? We're going on Friday and Saturday, the twenty-first and twenty-second. You *need* to come!" Excitement filled Faith's voice. "It's going to be *so* much fun! I told you about it, remember? Courage and Theo are going. *Please* tell me you're coming!"

Aneta's smile froze. After hesitating for a second, she shook her head. "Oh, no, no thanks."

Faith made a face. "Why not?"

"Well..." Aneta tried to think of an excuse. "I probably can't take off work. You all can totally go camping without me. I really don't mind."

"We are going in a week. You can definitely get off work. Courage took off work already, no problem."

"I don't know...I mean, I've never been camping before. I feel like I would-"

"No, no, that's *fine!*" Faith interrupted, still excited. "It's okay, Courage has never gone camping, either. You're not the only one. Theo has only done it a few times, but Bold and I have done this a *lot,* so it's not like we're doing it blind or something."

"Well...I don't really *like* camping."

"But you *have* to go." Faith protested.

Aneta sighed, wondering how to get out of the squad's camping trip.

"Aneta, pass me the tent poles, please." Bold called.

Glancing around, Aneta wondered where the tent poles were. She slowly spun in a circle, looking for whatever it was Bold needed.

Theo bent down and picked up something a few feet away from her. "I got it, Aneta."

"Those don't even *look* like tent poles!" Aneta protested, giving Bold and Faith a look. She already hated camping, and the humiliating realization that she did not know what tent poles looked like fueled her annoyance even more.

Faith and Bold quickly set up their one-person tents, chatting happily. Theo finished setting up his own tent shortly after, and began to dig a fire pit. Upon seeing that Courage and Aneta were still clueless, Faith and Bold set up the last two tents as well.

Aneta took a deep breath, trying to smile as she put her sleeping bag and suitcase in her small tent. She glanced at her ditty bag, wondering where she could take a shower. They were at a campground. It would have a shower.

"What do you *mean,* 'no shower'?" Aneta gave Faith an incredulous look. "It's a campground. It *has to* have a shower."

Faith shrugged as she pulled up her marshmallow from the flames, blowing it out. "I mean, yeah, it's a campground. But we don't have showers here. It's just a place for people to camp in the woods next to the river. Sometimes, when we used to go camping here for a week with Mom and Dad, I would go swimming in the river and kinda use a bar of soap as well... but I mean, that was in the summer. Right now, it's still kinda cold. Another week or two and it might be warm enough to-"

"Oh, I am *not* using the *river.*" Aneta's scolding tone made Faith snicker. Aneta humphed. "I *said* I didn't like camping."

"Oh, no, no, I'm *sorry!* Really!" Faith tried to keep a straight face, but she burst out laughing. After hastily composing herself, Faith placed her hands on Aneta's shoulders. "You are amazing for coming camping. Really. If you relax, then you'll feel *much* better tomorrow. We only have until tomorrow evening to enjoy everything. Just...relax and enjoy."

Feeling defeated, Aneta continued to toast her own marshmallow, leaning her elbow on her knee and putting her chin in the palm of her hand. She slouched sullenly. She hated camping.

Now that their conversation had ended, Aneta tuned into whatever Bold, Theo, and Courage were laughing about.

Groggy, Aneta slowly opened her eyes. It was still dark out. What time was it? The rain gently pattered on the walls of her tent. Faintly, she remembered how much she had woken up during the night to loud cloudbursts. She rolled over and moved her hand to the floor, looking for her watch. Instead, she ended up dipping her hand in a puddle of water next to her sleeping bag.

Aneta gasped in shock, then mumbled to herself in disgust. At that point, she realized her pillow was wet, along with half of her sleeping bag and her backpack. Fitfully, she clumsily detangled herself from her sleeping bag and marched to Faith's tent right next to her own.

She unzipped Faith's flap and frowned. "Faith. I. Still. Hate. Camping."

"What?" Faith, who had been sleeping soundly, could not focus yet. She slowly stirred and sat up. "What happened?" Her voice was barely above a whisper.

Aneta felt no regard for the other sleepers. "I'm *drenched!* Everything in my tent is *wet!* I *hate this!*"

Faith slowly stood up. "Oh, I'm sorry. Okay, well, let's move everything that might get damaged to my tent, and then in the morning, we can dry everything out on the line."

"*Oh* no. I'm shoving everything into my car, and I am driving *home.* I am not about to settle for anything else."

By that time, everyone else was up. From the inside of his tent, Theo asked what had happened.

"I got soaked," Aneta crossly said. "And now I'm going home.. I'm going to the bathroom, and then I'm packing everything   up."
Stomping off in the dark, Aneta found her way to the porta-potty and grumbled the entire way there. When she finished up, Aneta slammed the door shut, stalking off again towards camp. She walked for a while before realizing she had gone too far. Frustrated, she looked around, trying to find the tents.

The rain was still lightly falling, and an early morning breeze caused her to shiver. Where was she? Tightly folding her arms, she hunched and walked around in her pajamas. She realized she should have grabbed her phone or flashlight, but she had left too quickly to remember them.

"Enjoying yourself?" Voice sat down cross-legged next to Aneta.

Aneta rolled her eyes. "Oh, please." She sighed. "I still hate camping. It is so annoying. I hate it."

"Well, you definitely have a right to hate camping. I mean, everything is wet. And you're cold."

Enraged, Aneta stood up and kicked at the wet leaves. Her bare foot hit a stick, and she yelped in pain. "Oh, I am so *done!* I hate the woods. It's dark out. I can't see very well. I can't see my way *back,* and I don't think I'll ever go camping again." Grumpy, she folded her arms and pulled them close to herself, still cold.

She gingerly began to walk around again, soon spotting her car and the squads' cars. She could now hear Bold and Theo talking.

"What's that noise?" Aneta asked after a moment.

Voice shrugged.

Aneta paused. She waited to hear it again. Distant, inconsistent shouts alerted her. She rushed back to where she had left her friends.

"Where are you going?" Voice hurried after Aneta.

"Something happened!" Aneta yelled. Now that she was closer, she could hear a sword clash against another sword. *Another sword?*

"What happened?" Voice asked again.

Aneta stopped at the clearing where she had left Bold, Faith, Courage, and Theo. Except Faith and Courage were not there, and Bold and Theo were standing five feet apart, angry, with swords raised.

A few scout demons, no doubt drawn to the fight while on patrol, were on the sidelines, cheering and laughing at the sight, with one slightly taller demon standing closer to the boys.

The big demon called out to the boys: "Lunge! Take him down! Let's get on with it!" Seeing Aneta, it egged Theo and Bold on more urgently.

Aneta quietly gasped and covered her mouth with both hands as Bold rushed in, igniting a full-blown duel. Her eyes widened, and she wondered what had gotten into the boys, and why they had not taken notice of the demons, and why the demons were there in the first place.

"Why are they even there?" Aneta asked herself out loud.

"Well," Voice shrugged, "I don't want to say why, but let's just say it'd be awkward for the host to tell her respondents to leave.".

Aneta turned, baffled. *"What?"*

"It's kind of a rule of thumb. You can't really tell your guests to leave if you invite them."

"I *invited* them?" Aneta looked up, seeing the boys were still trying to kill each other. She pulled out her sword in case she needed it fast.

"Wait, what are you doing?" Voice tried to stop Aneta.

Without listening to Voice, Aneta charged forward. The small demons on the sidelines quickly scattered when they spotted her, but the larger demon who orchestrated the whole thing moved in front of Aneta to block her.

At that point, Aneta recognized it: Complaint. Raising her sword, Aneta shook her head once. "Oh-h no, you are *not* doing this." She spoke mostly to herself in disbelief, but Complaint took it personally.

"It would be best for you to leave, Aneta." It scowled at her.

"Over my dead body." With a short swing, she slit Complaint and rushed through the misting vapor of the dead demon to jump in between the boys.

"What on earth are you *doing?"* she cried out.

"Get out of the way, Aneta!" Bold glared past her, focusing on Theo, who also had fire in his eyes.

"Stop it! Stop it this *instant*! What do you think you're doing? Why are you fighting? Where are Faith and Courage?"

Neither of the boys answered her. They stood silently, still full of rage.

Aneta sighed. "It was me, wasn't it?"

Theo stepped forward, gripped Aneta's shoulder, pushing her out of the way. His sword narrowly missed Bold's face.

"Stop!" Aneta shouted. "Before someone gets-"

Bold cried out in pain as Theo sliced his arm. Before Theo could get any further, Aneta stepped in again and parried Theo's next strike, her sword clanging sharply against his.

She locked eyes with Theo. *"Stop."*

Theo held his position against Aneta, deciding what to do. He reluctantly backed off. He walked away a few feet and turned around again, watching Aneta and Bold.

Aneta glanced to both of them. "Look. I'm sorry. I complained. I... I've been complaining a *lot* lately. And I probably invited Complaint here."

Bold eyed Theo. "Faith and Courage went to find you," Bold informed Aneta.

"Meanwhile, Bold was wondering why he didn't see anyone else praying this morning." Theo stopped glaring at Bold and looked at Aneta. "He said we were complaining too much. It spiraled from there after the girls left."

Aneta knew there had to have been something else that they were not telling her. She put that aside. "How can we do anything when we are complaining or fighting? Complaint was standing *right here.* You could have gotten rid of him first. But now, the demons have gone. Bold, push up your sleeve. Your clothes are going to get stained."

Theo did not move for a moment, then finally relaxed. "I'll get you another shirt, Bold."

Bold nodded in thanks as Aneta wiped his bloodied forearm with a damp paper towel. Aneta sighed to herself.

As Theo came back with another one of Bold's shirts, Courage and Faith came back. Almost immediately, Aneta handed the job of nurse to the other girls and stepped away from the blood.

Theo pulled her aside. "I'm sorry I shoved you away, Aneta."

"I'm sorry I started everything." Aneta sheepishly admitted after getting back to camp. Everyone was now up and about in their pajamas. Their arguments slowly faded as she apologized to the uptight group, even though it was four-fifteen in the morning.

After sitting down on chairs and grabbing blankets, they all gradually admitted their own faults and smoothed out their problems.

Theo shook his head. "I'm... not even sure what actually happened. You left. Bold complained that you were too girly and said Faith should not have insisted you come along. I complained that they should have checked the fly on your tent. Courage told us to stop and went to help Faith move your stuff to your car. I'm not sure *what* happened after that. Bold said a few things. I said a few things. I don't know. Nothing I want to repeat."

"I'm really sorry, Theo. I should not have complained." Aneta looked at the other three. "I'm mostly out of my comfort zone. This is something I've never done, and it's intimidating to be the only one out of it."

After a few more confessions from the others, Bold and Theo grabbed dry wood and started a fire to make an early breakfast.

As soon as it was light enough to read, Courage pulled out her Bible and opened to Philippians. "'*Do all things without complaining and disputing, that you may become blameless and harmless, children of God without fault in the midst of a crooked and perverse generation, among whom you shine as lights in the world.*'

"I complained too," Courage continued. "I didn't complain out loud...but I was probably complaining longer than any of you in my mind. You know...the Israelites messed up a lot. They forgot a lot about what God did for them. They complained all the time. And God hated that. But...they did send the worshippers before them in battle. And those were some amazing victories. Maybe...we all should practice praising God instead of complaining." After saying that, Courage put her forehead in her palm. "Ugh, I definitely need to practice what I preach."

Aneta nodded. "You have a very good point. I definitely need this too." She gave her friend a hug. "Thanks, Courage."

|Chapter 25: "Thank You, God."|

Aneta grunted as she shoved Offense away from Agony and Sorrow. The scraggly-looking demon again tried to pry the shields from the girls' hands. Aneta remembered how hard she worked to show Sorrow and Agony how to use a shield and armor, and that they had yet to learn when to actually put it to use. Fighting on her own, she had a difficult time keeping Offense away from the two girls.

Offense was not a typical demon. It did not shriek and growl and hiss as it fought. It was mostly silent, except for its raspy breaths and an occasional squeaky grunt. It looked different too. Most demons were larger, clad with rubbery black armor, although their bodies were more similar to a materialized sooty smoke. Offense still looked the part, but it wore no hellish armor. It needed none, for it slipped in and out of whichever place it pleased. At one point, when Aneta grabbed its arms to pull it away from Agony, she almost yelped in surprise, feeling not typical, coarse skin, but a sliminess that made her lose her grip.

With an annoyed exhalation, Aneta wished Sorrow and Agony would help her, but the girls did not know to do so. On top of that, Aneta realized the girls did not know Offense was there in the first place. She was on her own.

Aneta struck out with her leg to trip Offense, but it dodged, jumped and clambered onto the girls' backs. Aneta rammed her shield into the pesky demon, making it leap away again, but that motion also caused Agony to lose her balance and trip.

She was about to apologize, but Offense spun around again and darted for Sorrow, who was still standing. Aneta ended up tripping as well, and before she could stand up, Offense had ripped the shields from the girls' hands and run off, seemingly done with its job.

Aneta slowly stood up, aching and tired from the squabble. She silently thanked God that the girls had worn their armor. It would not be too much work to get the girls two more shields, and quite possibly swords as well.

To Aneta's dismay, Sorrow and Agony quietly and politely removed their armor and walked away. Sorrow took off her crown and set it on the ground, nodding to Aneta in thanks. Agony took off her crown as well, but held it in her hand as she and her sister walked away, leaving Aneta behind.

Knowing she had been defeated, Aneta sat back down in disappointment. Her right calf had a gash in it, and she straightened her leg to let it relax. With a frown, she pulled up her other knee and sighed, resting her chin on her arms.

When Courage and Aneta were working together the next day, Courage asked how the Bible study went.

Aneta sighed. "It...completely failed. Our last Bible study went okay. But that day we didn't talk about modesty. They had lots of questions about God. But yesterday, I got around to modesty. And...I couldn't tell most of the time what they were thinking. I have no idea how well I actually did...or if I made sense."

Aneta stopped folding towels and sighed again, mentally exhausted. "When I stopped talking, Sorrow stood up, said thanks, and left. I couldn't really tell what Agony thought about it, but I knew Sorrow was done. I doubt she is coming back to church in general." Aneta humphed as she plopped a load of dirty laundry into a hamper. "I *hate* this. You or Faith should have done the Bible study! Not me!"

Courage remained quiet for a little bit before speaking. "You know, Aneta, if they are offended, then let them be offended. But *you* should not get offended in any way at them. That is not how it should work. All in all, you need to remember that complaining doesn't do much."

"What else am I supposed to do?" Aneta turned red, and avoided looking directly at Courage for too long.

"Well, maybe we should praise God. Remember? God has done a lot so far, and I'm pretty excited to see what else He will do. And the Bible does say to thank God in all circumstances."

"Kinda hard when nothing good is happening," Aneta mumbled.

Courage quietly breathed in and out, with her eyes closed, before speaking again. "When we thank God about something in the midst of our bad circumstance or situation, it shows that we are trusting Him. Because then, we are saying that we are just fine with whatever happens, because we know that God has His hand on everything. That is something God loves."

"You know, I don't want to admit it, but you're totally right." Aneta started off with a frown, but when she finished speaking, she had managed a small smile. "Thanks, Courage."

As Aneta continued throughout her day at work, she tried her best to stop thinking about her Bible study with Sorrow and Agony. As she walked back and forth, sorting laundry, tidying rooms and suites, and cleaning bathrooms, her mind kept wandering to what happened the previous night. It took a while, but she finally drowned out her embarrassment with thanks.

Right before ending the day, she came across a huge spill of milk on the carpet in the hall. Aneta offered to clean it so Courage could go home on time. She then spent the next half-hour cleaning it up. As she checked out for the evening, Theo called her, telling her that Advisor and Affection had invited them over for dinner, along with the rest of the squad.

Aneta walked home in a good mood, ready to change and be on her way to Advisor and Affection's house. However, she got to her apartment, and while absent-mindedly looking in her refrigerator for food before realizing she was going out to eat, Aneta noticed that the light inside was off. With a small gasp, she felt the jug of milk. It was nearly warm. With a groan, she began to wonder why the refrigerator wasn't working. How had she not noticed that morning? She tried to look behind it, but she couldn't move it very well.

With a sigh, she attempted to push it out of her mind and focused on getting out the door again for dinner with the squad. As she walked quickly down the sidewalk, she took a deep breath, deciding to thank God as she walked by the town park.

"Thank You for...showing me that my fridge doesn't work." Aneta sighed. "Now that I know, I can get it fixed. And my food should still be cold enough by the time I get back, so that is-"

The sidewalk blurred and Aneta barely caught herself with her hands. She grunted. Painfully grimacing at her skinned palms, Aneta glanced behind her to see that she had tripped over a raised piece of concrete. Clearing her throat sheepishly, Aneta straightened up and kept walking. She did not get far.

"You okay?" someone asked behind her.

Aneta turned her head. She opened her mouth to reply, but she only stuttered when she saw it was Devious. Had he been following her?

"May I help you?" she asked, not bothering to hide her skepticism.

"Oh, no. Thank you, though."

Aneta nodded, inwardly complaining that she was starving, having had only a small lunch, and wanting to get to dinner as fast as she could. To her dismay, Devious kept talking, making her uncomfortable.

"May I walk with you?" Devious offered. "Sometimes...it is quite dangerous to walk alone in town."

Slightly jumpy, Aneta silently prayed for protection. Even if she declined, would he still follow her? Why *was* he even following her, or attempting to do so?

"Well, I'm in quite a hurry right now." Her hands still burned as she clasped them together. "And my destination is right around the corner. You don't have to worry about it." Out of the corner of her eye, Aneta spotted a little girl in the park on the swings. She exhaled, realizing it was Rise. That meant Wonder and Candid were not far. What would happen if Devious saw them?

"But..." Aneta shrugged, hoping it was not a bad decision. "If you want... you can walk with me until I get there. I...wouldn't mind at all." Aneta minded Devious' movements. She did not want to get too close to him.

"Ah, well then." Devious smiled. "Let us hurry."

Aneta nodded, looking to the ground. What was he planning? She thanked God for protecting Candid, Rise and Wonder, and herself. *I'm really hoping You will protect me, I'm thanking You ahead of time.* Aneta's thoughts became scrambled.

"Aneta, what are you doing?" Devious asked suddenly.

The two of them kept walking. Aneta looked ahead. She only needed to get past the intersection about one thousand feet ahead, and then Advisor and Affection's house would be right there. She only had to get there.

But his question scared Aneta. "Sorry? Come again?"

Devious walked in front of her and folded his arms. "What. Are. You. Doing?"

Aneta smoothly unsheathed her sword as she figured out an answer to his confusing question. "I would ask the same question. What are *you* doing? You don't have the authority to stop God's works. You can't do very much."

With a hearty laugh, Devious shook his head. "I can do anything I want. But what are *you* doing? Are you...*thanking* God for your defeat?" He chuckled again. "What is that supposed to accomplish? Is your God a god of losing? Now that would make sense."

Aneta's blood boiled. "*I laid me down and slept; I awaked; for the LORD sustained me. I will not be afraid of ten thousands of people, that have set themselves against me round about.* God protects His own, and He wins. Every. Time. You are allowed to forge weapons against me, but you are not allowed to win in the end. I have that privilege over you."

Devious acted indifferent. "Well, I see you have not changed. You still hold on to Him. But I'm afraid you won't win. I have work to do, and I will not allow you to interfere." He let the end of his whip drop to the ground as he uncoiled it from his hip.

Aneta sighed, wondering how many more times she would have to fight him. She slid one foot behind the other, ready to fight. She eyed the dagger in his boot. She kept that in mind. On top of that, her stomach growled. She gulped and almost complained, but reverted and thanked God that He would protect her as He promised in his Word.

Devious made the first move. He immediately set two hidden demons on her, then entangled her feet with his whip. Aneta fell again on the concrete, grinding pieces of dirt and chips of concrete into her skinned palms. She turned, still on the ground, to fend off the two demons who leapt at her. She sliced one right away, but the other lunged and locked its jaws on her arm.

She yelled in pain, switched her sword to her left hand, which was free, and hit the demon's legs. It squealed as it vaporized with the other demon.

Without thinking too much about it, Aneta said, "Thank you, God." Relief flooded her. She could fight again.

Devious retracted his whip, disgusted at her persistence.

"My God is an awesome God," Aneta declared. "What makes you think you can possibly defeat Him?"

Replacing his whip, Devious yanked out his dagger. He tried to plunge it into her chest, but she deflected the attack and sliced a big gash in his leg, cutting through his boot.

Her heart fluttered as she rejoiced, and as Devious continued to swing at her, Aneta remembered the psalm she had studied that morning.

"O LORD, how excellent is Your name in all the earth, who had set Your glory above the heavens." Aneta smiled. "How much damage can you do when God is by my side?"

Devious' face fell and whitened. Aneta swiftly drove her sword forward, not giving him any chance to move Devious immediately disappeared as her sword struck his body.

Aneta let down her sword, worn out. She glanced at her right arm as she put her sword back in her sheath. Her shirt was torn, and blood was seeping through. She grimly smiled at it.

Aneta glanced to her side, waiting for Devious to reply. She gasped, seeing that he had left. Where did he go? She shot a glance behind her, looking at the park. Rise and Wonder were on the slide, and Candid was sitting on a bench. Devious was nowhere to be seen. Joyful, Aneta grinned and hurried to dinner.

When she opened the door to Advisor and Affection's house, Faith waved with excitement. There were three other people there, other than the squad.

Affection smiled. "Come in, come in, Aneta. This is Valor; you may remember him. He came to a church service at our house, remember? He just moved here with his parents, Hope and Keen. They will be joining us for dinner, and they will be at church tomorrow night as well!"

Aneta warmly greeted Valor and his parents. "Good evening. I'm really thankful for you! It will be great to see you there."

Advisor handed Aneta a plate of food he had set aside, and she proceeded to eat with the others at the table.

On Wednesday night, Valor and his parents came sure enough, and Valor brought a friend as well, who decided to come again on Sunday. A week flew by for Aneta, as she was busy getting Bold and Theo to fix her refrigerator, along with a leaky window after a storm on Thursday. On Sunday, she was in a particularly good mood when Valor came with his friend, and his friend's brother.

Before Aneta sat down for the service, Affection scooted next to her, subtly pointing out a man who had just walked in the doors.

"Do you know who that is?" Affection whispered.

Aneta slowly shook her head. "No, who?"

"That's the *mayor!* He is the one who shut down the other churches...don't tell Theo until after the service, of course...but I think the mayor will do that for us afterwards."

Aneta's stomach twisted. "Do you think he'll shut us down?"

Affection did not give her a promising look, and hurried back to her seat when the music began to start.

Beginning to fret, Aneta let her mind wander through different possibilities of what might happen. Would the mayor take the stage during the middle of the song service or the sermon? Would he quietly tell Theo to halt services?

Trying to slow her thoughts, Aneta gently breathed in and out, focusing once again on the service, praising God for the time they had to have church.

When church ended, Aneta started for Theo, seeing the mayor had immediately pulled him aside. However, Fair and Diligent interrupted her to ask a question. When she answered and moved on, the mayor had already nodded to Theo and left the sanctuary.

"What did he say?" Aneta pleaded.

Theo's face was still pale. "I- I don't...that was the mayor. He said he liked the church service." He was slightly dazed.

"Wait, *really?*" Aneta gasped.

"He said he was curious after he heard about a bunch of young people starting a church. He said he decided to come here to check it out, and he chose to let us keep going! This...this is-"

Faith hurried up to them. "What did the mayor say?"

"He liked the service!" Aneta blurted out.

Bold popped up next to them as well. "Really? That's awesome!"

"Can we keep having services?" Courage asked, two pews away.

"Yes!" Theo finally replied. "He wants us to keep doing this!"

Aneta hugged Faith tightly, feeling overwhelmed with happiness. She finally exhaled, not realizing she had held her breath. Maybe she could plant a church. Maybe she could mentor others, and help the church grow.

Maybe she really could.

"Thank you, God."